THE MOON REPRESENTS MY HEART

THE MOON REPRESENTS MY HEART

PIM WANGTECHAWAT

BLACK STONE
PUBLISHING

Printed in the United States of America

First edition: 2023
ISBN 979-8-212-34003-8
Fiction / Family Life / General

Version 1

Blackstone Publishing
31 Mistletoe Rd.
Ashland, OR 97520

www.BlackstonePublishing.com

You ask me how deep my love for you is,
how much I really love you.
My affection does not waver,
my love will not change.
The moon represents my heart.

Teresa Teng, "The Moon Represents My Heart"

For my father and grandfathers,
who gifted me this story.
And for my mother and grandmothers,
who gave me its wings.

THE WANG FAMILY TREE

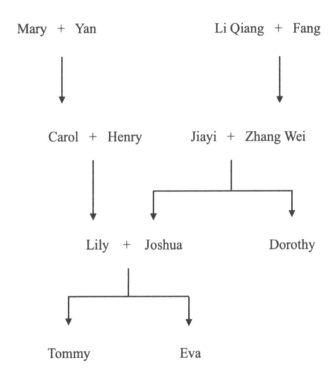

PART ONE

万事开头难

ALL THINGS ARE DIFFICULT AT THE START

Everyone who time-travels describes their experience differently.

For a scientific and extremely logical man like Joshua Wang, it is merely "a dark, swooping sensation"—a "blip" in time in which your body is simply uprooted from the ground before appearing somewhere else. His wife Lily, more artistic and romantic by nature, compared it to the feeling you get when you realize for the first time that you're falling in love—"a kind of thrill," "a rush of adrenaline." Like when you're hurtling toward the ground on a roller-coaster ride, terrified, but incredibly, wonderfully alive. Their son, Tommy, compared it to an exquisite football goal—a volley from outside the penalty box or a curving strike delivered from halfway down the pitch when the goalkeeper is off his line. His twin, Eva, did not use words at all. She painted instead:

a gorgeous sunset over a rippling blue ocean, a dark rainforest, with shadows lurking everywhere.

But despite these differing descriptions, all time travelers seem to agree on one thing: the experience comes with a sense of profound vulnerability. A loss waiting to happen. As Lily liked to put it, "You are holding something precious in your hands but are afraid that one day it will slip through your fingers. And that no matter how hard you try, you can never have it back."

JOSHUA, LILY, TOMMY, AND EVA

1972 / 2000

The last time the Wangs traveled back in time together as a family, the twins, Tommy and Eva, were eight years old. Joshua, their father, and Lily, their mother, were both thirty-one.

The trip was to Hong Kong on March 21, 1972, to meet Joshua's idol, Bruce Lee, the night before the premiere of his film *Fist of Fury*.

At around five in the evening, precisely as planned, in a narrow, secluded alley by the Hyatt Regency Hotel in Kowloon, the Wangs appeared out of thin air, quiet as a breeze. Not one by one, but together, holding each other tightly by the hand.

They were all dressed in the seventies-style clothes that Lily had meticulously prepared over several months so that they would resemble "the sort of wholesome, upper-class Chinese family that wouldn't look out of place in a fancy hotel."

For a while, they stood conversing with each other in low voices, the parents bending down to make sure that there was color in their children's cheeks, that their hands and legs weren't shaking or trembling from the trip. After all, they were still new to time-traveling. How are you feeling? they asked over and over again in hushed whispers. Are you okay?

Eventually, the four of them made their way to the hotel's entrance. After a nod from Joshua, they walked through the double doors as if they were guests there, passing the doorman, who doffed his cap at them, and the two concierges guarding the lobby, and headed straight into the restaurant.

The children, who were told to act natural, stared at their feet the entire time.

Sit up straight, Eva, don't slouch, said Joshua, looking at his wristwatch.

Darling, should we order? asked Lily, flipping through the menu. It will look strange if we don't. Did you bring the money?

Of course I did.

Can we have the ribs, Mum? asked Tommy.

Yes, the ribs! cried Eva.

And barbecued pork!

And garlic fried rice—

Also those beans with minced pork—

Mantou!

Quiet, said Joshua. Tommy, Eva—we're not here for the food. It doesn't matter what we order.

Lily lifted an eyebrow. So does that mean you don't want the duck?

The duck?

You always want the duck—

It doesn't matter if we get the duck—

Mum, the ribs—said Eva.

You always want the duck, so I just *assumed*—

Tommy asked, Can we also have what Dad brought from—

The food is only for show—

The ribs!

But we have to *eat* the food—

Get the fucking duck then!

Silence.

Lily flattened the menu against the tabletop. Eva covered her face with her hands. Tommy, who was play-fighting with his chopsticks, dropped them onto the plastic plate as though they were hot.

Joshua, said Lily, in a voice that said, *Joshua, this will not do.*

But he looked down at his wristwatch once 'more. It's almost time, he said.

Their glances strayed to the door . . . still no Bruce.

Lily, order whatever you want. Tommy. Eva. Joshua looked at his children with that gaze that made Eva burn red and Tommy squirm. What's the sentence I taught you again?

The two children chanted together under their breath in clipped, rehearsed Cantonese: We are big fans of yours, Mr. Lee. We watch your movies all the time. Please, may we have your autograph?

Lily scoffed, leaned back in her chair, and lit a cigarette.

When Joshua glared at her, she shrugged and said, One of the perks of the seventies.

Joshua turned back to his children. Say it one more time.

We are big fans of yours, Mr. Lee. We watch your movies all the time. Please, may we have your autograph?

Good. Again.

We are big fans of yours, Mr. Lee. We watch your movies all the time. Please, may we have your autograph?

One more time.

The trip had taken nearly a year to plan, during which Joshua lost his temper multiple times and Lily abruptly left the house to take many long walks by herself. Tommy burst into tears four times (he kept count himself), Eva only once, but the number of shouting matches she had with her father nearly reached double figures.

In Joshua's office, the mountains of books, documents, diagrams, and black-and-white photographs continued to grow taller and taller. Every inch of the blackboard at the far end of the room was covered with numbers and scribbles. Post-it notes glared down from windows and lamp shades, saying things like, *1971 or '72?*, *What about Linda?*, *Find safe place for arrival*, and *Turn of the millennium—effect?*

In February, three months before the trip, in addition to the vintage clothes strewn all over the place, a huge piece of paper was stuck to their living room wall. At the top was Lily's handwriting: *Rules for Hong Kong 1972 Bruce Lee Trip.*

The rest was written in Joshua's untidy scrawl:

24 hours is the limit. Consult your watch often. If you start to feel unwell, let Mum and Dad know immediately.

Stick together. If lost, try and find your way back to arrival point.

*While traveling, do not, under any circumstances, let
go of each other's hands.*

*Do not tell anyone who you are or where you've come
from!*

Memorize your false identities and follow the plan!

The twins, who had only traveled once or twice before by
themselves, were tasked with remembering these rules word
for word. Particular attention was paid to the first one. Years
ago, during many of their earlier trips together, Joshua and Lily
were able to prove their theory that the body can only endure
a limited time in the past before beginning to deteriorate. The
children were told that any signs of illness—whether it be a
fever, a headache, or even a slight cough—should be flagged
at once. This meant every Saturday and Sunday evening, the
entire family would go down to the South Bank for what Joshua
called "required physical preparation," which was, in reality, an
exhausting, energy-sapping run from the National Theatre to
the Globe Theatre and back again. Watching Bruce Lee movies
after dinner also became part of the "education," and Cantonese
lessons were increased from twice a week to three times a week.

The night before the trip, having sent the children to bed,
Lily found her husband sitting on the floor in their living room,
sheets of paper surrounding him in a wide circle like a halo.

She poured herself a glass of wine (Joshua had stopped
drinking years ago) and joined him on the floor, squeezing
into a little space next to a photograph of Bruce Lee and his
blonde-haired, blue-eyed American wife, Linda.

It's her birthday tomorrow, you know, said Joshua, pointing to Linda.

Tomorrow, of course, would be March 21, 1972, as well as May 2, 2000.

Lily rested a gentle hand on the woman's face: And what a present she's getting—us.

If all goes according to plan, that is.

It will go according to plan, said Lily, sipping her wine.

How do you know?

She leaned against his shoulder as he turned sideways to scribble down some calculations on a piece of paper.

Confidence, she said. Experience. Intuition. Fate. I don't know.

Arrogance?

She chuckled. Yes, that too.

The only sounds in the room were of a pencil against paper and the ticking clock.

Above the fireplace was a painting Lily had done: a magnificent stag against a green background. The creature's head was turned away so you couldn't see its eyes, only the back of its head, ears, and antlers. Lily sipped her wine and stared at it, remembering the day in Richmond Park when she'd painted it and thinking about how she should have made the green much darker.

Later, Joshua spoke, breaking the peaceful silence.

We're the first family to travel back in time together, he said, not for the first time.

The very first that we *know* of, she corrected him.

That we know of, yes. But still. He let himself smile a little. A pioneering feat.

I love you, she said, quite unvarnished.

The Big Moment came just when the duck arrived at the table: Bruce Lee walked into the restaurant with Linda and his studio head, Raymond Chow, the door swinging shut behind them to block out the noise of hurried footsteps, screaming, and frantic whispering.

Every waiter in the room snapped to attention. Lily put out her cigarette in the ashtray while Joshua uncharacteristically jumped to his feet.

Later, Tommy and Eva would not be able to recall much of what happened next. But they would remember the feel of their father's hands on their shoulders, how heavy and firm they felt as he guided them to stand in front of the iconic actor. They would also remember how their mother reached forward to shake Linda's hand, and then how Bruce looked down to grin into their stunned faces.

Joshua and Bruce conversed in Cantonese as if they were old friends. Then Joshua said, Tommy. Eva. And the practiced sentence dropped from their lips, easy as anything: We are big fans of yours, Mr. Lee. We watch your movies all the time. Please, may we have your autograph?

Bruce laughed and the sound was bigger than life itself.

You look just like my daughter! he said to Eva in English. Did you really see my movies?

Yes, sir! Eva went into her kung fu stance, sending Bruce into more raucous laughter.

And what about you, young man? He ruffled Tommy's hair. Any moves for me?

Tommy found himself shaking his head mutely. Bruce beamed and crouched down so that they were level in height.

You look just like your father, he said, glancing up at Joshua, who was standing right behind Tommy.

Bruce was right: father and son did look remarkably similar. The same slight build, angular cheekbones, a sharp nose.

Does *your* son look like you as well? Tommy blurted out.

Not as much as the two of you. Bruce ruffled Tommy's hair again. Now . . . you say you want my autograph?

After they had gone back to their table and finished their meal, after they'd returned to their arrival point and traveled back to May 2000, Eva would not be able to stop talking about how she made Bruce Lee laugh, and Tommy would go on and on about how "cool" he looked. Even after being told to go to bed, Eva sneaked into Tommy's room, and they spent nearly an hour whispering to each other excitedly about what else Bruce had said and done.

Joshua, however, remained silent for the rest of the evening.

When husband and wife went up to bed, Lily finally asked, Josh, is everything alright? You can tell me if it's not.

At first he did not answer. Then he took her hand under the covers.

The sun's coming out tomorrow, he said.

The sun?

If we wake up early, we can drive to Ruislip and give the kids a day at the beach.

There was so much about the trip that Lily wanted to discuss with her husband. All sorts of things, from technical calculations to bell-bottom jeans, Hong Kong high-rises, other men's wives, and how much she'd missed smoking; but she knew him too well. So she kissed his cheek and told him a beach day sounded nice.

The next morning, Joshua woke just after the crack of dawn.

When the rest of the family eventually came downstairs, woken by the smell of fried eggs and garlic, they found breakfast ready in the kitchen: congee with fried mushrooms and thin slices of ginger, and omelettes stuffed with minced pork and onions.

We're going to the beach, Joshua declared to his children in a tone that brooked no argument.

And so an hour and a half later, the Wangs were at Ruislip Lido, west of London.

Joshua and Lily, in shorts, loose-fitting T-shirts, flip-flops, and sunglasses, sat on separate towels as the sun glared down at them, casting harsh shapes on the sand. He had his newspaper in his hands, she a hefty history book about female spies in World War II. Occasionally, they would look up from their pages to make a comment on what they had just read or to look over at Tommy and Eva in the shallows.

The twins were jumping over waves—giant, powerful ones that sometimes knocked them off their feet and sent them plunging under for a few seconds. They always reemerged spluttering and laughing, red-faced like babies. Other times they held hands and leaped as one, and from where their parents sat, it would momentarily look like two small figures suspended in midair, flying.

This is nice, Lily eventually remarked, watching them.

Joshua glanced up from his book. What's nice?

Today. Today's nice.

And yesterday?

Yesterday too.

He allowed himself a smile. What do you want to do for dinner?

Do you have something in mind?

Much, much later, when all the years had become indistinguishable to all four of them, this would still be the day they would remember as "a good day."

TOMMY AND EVA

NOVEMBER 2004

Aside from the same black hair, Tommy and Eva at twelve no longer look very much alike.

She has started to grow into a shape some people might call "chubby," her cheeks and chin fuller, her arms and legs thicker than they used to be. She wears glasses now (she can't see at all without them). When not at school, she spends most of her time drawing, reading, journaling, and drawing. Her go-to spot is the sofa in the living room, where she sits curled up with a novel or a sketchbook, her knees drawn up nearly to her chin, utterly engrossed in another world.

He has started to elongate into a shape some people might call "athletic," his cheeks hollowing a little, his arms and legs more muscular than they used to be. He wears cool clothes now (fashionable sneakers and T-shirts with hip slogans or graphics emblazoned on them). When not at school, he is at the nearby football ground, playing for a local youth team as a left winger. Or he is on the sofa in the living room, where he sits next to his sister, his long legs stretched out, playing FIFA on the PlayStation as though he doesn't have a care in the world.

But then, of course, in November, The Experiment happens.

———————

One early November evening at five o'clock, when it is already pitch-dark outside, Eva looks up from her copy of *The Secret Garden*. Her eyes on the clock above the fireplace, she remarks in a puzzled, surprised tone, "They are two hours late."

Tommy assumes an unbothered expression and directs Michael Owen toward the Chelsea goal. "So? They've been late before. Remember when Mum took Dad back to Liverpool?"

"They were an hour late then."

"Or that time when Dad took her to the Walled City?"

"That was an hour too."

"They've been late before."

"Yes, but—"

"—but not two hours, yeah, I heard you the first time." He pauses the game. Flicks his eyes up to the clock. "They've never been in the nineteenth century for longer than a few seconds before. This is a first. Of course they'll want to stay as long as they can."

"Should we let someone know?"

"Who? Our neighbors?" He laughs and resumes the game. He puts on a whiny, childish voice. "*I'm sorry, but we're time travelers, and our parents are late coming back from their trip to the Victorian era and we're afraid something bad might have happened to them.* Oh, yes, that would go down well."

"Don't make fun!"

"I'm not maki—"

"Yes, you are!" She snaps her novel shut and looks around the living room, her eyes wide behind her purple-framed glasses. "Should we call Ah-ma?"

The woman they call Ah-ma is Grandma Carol, their mother's mother. Ever since the twins were little, they have called her Ah-ma—the word for "grandmother" in Teochew, the Chinese dialect their mother's family speaks. Lily's father passed away before the twins were born, making Ah-ma their only close relative living in England. She, however, does not know The Secret of what they can do; Lily has always been adamant that she shouldn't.

"They're only two hours late," Tommy says again. "Give them time."

"But, Tom—"

"Give them time."

But an hour later and still nothing.

She slips away from the living room. He, still captivated by his game, ignores her. A few minutes later he hears chopping noises from the kitchen. Later the sound of the stove switching on and then the sizzle of garlic in hot oil. The scraping of the spatula against the frying pan. The familiar scent of home.

A short while later she pokes her head into the room. "I made dinner," she says.

He pauses the game and follows her into the dining room to find two bowls of rice, two pairs of chopsticks, a plate of stir-fried cabbage, and the rest of the barbecued pork their father had bought from Chinatown yesterday.

He mumbles his thanks and sits down. They eat together in silence, trying not to look at the clock.

———————

The next day is a Sunday.

Having gone to sleep at four in the morning, they both wake at noon and come down to sit in the kitchen together, he on the countertop and she on a high stool, buttering toast and sharing swigs of orange juice from the same carton.

Ideas and theories are thrown out. Maybe something's happened. Something's definitely happened. Perhaps they're stuck. Perhaps they've traveled to the wrong era. Or they haven't traveled at all and they are trapped somewhere in the space between now and then, lost in that weightless darkness they have all experienced. But neither one of them wants to voice or even think about the implications of the fact that the body cannot cope with spending much longer than twenty-four hours in the past.

"We can try and go get them," she suggests.

He shakes his head. "We can try, but I don't see how it will work."

"We can try," she says again.

He shakes his head and slips off the countertop. He grabs a plate for his pile of toast.

"We wait," he says.

———————

Sunday bleeds into Monday, Monday into Tuesday and Wednesday, and neither of them has left the house or acknowledged the fact that they haven't been to school or, in Tommy's case, football practice, or, in Eva's case, their local bookshop.

When they're not sleeping (and waiting), they spend their time on the sofa. He plays FIFA and she, avoiding journaling, begins sketching a picture of a peacock with two heads. They take turns heating up leftovers or cooking meals from whatever is left in the fridge—four-day-old lemon chicken, stewed pork in brown sauce, morning glory stir-fried with oyster sauce, omelettes stuffed with tiny pieces of spiced sausages. After they run out of rice and groceries, they turn to their supply of instant noodles.

On Thursday, while Tommy is frying the last of the sausages with two packets of noodles, he suddenly stops. Eva puts down her detailed sketch (the peacock with the two heads now has a plumage full of eyes, hearts, and lightning strikes) and raises an eyebrow. "Do you have an idea?" she asks.

"It's time we tried to find them," he says.

After dinner, they make their way into their father's office, which is in an even messier state than it was during their Bruce Lee family trip four years earlier. The entire floor and all four walls are covered with documents, photographs, paintings, and huge books. Somehow the lights are not working, so he throws open the curtains, but it is already dark outside, so it doesn't make much difference.

The twins stand facing each other in the middle of the room. A nod from him and they reach out to grab each other's hands.

Heads bowed. Eyes closed. Concentrate.

Inhale. Exhale. Inhale. Exhale. One, two, three, just like always.

The beating of their own heartbeats. Boom, boom, boom. Almost silence, but not quite. Not quite.

After what feels like days, he says, "Open your eyes."

From the tone of his voice, she already knows: they are still in the same place. And when she opens her eyes to look into his, she sees tears glistening there.

Tommy wakes first on Friday. It is three in the afternoon and outside the sun has already begun to set when he crashes on the sofa, exhausted from sleep.

For a moment he looks as though he might reach for the remote and the joystick. But then he changes his mind, runs his hand through his hair, and tips his head back against the cold brick wall. He stays like that for a few minutes, looking up at the ceiling. At the empty fireplace. At the ticking clock. At his mother's painting of the stag with its face hidden from view.

Eva joins him later with the last of the instant noodles separated into two bowls with two pairs of chopsticks. He moves to make room for her and they sit facing one another, each with their back against an armrest, their toes almost touching. Their warm bowls of noodles, seasoned with processed chili and coriander, are cradled in their hands.

Her eyes are red. "It's time we called Ah-ma," she says.

And this time he nods.

There is no funeral. (There is no point.)

They tell everyone that it was a car accident. (Easier and simpler to explain to those who don't know.)

Lawyers in expensive suits show up at the house. (Ah-ma meets with them in the living room.)

Tommy's football coach comes to check up on him. (He doesn't go back to training.)

Their father's colleagues from the university send flowers and a card. (Eva puts the flowers in vases but forgets to water them.)

Ah-ma goes to their school for a meeting with their teachers. ("Take as much time as you need" is something they hear over and over again.)

Ah-ma goes shopping for groceries and the fridge is stocked again. (But the food tastes a little bit different now.)

Their father's office is tidied up overnight: all the papers are stacked neatly into envelopes and small paper boxes, and the few vinyl albums he treasures are stored in the attic. (But their mother's studio is left as it is, with her paintings and brushes and colors, and the fairy lights draped around the windowsills.)

The word "dead" is never used. (They are just "gone.")

Ah-ma says, "I lost a daughter and a son-in-law to stupidity."

Ah-ma says, "I cannot believe that no one has ever told me about any of this."

Ah-ma says, "I cannot believe that you all lied to me."

Ah-ma says, "I cannot believe that this is real."

Ah-ma says, "I cannot believe that this is real."

Ah-ma says, "I cannot believe that this is real."

Ah-ma says, "This will never happen again."

Ah-ma moves in on a Tuesday. Her house in Primrose Hill, the one Lily grew up in, is rented out. She takes over Joshua and Lily's master bedroom. Black-and-white photographs of her loved ones who've passed away begin to appear on the walls: her mother, Mary, and her husband, Henry. Lily as a little girl in pigtails stares at her children whenever they make their way up the stairs.

Ah-ma hangs up the paintings her husband had bought at auctions to impress his white lawyer colleagues whenever they came around for a visit—paintings of mountains and lakes done with Chinese brushes, every line curved so exquisitely, Eva is left enraptured. Chinese characters adorn the edges of the frame.

"What do they say?" Eva asks.

Ah-ma clicks her tongue. "Your grandfather and I have never known," she says.

Ah-ma moves the sofa to a new spot.

The Chinese calendar their father had hung up in the kitchen now hangs in the living room.

She brings her own armchair and sets it next to the window where their mother's bookcase used to be.

She does not let them sleep in beyond ten o'clock.

She does their laundry and folds their clothes on the kitchen table instead of in their bedrooms.

She does not cry.

Eva wonders: How can you not cry when you've just lost your daughter?

How can you not howl and tear your hair out like a madwoman?

Isn't that what all of us are meant to do?

She doesn't know.

But Ah-ma cooks for them every day without fail.

Ah-ma says, "I'm here for both of you if you need me, but things are going to be very different around here."

Ah-ma says, "This is all very unfortunate, but other people have had it worse."

Ah-ma says, "Look around. You still have a good life."

Ah-ma says, "You can't stay in the house all day."

Ah-ma says, "You can't not talk to anyone all day."

Ah-ma says, "It will get better with time."

Ah-ma says, "You will learn to live and get on with it."

Ah-ma says, "You will learn to get on with it."

Ah-ma says, "You will get on with it."

Ah-ma says, "We all will."

It's been four weeks, three days, and infinite minutes.

It's one in the morning, with the rain falling down steadily outside in a humdrum rhythm.

Tommy sleeps with his curtains open. The moonlight and streetlights keep making strange shapes on his wall:

"A bear," Eva says, "a moose, a dolphin, a knight with a heart-shaped shield." "A tower," he says.

"Do you want to sleep in here tonight?" he asks.

"Just for a little bit," his sister says. "If you don't mind."

"I don't mind."

He turns just in time to see her rub her eyes with the back of her hand.

"Are you crying?" he asks.

"No. I'm just angry. Do you think they'll come back? One day?"

He stares hard at the shifting shadows. "I don't know."

"A fire-breathing dragon," she says. "An alligator with a severed tail, a rose, a sleeping kangaroo."

"A nose," he says. "A glass knocked over with the water spilling all over the tablecloth."

Although it feels a little bit childish, she takes his hand over the covers.

"I can't believe," she says, "that it will be Christmas soon."

JOSHUA

1977

Even years later, when he was a grown man of particular status and stature, Joshua Wang would still dream of the Kowloon Walled City and the path he took every Saturday morning as a little boy from his parents' restaurant—ground level, with direct access to the streets of Hong Kong—to the flat that belonged to his paternal grandmother, Fang.

He would not remember much else about his childhood home. Not the sound of rain against zinc rooftops or the position of his mother's favorite chair in their cramped living room. But he would remember this: the path.

Left after leaving the restaurant, along the path packed full of low-level offices and construction workers sitting on small plastic chairs, with chopsticks spinning in their hands, and loud voices raised to match the clinking of bottles, the spatulas rattling against frying pans, the two hired waiters shouting orders to his father in the kitchen.

Then right up a flight of stairs, past a dental clinic with its array of false teeth—gold, silver, black—displayed in a red-colored tray in the shop window.

Walk to the end of the almost pitch-black corridor with the corner shop, the way before him lit dimly by white fluorescent bulbs that hung from the ceiling. The owner of the shop was a stick-thin man with a large mole on his upper lip who would take a broom to children who came in to steal sweets and alcohol.

Up two flights of stairs. Duck past the thin stream of water dripping down from the ceiling, past the path his mother took every morning to fetch their drinking water and do their laundry.

Turn right at the junction. He had never gone down the dark corridor to the left, where women in kimonos sometimes peered out from dimly lit rooms, with smoke unfurling from their cigarettes like strings of silk.

The old man. Curled up against the damp wall, smelling of piss, twitching, often with a needle sticking out of his forearm. In his dreams, Joshua might stop and feel the man's forehead. There were times when his dream-self would even embrace the man, hold him close as if he were his own flesh and blood, while both of them wept like children. Other times he would walk right past him. (All of these encounters would make him wake, much later, with a deep pain in his chest.)

After the old man, a flat with a pretty little girl who gave him his first toy, his first kiss.

A flat with an old woman who would look at your palm

and tell you when you would fall in love and how many children you would have.

A flat with a lanky boy his own age whom he used to be friends with as a very small child. Later, they pretended not to know each other, not since the boy's older brother returned from jail.

A flat with an English lady who never walked past the old man with the needle without stopping to offer a kind word.

A flat that always remained empty.

Then his maa-maa's.

For as long as he could remember, there was a picture stuck to her front door: three smiling fat men, shirtless, sitting under a bamboo tree with a tiger curled around their feet, done in the Chinese style with a fine, sharp painting brush.

It used to make him laugh. But he never once asked his maa-maa what it was supposed to mean. He always assumed it was from a magazine or a calendar, and his maa-maa, finding it funny, had cut it out long ago and pasted it to her door as though it was her unique way of saying to him: This is so you'll always remember where to find me.

His maa-maa was a very small lady, white-haired and extremely wrinkled. After her husband died and her children moved out, she continued living in this flat by herself, except when they were able to find a tenant for her very small, windowless second bedroom.

Every Saturday, whenever Joshua came around, she would kiss him on the cheek and beckon him to sit down at the wooden dining table her husband had built for her when they were just newlyweds. Joshua's father, her eldest son, would only visit once a month. And that's already too often, Joshua heard his father grumble to his mother one day.

The rice, his maa-maa would say. And Joshua would produce the small, still-warm plastic bag his father had pushed into his hands earlier that morning. Their restaurant had a big rice cooker, while Maa-maa had only a stove.

Sit, she would say next, handing him a bowl to put the rice in. Then breakfast, usually dumplings and stir-fried morning glory or pork in brown sauce. Then tea that was always too scalding.

In his memories she was the best cook he had ever known. He sometimes wondered if this was actually true. Or if it was just because he was a child at the time, and everything one loves as a child tends to endure into adulthood as one intact, perfect thing.

His favorite dish of hers was the pork ribs, fried in bubbling oil with garlic until the skin turned golden brown. He recalled how, when he picked one up with his chopsticks, the meat was so tender it would fall off the bone. But he would later forget the taste of it. He had tried to recreate the dish himself numerous times over the years, though it never turned out exactly the way she used to make it.

Eat up, she always told him, so you can grow up as strong as your je-je one day.

Eat up so you can grow up to be as strong as your je-je one day. This was something Maa-maa said often and fondly, for stories about Joshua's grandfather were, besides her grandchildren, one of the few joys she still had left in her life.

Your je-je was the love of my life, Maa-maa said. I miss him every day. But like the sun and the moon we are always together, even in spirit. Some people can go through their entire lives without finding someone they love this much. I hope your karma is good and you will be as lucky as me one day.

Joshua, being a child, never quite understood what she meant, but he would smile because he could tell that she was very sad every time she talked about Je-je; her lips would tremble and she would blink more often than she usually did.

Je-je was born in mainland China, Joshua knew. One day, when he had grown into a young man, Je-je smuggled himself into Hong Kong on a fishing boat. He made his way to the Walled City, where he had heard that the rent was cheap and where he, as an undocumented immigrant, could disappear.

It was here that he first laid eyes on Maa-maa. She was the young daughter of his landlord, who always poked her head into his room, asking if he wanted to join her and her family for meals. She made fun of him and made him laugh. He could make her blush. There was a sweetness there, she told Joshua, the first time they locked eyes.

I sewed dresses with my mother for a living, Maa-maa said. And every day your je-je would go into a room with no windows that smelt of chemicals and cut big sheets of plastic into smaller pieces of plastic so that we could earn enough money to buy our own flat.

Did he have lots of friends? asked Joshua, who did not have many friends.

Yes, he did, Maa-maa replied, proud. The people who lived

in these flats along this corridor, they're all gone now, but he used to know all of their names. We would have big parties and cook together in each other's kitchens and sit down for meals or mahjong every week.

Sometimes she would dab her eyes with a napkin. He had a twinkle in his eyes, your je-je, she liked to say. He could make everyone laugh. It makes me sad that he never got to meet you.

When Joshua turned eight and thought himself grown enough for serious topics, he asked her how Je-je died.

Maa-maa put down her cup of tea, then ran her right hand over her left as though remembering another person's hand there. Her voice shook a little. A heart attack, she said. While playing pool. He made a shot, put his hand on his chest, laughed, and then . . . that was that.

She went into her bedroom and came back a few seconds later with a photograph. This is us the day we moved into this flat, she said quietly, pushing the photograph into his hands. You have his smile. Have I told you that?

That night Joshua stared at the photograph for a very long time until he could recall every single detail with his eyes closed:

The very same flat he had visited that morning, but with the furniture in different places, the wooden dining table in front of the small TV instead of the sofa.

A window to the left of the picture, overlooking a rooftop filled with clotheslines.

The wallpaper, cream-colored and dotted with flowers, old and peeling, left behind by the previous tenant.

His maa-maa, young and smiling, in a rose-colored dress.

The young man with his left hand around her waist, hair slicked back, and wearing a smile that looked very much like the one Joshua himself saw every time he looked in the mirror.

He clamped his eyes shut tighter. Breathed in. Out. In. Out.

First the sensation began
    in his fingertips,
    raising goosebumps on his arms as it traveled up to his shoulders, his neck,
    until his lips began to tremble.
    It spread to his head.
    A cold, refreshing feeling, as if someone had
    splashed him with a pail of freezing water.

His toes seemed to dance.
    A peculiar heaviness, not unpleasant, settled on his chest.
    Should he scream? Cry? Laugh?
    No. He curled his fingers into fists and
    spoke the photograph into existence in his mind's eye.

Darkness.

Or was it . . .
    light
    in a different kind of universe?

Silence.

Water. Dripping.
 The sharp smell of something charred.
 White fluorescent light tapped on his eyelids.

Then . . .
 a voice:
 Hey, boy! Boy! Move, will you? You're blocking my way!

He opened his eyes.

And saw eyes that were similar to his own.

———————————

Once upon a time there was a boy who watched the Kowloon
Walled City change.

He would loiter on stairs, sometimes on rooftops, at junctions
where paths led down to
 dark and damp corridors that twisted and turned into each
other like one big giant maze.

The boy learned how to breathe through the smells of fumes,
rubbish, unwashed bodies,
 and food cooked over fire that was cranked up much too high.

Was he an orphan? A thief? A ghost?
 No. A traveler, perhaps.

A visitor.
Just a boy.

The boy moved like a monkey: quick, light-footed, fleeting, as though
    the world could never catch up.
    No one knew his name; not many even knew he was there.
    Those that did, however, grew old before his eyes, then grew young again.

And there was that one question the boy would always ask,
    as Hong Kong turned from decade to decade
    and the people in the Walled City turned with it:
    Please. Where can I find a man named Ah-Li Qiang?

Sometimes the boy would meet the man with
    eyes similar to his own, with a smile almost identical.

The man with the smile never seemed to take the boy seriously when they talked.
    If they ever talked much at all.

What is this nonsense? the man said, laughing. Oh, you're my grandson, are you?
    He poked his friends in the ribs. Clasped a hand on their shoulders.
    What do you make of this boy, eh, brother? He says we are related.

Personally, I don't see a resemblance. I am much better looking.

And what is it that you just said? That I shouldn't play pool?

The man laughed uproariously. Do you hear that, brother?

We have a comedian on our hands. I shouldn't play pool? *Pah!*

Who are you, little one? Telling me not to play pool!

Me? Dying from a heart attack?

You can predict the future now, eh?

The man laughed some more.

So the boy simply stood and pleaded.

But like most pleas made by children like him,
they went unheard.

———

There was a Saturday when Joshua did not come to Maa-maa's flat in the morning with rice. Instead, he came late, close to noon, and did not even utter a single word after she had scolded him for his unexplained tardiness.

He stared at the food she had heated up for him as though not really seeing it: his favorite, fried pork ribs, with a small side of stir-fried cabbage that she told him his je-je used to have every day with congee for breakfast.

What is wrong, child? She asked him when he simply sat there, staring.

Nothing, he said. He picked up his chopsticks and tried to give her a smile.

It had been three months since she had given him that

photograph. He had become obsessed with it, asking her questions about his je-je almost every day. Most of them, she began to notice, were about the day he died. What was he wearing? What day and year was it, could she remember? What was the weather like outside? Where was the pool game? At Ah-yan's? Who was Ah-yan?

She told him everything she could recall, which wasn't a lot, and it left him disappointed. As much as she loved her grandson, she could not bring herself to tell him that what she remembered most was not the event itself, but how she felt when she heard what had happened: like life had ended. Like the sky would always be dark and rainy for the rest of her existence.

She began to notice dark circles under his eyes. His skin had become pallid, almost tinged with gray. She did not take her seat opposite him like she used to, but walked over and touched his cheek as though checking if he had a temperature. Child, what is the matter? She asked again.

He shook his head. Nothing. He turned away from her touch and picked up a rib with his chopsticks, thinking that if he could just eat her food, she would believe nothing was wrong. But to his horror, tears sprang to his eyes. A betrayal by his young, untested body.

Oh, my love. Her arms came around his shoulders, and then he was weeping uncontrollably, like he had never wept before or since. What is it? You can tell me.

No matter what I do, he cried, he stays dead.

TOMMY, EVA, AND CAROL

OCTOBER 2005

Hope is dangerous.

Hope persists, even in the face of logic, sense, and everything that is orderly.

In that house on Kennington Road, south of the River Thames,
    hope lives
    still
    in every crevice, every seam, every brick, every shadow,
    weaving dreams out of thin air,
    a seamstress with nimble fingers,
    painting lovely, lovely scenes of infinite maybes.

Maybe they will come back,
    she whispers to you when

no one is listening.
Not even yourself.

Maybe they are not gone.
They are simply away.

But then you shake yourself awake, disentangling yourself from her grip.
And she is nothing but a blade.

For Tommy, the past seeps into the present at the worst possible moments.

His mother still greets him in the kitchen every morning when he comes downstairs for breakfast; she sits at the counter, sipping her tea, telling him to tuck his shirt into his trousers. She is there when he leaves for school, moving around in her studio, paintbrush in hand, yelling over her shoulder at him to be home on time. She is on the sofa after dinner, flipping through a book or a journal. In his doorway before he switches off the light, wishing him goodnight. She is even there when he falls asleep, trying to dream of nothing. There when the darkness pulls him into the past, a constant presence out of the corner of his eye.

But his father . . . With his father it is not that simple. It never was.

His father does not inhabit the house like his mother does. Instead, he comes wrapped in fog and memories, ambushing Tommy whenever his mind strays and even when it doesn't. His father at their table in the Hyatt Regency Hotel in Kowloon before Bruce Lee walks through the door. The expression on his father's face, stern and almost always disapproving, lurking in the back of his mind. Always lurking. The downward curve of his mouth, the hardness in his eyes.

Sometimes Tommy is back in their car and those eyes find him again, meeting his through the rearview mirror. Sometimes he is a little boy, at his desk doing his math homework, and his father looms above him, demanding. Always demanding. "Focus! Why is it so hard for you to get this? Focus! You're not listening!" And Tommy shakes with fear because that's what he has always done. Just looking into those eyes feels impossible.

The good day, though.

He tries to concentrate on the good day. Conjure up the feeling of his father's firm hands on his shoulders as Bruce Lee beams down at him. Or the strength of the waves as they rush at him before he and Eva hold hands and jump. He looks over his shoulder, and there they are, his mother and father on the beach, waving . . .

But the good day hurts as much as the bad. Sometimes even worse. And so, he brushes all of these memories aside with the same adeptness he used to display when he took the ball past three defenders on the pitch.

Why dwell on them? He tells himself. What's the use of memories, even happy ones, when all they do is make you sad?

———

"Your mother told me you're a footballer, isn't that right, Thomas?"

Thomas. That's what Carol has always called her grandson. It's true that his charming smiles and nonchalant manner are different from his father's, but there is a guardedness about him that reminds her too much of the man her daughter had loved.

Carol remembers well the coldness that Joshua emitted when she first met him. "Are you absolutely sure?" she had said to Lily, after pulling her daughter aside before the wedding at the town hall. "Joshua is not the kind of man your father and I ever imagined you marrying."

Carol's husband, Henry, had agreed. "He does not seem right for you."

Her daughter's eyes had flared. The memory still stings, even now, years later. "I knew this would happen," said Lily. "If it bothers you so much, if you can't support me, even a little, then maybe you should leave."

That anger in Lily's eyes, ever present since a teenager, is something Carol has never understood. For years, she and Henry tried to fathom the reasons behind it to no avail. "All we want," Henry used to say, "is for her to be happy and to have the best life we can give her. Why can't she see that?"

"I know, dear," Carol always said in response, shaking her head. "She is too spoiled. Too ungrateful. This anger she has for us"—she tsked—"it is very unfair."

That same anger, Carol notices, is now swimming in her grandson's eyes.

He is on the sofa in the living room, playing FIFA. It is a Thursday night. A school night. He does not even afford her a look.

"Yes, I used to play for my school," he answers in a tone that borders on defiance. "So what?"

Carol uncrosses and crosses her arms. "But you don't anymore." It's not a question.

"I might. You know how it is . . ."

"No, I don't know how it is." She almost says, "You are just like your mother," but stops herself just in time.

He pauses the game and looks at her, properly this time. Like his father, he tries to add steel to his voice. The effect, however, is not quite the same. "No, Ah-ma," he says coldly, childishly, "I don't suppose you do."

"Thomas—"

"Tommy."

"Thomas. That is your name, and that is what I'll call you."

"I prefer Tommy."

"Thomas is a perfectly good name. It was your grandfather's middle name. My husband's. He did everything for this family. This house we're living in—"

"Was because he worked himself to death, yes. I've heard that story many times. I haven't forgotten."

There is a tense pause. Then Carol snaps. "Turn off your game, Thomas."

"Why?"

"Just do it."

With an air of wanting to get this over with as soon as he can, he complies. Carol walks over to the sofa but doesn't sit down. She doesn't even attempt to be friendly.

"You weren't in your bed last night," she says. "Or the night before. Or the night before that. I know both you and Eva have been . . . traveling . . . even though I've already told you that doing so is now forbidden in this house."

That hurtful, inexplicable anger again, blazing in his

gaze. He curls his hands into fists. Digs his nails into his palms.

"As long as I'm here," Carol continues, "there will be no more of that. I know your parents did things differently, but that's what got them in trouble."

"They're not in trouble—"

"Do you understand what I'm saying?"

Tommy unclenches his hands. Then clenches them again. He thinks he's so grown-up, Carol thinks. This child that my child has raised.

"My dad told us that what we can do is a privilege," he says. "Not everyone has this gift and we shouldn't waste it. We must nurture it."

"Your dad thought he was the cleverest man alive," says Carol. "But he was the most foolish. And now my daughter is gone." Her voice breaks, a moment so tiny, she almost misses it herself. She puts a firm hand on her grandson's shoulder. "No more, Thomas. Do you understand me? I do not want to keep repeating myself. This is for your own good. No more."

It is different with Eva.

When Carol first enters her room, for one frightening moment she thinks she must have stepped back in time herself and it is Lily's bedroom, back when Lily was a little girl who ran to her whenever she scraped her knee or got scared of the dark.

Drawings and paintings cover every surface of Eva's walls. Colorful images of imaginative creatures, like a pink unicorn with two pairs of wings, a griffin with a flower crown, and a stag and a doe with their heads bent together in the shape of a heart.

But more than anything there are sketches of people—women, men, children. Some are turned away, their faces hidden from view, sad, despondent, and lost. Some are looking right at Carol, eyes burning, searing straight into her soul.

Eva stirs from her bed, where she's been sketching. "Ah-ma? Is it time for dinner? I'm about to head down—"

The question slips out before Carol can stop herself. "What is that?"

Eva gets to her feet. "What?"

"That."

A sketch of a woman, right above Eva's window. Her long black hair reaches the small of her back in one thick braid. Her face, lined and harsh, is as still as a stream on a hot summer's day. Not even a ripple in it. Holding on to her right hand is a child—a little girl with large, round eyes, eyes that send a frightening jolt through Carol's body.

Carol steps toward the sketch, her hand stretching out as if to touch a sacred object. "That's your great-grandmother Mary. My mother. And that's . . . that's . . ." Her hand moves over the image of the child. "That's me." She turns to her granddaughter, hurt twisting around in her expression. "What is this, Eva?"

"I've been meaning to tell you, Ah-ma," says Eva in a very small voice. "I saw them."

"You mean you saw them in your dreams?"

"No. Not in my dreams." Eva keeps her eyes on her feet. "Do you remember when we told you about what we can do? How none of us can really go back to before the twentieth century but we all have different abilities? Mum was the best at traveling back to specific dates, but only in England, and Dad could only go back to Hong Kong. Tommy's travels always take him back to London before 1950."

"But what does that have to do with *this*?" Carol's lips curl. She rips down the sketch but cannot bear to look at it.

"This is me, Ah-ma," says Eva. "This is how it works for me. I see people from our family, almost like they're in a dream. I see their faces, hear their voices, even those I've never met before, and I travel to where they are, when they are. That was in Liverpool where you grew up, wasn't it?" She gathers up her courage and takes the sketch from her grandmother. She points to the woman in it. "Ah-lao-ma Mary. My great-grandmother. Your mother. I think she called to me. I heard her voice. I closed my eyes and there she was. And there you were too."

Carol does not know what to say. She spots another sketch and tears it down. This one is of the same woman, her mother, but instead of a younger Carol, there is someone else in the picture with her: a tall man with his hands resting on her mother's shoulders. The man's eyes are kind and he wears a wide, radiant smile. A peaceful smile.

"This man with my mother," Carol whispers, her eyes lingering on his face. "I don't know this man."

Eva takes a step forward. "Ah-ma, that man is your father."

Eva tries to tell Carol all the things she does not want to hear:

A man standing on the prow of a ship.

The same man floating in the ocean, holding on to a plank

of wood. The world on fire all around him. Screams. Death. So much death . . .

The man and the woman with the long braid kissing under a bridge.

Them with a baby girl. Them in a little flat with the rain falling through

a hole in the roof. Eva hears the man tell the woman in Cantonese:

You have given me a life here.

The man marches down a street with other men, their fists raised, shouting.

The sound of whistles, clubs beating down on bodies.

Shackles. The dank smell of a cell. Darkness.

Then . . . the sea air. As salty as tears.

A new shore. A new life.

But a whole other life, lost forever.

"Mum mentioned that you never knew your father, Ah-ma," Eva tells her grandmother. "She said you and your mother never knew what happened to him. One day he just . . . disappeared."

"I know that he's a mariner from China," Carol replies, her mouth dry. "He fought in the war. He and my mother met in Liverpool. They had me. Then he left and we never heard from him again. Men are unreliable. They are often fickle and weak. Your grandfather was the only one who was different."

Eva's voice wavers. "Ah-ma, your father didn't leave you. I've been trying to tell you. He was taken. The government, they didn't want Chinese men like him to remain in England after the war, so they arrested him and sent him—"

"No." The word cuts Carol's tongue as it slips out. "No more. I won't hear it. Is this what you've been doing, even after I've moved in?" A horrible realization grips her. "Have you been seeing your father too? And your mother?"

"They call to me sometimes. And I go." The tears gather in Eva's eyes. "But I don't approach them or talk to them. I can't change anything about how they . . . how they . . . so I just stay away and watch them from afar. It helps me."

"It *helps* you?" The old woman clicks her tongue. "My dear, you are delusional. How can it help you?"

"It comforts me. It helps me to know that they are not really gone."

"But they are gone."

"Ah-ma, don't *you* want to know *your* father?"

Eva reaches out to take her ah-ma's hand. It is the first time she's ever done so. And for Carol, the gesture seems to say: I am giving you the world. Everything you've ever wanted.

But why does it taste like poison?

Sometimes Carol dreams of her mother, Mary, as she was: strong, healthy, unshakable. Sometimes Carol sees her in their one-bedroom flat in Liverpool, with the curtains open and the gray, overcast sky outside. Sometimes she sees her at the stove in their tiny kitchen, making fried rice. Or in the bathtub, her cracked hands cupping water to pour over her tired face.

"Don't you want to know your father, Ah-ma?" her grand-daughter asks.

Eva keeps telling Carol that she knows almost everything that happened. She offers Carol old newspaper clippings, black-and-white photographs, and stories she has seen during her travels. Eva tries to tell Carol about how the man who was her father had started a protest to demand equal wages for Chinese sailors after the war ended. About the prison cell he was kept in and the day he was deported back to China without a word to his family in Liverpool.

"Ah-ma, don't you want to know how much he missed you and Ah-lao-ma Mary?" Eva asks. "Don't you want to hear how hard he tried to find both of you again? What his life was like afterward? What his laugh sounded like? What a good man he was?"

And Carol shakes her head. "I don't need to know anything else about my father," she says.

Eva frowns. "I don't understand—"

Carol pulls her hand away from her granddaughter's grip. "You don't remember your ah-lao-ma. When she died, you and Thomas were too young. At the end she didn't remember how to get to the park even though it was right across the street from our house. She didn't remember my father, the man she told me she loved. She didn't even remember me. She, my Henry, and now your mother . . . all gone." She shakes her head. "What are memories even worth in the end?"

―――――

Sometimes Carol dreams of Mary as she once was: strong, healthy, unshakable. Sometimes she dreams of a man standing behind her, his arms around her waist, his chin resting in the crook of her neck. Of blue skies and the open sea stretching as far as the eye can see.

She hears the cries of seagulls, of ships coming into dock.

Sometimes, in her dreams, the city of Liverpool is her entire world again. And her life begins anew every night when her mother walks in through the door, finally home from work.

But then she wakes and her daughter is dead. And the loneliness of her childhood stings just as much as it used to.

JOSHUA

1978–1986

It was always Hong Kong.

He tried to visit other countries, other cities.
　　He'd lie in bed conjuring photographs of places like
　　Paris, London, Istanbul, and Quebec on sunny, rainy days.
　　But it was always Hong Kong he saw when he opened his
eyes.
　　The same heavy heat, the same sun, settling on his skin:
　　a familiar, loving, sometimes suffocating embrace.

After a while, he stopped questioning why.
　　Perhaps it was the spirits. Or science.
　　Or just the way "it" worked.
　　Like how knowing specific dates and times did nothing.

Only visualization.

He became a master at it: memorizing what he saw and heard

    and then recreating the whole picture again from scratch

    as he lay in bed in the middle of the night. It was almost like painting:

    the exact shapes of the buildings, rising toward the sky;

    how damp the roads were from the rain; even the shoes of a random pedestrian.

He shared a room with his younger sister, Dorothy,

    a sheet hanging from the ceiling separating his bed from hers.

    This meant he had to make sure he wasn't gone all night.

    That everything he wrote down or read was carefully hidden.

But, of course, secrets could not live in such a small flat.

    And so, whenever his family members looked at him,

    there would be something hard in their gaze. A judgment.

    Unspoken, of course, like most things between them.

    They assumed he had girlfriends or, worse, had joined the triads.

    His mother would sometimes reach out and touch his cheek,

    a small gesture that contained the universe, and there would be

    tears in the corners of her eyes. His father glared at him in the mornings

    when he emerged from his room, exhausted.

Who are you? said his father's silent stare.

    What have you done with my son?

He never thought to correct their misconceptions.
    He preferred it like this: safe and isolated and secretive,
    as though "it" could go on forever and ever,
    like a love song
    between lovers in a bed in a room with no window.

His maa-maa was the only one who knew. How could she not
    when he cried and begged for her forgiveness
    because there was nothing he could do to reverse what
would and had already happened
    during that pool game.

On that very first day, after he told her how he had
    stood in the doorway and seen his je-je laugh for the very
first time,
    she asked him, What does it feel like?

He pressed his lips together.

Light, he said.
    Like lanterns floating in the sky on Chinese New Year.
    Warmth.
    Sweetness.
    Dizziness.
    And then this heaviness inside his chest
    that sometimes squeezed his heart and made him want to
    sit down on the ground for a while
    with his head in his hands.

Miss Cindy, his English teacher,
   came from a good, well-off Hong Kong family;
   you could just tell. She had an overseas education
   and a sweet, optimistic outlook on life that landed her
   a job at this school for children who weren't
   from good, well-off Hong Kong families.
   Miss Cindy was the one
   who gave him his English name while Jesus Christ
   stared down at the entire class benevolently
   from a picture on top of the blackboard.

Others were Barry, Peter, Tony, David, and Christopher.
   But he was Joshua.
   Joshua. He said the name out loud,
   and felt a satisfying weight pressing down
   on his tongue.

He stayed behind after class, curious,
   swaying on the balls of his feet until she noticed
   and beckoned him over. Miss, who is Joshua?
   he wanted to know. What does the name mean?

Ah! she beamed, for she was the sort of teacher
   who viewed students asking additional questions as
   a personal accomplishment. A badge of honor.
   Let's see, shall we?

Theirs wasn't a good school.

Their library hardly qualified as a library,
only one long bench and seven bookshelves
in a room with one window; but, of course,
there was a Bible. She sat with him
and took him through the story, verse by verse.

So that's you, she said. Joshua.
   He led the Israelites into the Promised Land.
   He was a warrior. A leader.
   He and his people marched for six days, and on the seventh,
   brought the Wall of Jericho crumbling down.

I'm Joshua? he asked, staring transfixed at the
   embossed volume of scripture before him.
   Yes, she said, pleased. That's you.

Miss. He looked up. Enlightened.
   These books in here.
   Can I take them home?

———————

To cut out the photographs,
   he borrowed the scissors
   that his mother used to
   cut threads and pieces of cloth
   and to trim his hair when it got a bit too long for school.
   He had to be discreet, of course: late at night with a flashlight
   under the covers. History books, mostly, the ones with
photographs or

extremely detailed descriptions. Was the sky gray on that day? Smoke
billowing from chimneys? Carriages. The neighing of horses
and sturdy boots against the cobblestoned streets. The scent of tea
as it was poured into tiny cups. The sound of gunfire ringing from all directions.
The sky opening up and bombs
raining down in shards of orange, red, and black.

He knew he could get Miss Cindy in trouble
for allowing him to take these books home,
for not knowing that he was using his mother's scissors on them.
But no one understood, he thought.
What he was doing was important
and worth every sacrifice.

His sister began to ask questions after a while,
when the wall on his side of their bedroom
started to become covered with photographs and texts.
The world, he told her,
is so much bigger than the Walled City.
I want to see it all.

He had always known that he was
smarter than his friends. But
I want everything,

he began to learn, was something
a boy like him—with where he came from
and who his people were—was not meant to say.

Instead, what worked better, he came to realize,
was working twice as hard. And asking in
subtler ways—ways that "they" would not deem
threatening or
overreaching.

Boys from the Walled City aren't usually very intelligent,
a teacher told him once, singling him out during a talk.
But your teachers say you're different.
He was a guest speaker, the kind that the school brought in
every once in a while to "inspire the youths,"
a well-to-do man in well-to-do clothes,
speaking fluent, perfect English.

It took everything in Joshua
to stay silent.

His eyes strayed to Miss Cindy, standing by the window,
as the man droned on. She furrowed her brows,
pursing her lips. Sir, she began,
but the man had already brushed over his previous remark,
continuing on with his lecture as though
the matter of who Joshua was or wasn't
was as important as
a fly on the windowsill.

Miss Cindy asked Joshua to stay behind after class.
    Her eyes were fiery when she
    looked him right in the face and said:
    Joshua, bring your books to my office after school.
    I'm going to help you in any way I can, if you want me to.
    Do you want this?

Yes, he said,
    I want this.

He kept a black notebook in which he documented
    every blip, every trip, every time he lingered somewhere
too long
    and returned out of breath, his heart hammering in his chest
in a rhythm that screamed
    doom, doom, doom.
    His notes mimicked those he found in the volumes of
science, history, and mathematics
    he could not afford to buy but pored over in his school
library and bookshops.
    There were diagrams and sketches he drew from memory
right after.
    And then the numbers—hours, dates, times—
    both those he could visit and those he couldn't,
    until they grew and shaped into
    rules.

Sometimes, in the early hours of the morning,

just after a trip, when he felt sedated and content,
he would allow himself to fantasize about showing this notebook to Miss Cindy.

He imagined the expression on her face when she knew
the truth.

All the places and times in Hong Kong he could show her.
And all the possibilities opened up before him one by one,
a sweet, juicy fruit
ripe enough for eating.

———

Around the time he turned thirteen,
everyone in school found out that Miss Cindy
had a boyfriend. The rumor started when someone
saw him picking her up from school one evening.
He was white and dark-haired, an American whom she had
met while studying abroad.

One day, when she met Joshua for their usual after-school tutor-
ing session,
he saw the tiny diamond ring on her wedding finger,
and he knew.

I was going to tell you something, he told her.
But it doesn't matter now.

Doesn't matter?

She put down her pencil.

Scrutinized him for a moment and then looked as though she might cry.

He hated the sight of people crying because of him.

Always had.

He kept his gaze on his textbook.

The words and numbers threatened to blur together in front of his eyes.

You'll be gone soon, he said.

She did not contradict him.

But she understood.

He was right and they both knew it.

Joshua.

She said his name in a way

he thought sounded very much like she owned it.

And, in a way, he reckoned she did.

Before I go, she said.

I have a gift for you.

A gift?

A school, in another district.

A future.

If you want it.

But you have to work very hard.

Harder than you've ever had to work before.

He couldn't get the words out fast enough.
    I want it, he said.
    I want everything.

He stood in the departure lounge
    on an early Saturday morning. There was a
    thin pink line running along the edge of the horizon.
    He was only fourteen,
    but after the third time he saw the same plane
    taking off into the sky, he told himself,

Enough, and that was that.
    Done. A chapter, closed. Forever.

He had always been good at
    leaving things in the past where he felt they belonged—
    in pieces, in fragments.

A year later.
    Wearing a new uniform,
    with a new haircut,
    he walked into a new building in a new neighborhood.
    The building was made up of classrooms that smelt of
    old books and ink and corridors that twisted into and away
    from each other in a way that was reminiscent of his Walled
City home.

There were shields on the walls, certificates, awards,

portraits of people who looked seriously into the camera,
into his eyes, as though they were gatekeepers of
a deep, sacred secret he would never be privy to.

That, too, was the look his classmates gave him at first.
 Classmates from both Hong Kong and abroad, who arrived
at school
 in fancy cars, with chauffeurs, their schoolbooks kept in
designer bags.

Then the look changed into something else he could not quite
place.
 Was it apprehension? Scorn? Fascination?
 Who was he? An exotic species that had escaped from
the zoo
 and was now running wild in a metropolitan city?
 A case study? A joke? A movie character?
 To be pitied, preserved, lifted up
 by people who fancied themselves his
 friends, benefactors, helpers,
 concerned lovers who wanted to give him kisses
 in dark corners and flaunt him to family and friends,
 as though he were a symbol of something
 they longed to be in a new, progressive world?

You're different now, his sister said to him once.
 His father looked at him with calculating eyes.
 (Disdain? Jealousy? Anger? Or simply
 an undecipherable, cold detachment to a thing
 he no longer understood nor cherished?)

His mother gave him larger portions at mealtimes.
He was too young to make sense of it,
but was also young enough to understand
that there really might not be any sense to any of it.

It was what it was:
    a breaking apart.
    Like how it was whenever he closed his eyes
    and felt his body cleaving away from
    a time, a place.

Math, though.
    Math made sense.
    Math and the black notebook
    filled to bursting with what he felt
    was his entire life.

EVA

Eva dreams in colors.

Orange light. Pink and purple sky.

The brown autumn leaves, falling.

Dark red, tinting the edge of the horizon.

She hears her mother's voice, barely a whisper, so low she can't even make out the words.

But, still, it is unmistakable. And with it comes memories of what feels like a different life—a life in which the presence of her mother felt so natural, like the air itself.

There is nothing Eva can do; time cannot be reversed or altered.

But she cannot resist closing her eyes and drifting away.

She goes to stand opposite their house, years ago, and watch as she herself as a little girl appears through the door, with Tommy close behind.

Then her mother. Then her father, twirling car keys in his hand.

It is autumn, just a few months before Christmas, and she remembers how excited she was that year to hang up the lights. But as hard as she tries, she cannot remember where they were going that evening. To the cinema? A shopping mall? Dinner somewhere?

She watches as the four of them get into the car. Her father starts the engine, his inscrutable eyes trained on the rearview mirror as he backs the car onto the road. She watches until the car disappears, speeding away toward an evening that felt so ordinary back then, yet feels so magical to her now.

———

When Eva comes back to the present, she grabs a new sketchbook and a charcoal pencil and curls up in bed.

Lines upon lines, none of them straight, but every one of them, either heavy or light, all curving and intensely drawn. First, the shapes of their faces. Then the eyes, the noses, the mouths, the hair. Before long, her parents are staring up at her. A little bit of something. A little bit of nothing. Anything.

She sticks the drawings up on her walls with the rest and looks at them until she falls asleep.

She dreams again, but this time at least she knows what awaits her when she wakes.

———

The next evening, Eva comes home from school and finds empty spaces on her bedroom wall.

All the portraits are gone.

She goes to her ah-ma, angry and crying. "This doesn't change anything," says Eva. "It doesn't stop me from going back."

"It is for the best," Carol says. "You and your brother are playing with fire. Your parents' fate should have taught you that much. They should not have encouraged you. One day you will understand and you will be grateful for what I'm trying to do."

"I won't! Ever!"

Carol's voice lashes out like a whip. "Stop wailing, Eva! You are not a child anymore. You must learn how to behave. Now, wipe those tears off your face. Make yourself presentable. Dinner is in ten minutes."

Eva cries herself to sleep that night.

Even when Tommy knocks on her door and tries to ask her what's wrong, she ignores him.

When she sleeps, she dreams of the past: their entire family at the beach after the day they met Bruce Lee. She feels the sunshine on her skin and the taste of salt on her tongue. She remembers the warmth of her mother's smile. Even her father's silence feels almost like peace.

When she wakes, she sees sunlight streaming in through her open window. Her eyes search for all the familiar faces she was used to seeing every morning—her grandparents' and great-grandparents' and, best of all, her parents'—but, of course, they are gone.

The griffin she drew with her crayons seems to be winking at her: It's all a big joke, isn't it?

———————

Two nights after her fight with Ah-ma, Eva lies in bed as the moon peeks out from behind the clouds

and closes her eyes.

She tells herself that the drawings might be gone, but they are just drawings. She can always draw new ones. She can always find them again. Yes. Just like this.

Someone is calling her name. She can hear it as clear as day. "Eva. Eva, I'm here. Come to me, Eva."

The voice is sweet.

And when she touches her tongue to the roof of her mouth, she can taste the memory.

TOMMY AND PEGGY

1927–1936

The traveling is easier now, Tommy longs to tell his father. Somehow, it's become easier. Remember how I used to need photographs? How you had to make me research and memorize every minute detail for hours beforehand? Now I simply have to close my eyes and conjure up a feeling. You would be fascinated by the hows and the whys; it would be a proper experiment for you. You would take notes and ask me questions that I wouldn't know the answers to, but at least I would get to hear your voice.

The first time Tommy met Peggy Lee,
    he was nine years old.

Both of them reckoned she was around the same age,
although she was a lot smaller in size,
her head only coming up to his shoulders.

The photograph he used for the journey
was the one he found among his father's research papers,
filed in a folder marked, "England, 1920s–1940s."
It was of the Chinese-American actress Anna May Wong,
in Limehouse Causeway in East London.
Of course, when he chose the picture, he knew none of this;
he simply liked her smile and thought this would be
what his great-grandmother,
the old woman his father had spoken about more than his
own parents,
looked like when she was young.

When he opened his eyes, it was a gray, overcast day,
with smog in the air that came from what he now knows
were the factories by the docks. He was in the middle of
a road.
He couldn't see his hands when he held them up in front
of his face,
or the rest of his body when he looked down; there was
only concrete.

The buildings in the Causeway were all squashed together—
flats, shops, pubs, restaurants, boarding houses.
There were no English signs in sight,
only familiar yet strange Chinese characters that he could
not decipher.

Far away he heard a ship's horn cry out.

Then another, followed by a crack of thunder in the distance.

His mother had given him
the appropriate clothes to wear—a buttoned-up collared shirt,
thick woolen socks and shorts that came down to just below his knees—
and his first thought when he felt the rain tapping on his skin was of her.
She always complains whenever we get our clothes wet, he thought.
She wouldn't like this. She wouldn't like this at all.

He tried to recall his father's firm, steady voice:
Take in your surroundings and remember your research.
Find a place to hide before you become visible.
Go slow. There is no need to rush.

But then, as the tips of his fingers slowly began to appear,
three young Chinese men ran past,
their heads bowed to protect their faces from the rain,
their brown work boots thundering against the earth,
and he felt the smallest he had ever felt—
smaller than that time Dennis McKenzie
called him a "chink" in school and he responded by
pretending to laugh along with the rest of his classmates.

One of the men looked back, stared right through him,

and almost did a double take. *I must look like a ghost*, Tommy
thought,
    as the man shook himself and went on his way.
    A truck sped past, splashing water on him.
    Then again, far away, the ear-splitting sound
    of thunder.

His whole body trembled. And were these tears on his face?
    Or was it just the rain?
    Go slow. There is no need to rush.

There was a small alleyway to his right; he could see it
    out of the corner of his eye. Everything was a blur,
    his breathing quickening as though he was being chased.
    The voices inside his head grew
    louder and louder with every step. Am I safe?
    Will anyone see me? Where am I supposed to go?
    What should I do? How will I survive?
    Go slow. There is no need to rush.

Walk. Walk. Side-step.
    Run. Hide. Duck. The alleyway now.
    A little corner that the rain couldn't get to.
    A muddy stream of water touching the soles of his feet.
    The brick walls that surrounded him seemed to leak brown
and red.
    Aside from the rain, he could hear only the sound of his
own heart,
    pounding inside his chest as if it were desperate to claw its
way out.

He sank to his knees.
    Hands covering his face. Shivering.
    So these were not only raindrops then.
    Go slow. There is no need to rush.

For an eternity he sat there and stared at his hands,
    at the muddy stream pooling around his feet.

Then the sound of footsteps approaching.
    Someone moving.
    And there, in the same muddy stream,
    another pair of feet clad in tattered boys' working boots.

A voice, crystal clear and sharply curious:
    I thought I knew every Chinese boy in the Causeway,
    even all the ones on Nanking Street, but I've never seen
you before.
    Where did you come from?

He looked up and there she was:
    hair cut short to just below her ears,
    pulling a winter coat that was a few sizes too large around
her tiny frame.
    A little girl.

She gave an exasperated sigh.
    He realized that he hadn't offered a reply.
    Well? she demanded impatiently. Who are you?
    Are you lost?

Yes, he found himself saying.

Yes, I think I am very lost.

She looked at him for a moment,

and then her gaze softened.

Come on, she said. We'll get you somewhere warm.

The heat from her father's stove soaked into his skin.

It was mid-afternoon, he realized, seeing the clock on the wall in the kitchen.

The café was cold and empty, with the wooden chairs and tables stacked up against the walls.

What day is it? he asked. Sunday, she replied,

seating him at the dinner table after putting a lit match to the coals.

She began to chat incessantly. My father is sleeping upstairs, she said.

That's him you can hear snoring. It's just me and him.

My mother left when I was very young.

Do you not have a mother too? Is that why you are lost?

Would you like tea? Mantou? Or I can heat you up some broth. We also have bread.

What's your name? Who are you? Where did you come from?

His father's voice again: Remember. Never tell anyone who you are.

And so he answered: Somewhere in London. But I can't tell you where.

The second time he meets her he's twelve.

They both reckon she's around the same age, give or take a year
or two.
   It is after It happened. A month or so after, just around
Christmas,
      when he is lying in bed in the middle of the night,
      trying to forget November.

The image of a little girl
      in a small kitchen on a gray, rainy day
      comes to his mind.
      A comfortable warmth
      running through his veins.
      And so he closes his eyes
      and prays.

When he opens them again,
      it is the same alleyway, the one next to her father's café,
      but it is a different rain. A different day.

She appears behind him a few minutes later and stops in her
tracks.
      Don't I know you? she asks, in a winter coat that is
      a few sizes too large. He finds himself smiling
      for the first time in what feels like a lifetime.
      I thought you were a dream, he says.

Years later, whenever Peggy thought of Tommy,
    these were the words that came to mind:
    Beautiful. Funny. Charming.
    Lonely. Alone. Lost.
    Sometimes he looked at her like
    she could break apart in his hands,
    and that made her sad.

Years later, whenever Tommy thought of Peggy,
    these were the words that came to mind:
    Beautiful. Unpredictable. Chatty.
    Determined. Dreamy. Hilarious.
    Fun. Unrelenting. Stormy. Warm.
    Lovely. Delicate
    in the way her limbs move and create shapes in the air.
    But there is always something hard and steely
    in how she levels him, her father, her father's customers—well,
everyone, really—
    with her eyes.

Ever since It happened,
    Tommy finds himself closing his eyes at night
    and appearing in the alleyway next to her father's café more
often than he knows he ought to.
    The kids in school, they avoid him or they freeze in his
presence,
    not knowing what to say around him, as though
    every syllable might set him off. He has to be the one

to take care of them instead, reassuring them that, yes,
it is alright to act like nothing happened
or to behave as they normally would.
He has to be the one who gives them permission
to be alive around him.

But with her . . . with her he doesn't have to talk at all unless
he wants to.
She talks enough for the both of them.
And she has been there. Before.

My mother is Anna May Wong,
she likes to tell people whenever they ask where her mother is.
Anna and my father had a love affair when she came over
to film *Limehouse Blues.*
That's why she's never home. She is busy in Hollywood
starring in pictures.
Or sometimes she would say: My mother is back in China.
She is the most desirable woman in Asia and so she
can't cross the ocean to live in East London.
She'll make all the English men go crazy.
Or, My mother is a white woman—
a duchess who lives in a castle with the King of England.
Or, My mother is a ballet dancer from France,
who's dancing her way across Europe, wearing pink ribbons
in her long yellow hair.

He listens to her tales about her father,
the old man she loves so very much,
who spends his days cooking and doting on her.

She has dreams of buying them a house right by the sea.
She says, We will have the largest kitchen in England,
so he can cook as much as he wants, and I will write
and make money for us both. We will never
be poor again. And no one will ask
who my mother is ever again.
The way she says this—with a defiant, proud look in her eyes
and with her lips pressed firmly together—makes him feel
ashamed.
She knows who she is, he thinks. What she wants.
How she plans to bend the world to her will.
But what about him?
All his desires (mostly the ones regarding her)
feel horribly juvenile and insignificant in comparison—
only shameful secrets he does not dare utter out loud.

And so he sits in the café as she bustles around,
carrying cups of tea and trays of mantou and fried dumplings
from her father in the kitchen to the customers waiting in
droves.
Chinese dock workers, mostly, who consume their food
in a hurry
and leave with two or three cigarettes in the ashtray.
Sometimes there are merchants and businessmen in sharp
suits
who take time sipping on their drinks, flipping through
the day's newspapers.

And so he strolls beside her down to the bank of the Thames

on summer evenings, when the children are playing outside
on the streets
　and the fog is so thin on the river they can count all the
ships docked in the quay.
　She talks and talks, about anything and everything in her
life, and he thinks
　　he can spend the rest of his life just standing there, listening.
　　And some nights he lies sprawled on her bed and learns
　　to smoke cigarettes while she sits on the windowsill,
　　writing in a notebook so old and used its pages are falling
apart.
　　Her tongue sticks out a little when she is focused,
　　lost in a world of her own words, and this sight brings him
peace.

He has limited control over the year he sees her; he simply
closes his eyes.
　　And history is always perched on his right shoulder,
　　whispering dark premonitions in his father's voice.
　　They grow together, grow apart,
　　and then grow back together again
　　in a rhythm so chaotic he knows one day
　　she will ask The Question and everything
　　will unravel. Just like his ah-ma had told him:
　　This must stop.
　　But how can he stop
　　when all he wants is to always
　　be with her?

The Questions,
    when they come,
    are asked in moments that are
    small and separate from each other,
    like little jigsaw pieces
    scattered across a coffee table.

Both of them begin to notice
    in each other's eyes
    things about the other they themselves
    do not yet know.

And on a few occasions,
    she sees him and he seems younger than before.
    Then again, some years older.
    She runs a finger cautiously
    along the lines of his stubbly jaw.
    He sees the fear written there,
    on every line of her face,
    and he knows:
    She will ask. She has to.

(The First Question)
    You never show me your writing, he says one night,
    blowing smoke out of her window.
    Her head snaps up from the page and she
    gives him a broken look.
    What? he says, confused.
    I read you my poems, she says. You said you loved them.
    Don't you remember?

(The Second Question)
    She finds him in the alleyway
    and, for the first time,
    she is in a coat that is exactly her size,
    high-heeled ladies' boots that are black and sleek,
    her hair below her shoulders and neatly permed,
    her lips as red as blood, making him feel
    like a little boy in her presence.
    I like your coat, he finds himself mumbling. Is it new?
    She frowns. You've seen it before, she says.
    These gloves too. And this shade of lipstick.
    Don't you remember?

(The Third Question)
    When he is sixteen,
    he kisses her for the first time.
    They are lying together in her bed,
    watching the light from the moon and the
    streetlamps outside dancing across the ceiling.
    He grins after they break apart.
    I've always wondered, he says, what that would feel like.
    But tears fall from her eyes and he knows.
    He says, We've kissed before, haven't we?
    She nods and says, It was down by the river
    when a summer rain was falling.
    Don't you remember?

(The Fourth Question)
    I'm asking again, she says.
    Where did you come from?

And he knows he can't put it off any longer.
If he were to lie, she'd know, and he'd lose her.
He doesn't know much, but at least he knows that.

So he tells her
    and shows her
    by closing his eyes and
    slowly disappearing like a ghost she's seen in the pictures
    as the dawn's first light
    breaks in through her curtains,
    nearly drawing a scream from her lips.

He tells her more
    beside the water as a ship nearby
    unfurls its sails.

This doesn't have to mean anything bad, he insists.
    In fact it can be good for us. I can help you.
    I can help your father. I know things—
    things that will happen later,
    don't you remember?
    She tries to smile. And lets him kiss her
    with promises on his lips.
    For she is only fifteen
    and still has faith in promises.

(The Fifth Question)
    She asks for the whole truth:
    What happened to your parents?
    And he explains to her

as they lie in bed together,
him thankful for the night
and just the touch of her hand
tracing his.

In the silence that follows,
  she tells him that she understands.
  It's not the same, she says,
  but I know what it's like
  not to have someone
  who should always be here.

The question
  escapes from him
  before he can stop himself:
  And will you always be here?

Yes, she says.
  And in the moment,
  that single word feels
  as easy and as true
  as the way he
  brings her hand,
  still entwined with his,
  to his lips.

I'll always be here too, he says.

One day,
  when he is seventeen,

she simply turns around;
she stops him in his tracks
just by a look in her eyes.

I always miss you, she admits,
    whenever you're gone.

Later,
        he holds on to her hand
        as he slowly disappears.
        The last thing he sees
        before darkness
        is the warmth of her smile.

He never says, or even considers, the word "love."
        To him, the word is
        too crass, too crude,
        too inadequate
        for all that she means to him.

There is no agreement and no commitment;
        how can there be?

But he thinks:
        Maybe everything
        makes sense now.

Maybe all of it
        has led up to her.

JOSHUA

1987

"Bearing in mind the prosperity and stability of the entire Hong Kong, we wish to express a full understanding of the decision made by the British Hong Kong government to take appropriate measures to clear the Kowloon Walled City and build it into a park. Like other parts of Hong Kong, the Kowloon Walled City is a question left over from history."

Chinese Foreign Ministry (January 1987)

People change: they leave or let you down. It is one of the very few things about the world that stays the same. Joshua learned this at a very young age growing up in the Walled City. He just never thought that the world itself would change.

Be altered, destroyed, or pulled apart by a single statement read out on the news or a flyer stuck to the front of your door.

"The world" being these dark corridors. Every one of these small flats. The stairs that led up to everywhere and nowhere all at once. The almost pitch-black darkness. Water dripping down from the ceiling. But, most of all, the people.

Some made protest signs and joined the marching. Some threw things at the officials who came around, census in hand. But his maa-maa, upon hearing the news from his father, sank into her chair, closed her eyes, and stayed as still as marble for a very long moment. It was the first time Joshua ever saw his father reach out to take the old woman's hand.

Where will we go? his sister asked.

Wherever they tell us to go, his father answered.

His maa-maa opened her eyes. She looked into her eldest son's face and said:

This is my home. I will not be leaving this place.

———

Eighteen.

    The guidance counselor called him

    a prospect,

    a prodigy,

    to his face.

    Universities in the UK, she said,

    will be clamoring to have you as one of their own.

    Scholarships. Grants.

    You name it.

Do you want it?
She was not Miss Cindy and so he
said the words he had practiced to perfection:
I'd be very grateful.

Tears streamed down his maa-maa's face
    after he told her.
    You won't see me again, she said to him.
    Of course I will, he said, shocked. Maa-maa, I will come
back and visit.
    You might, my dear boy, but I'm afraid I will no longer be
here when you do.
    She covered his hands with hers.
    But you will see me, I think,
    in other ways.
    Like how you saw your je-je.
    His heart plummeted.
    Oh, how rare it felt
    for it to plummet in such a way.
    He never thought it possible before.
    He asked, Should I not go?

You cannot go,
    said his father, sitting at their dining table,
    smoking in a white undershirt, as his mother
    bustled about, pouring him tea, wiping bits of rice,
    bits of chili, off the brochures spread open before them.
    We need you here.

Here? Joshua scoffed, incredulous.
What for?
The restaurant, his father said,
although they all knew he meant The Eviction.
Who will take care of your maa-maa?
Who will take care of your mother
when we're driven out of our homes?

You, Joshua longed to say.
But the word died in his throat,
like so many words did in the presence of his father.
For a fleeting moment,
he imagined the oncoming demolition
as a giant fist
smashing through walls and slabs of concrete,
shards of glass flying and piercing his skin,
his maa-maa's living room a desert of dust.
He did not know how to feel.
Was this pleasure? Or pain?
His sister regarded him with a mixture of
disgust and pity
from the corner of the room.
That school, those people, his father said,
tapping his cigarette with his index finger.
They've made you selfish.
Put ridiculous ideas in your head.
Look. You're making your mother cry.

His maa-maa wiped the tears from her face
    with trembling fingers.
    No, no, she said, shaking her head.
    You must go.
    This is what's meant to happen.

Hong Kong at sunset looked different from above.
    Almost beautiful.
    The sky was blood red. Then orange.
    Behind him the pigeons cooed in their cages,
    flapping their wings in a soothing, conversational rhythm.
Lost
    in their own little world. He sat on the ledge and thought,
    This will all be gone soon.
    He touched his father's cigarette to his lips.
    (He had stolen it in a fit of recklessness.)
    Inhaled. Exhaled. Watched the column of smoke
    drifting toward the clouds floating before him,
    so close he could almost reach out and touch them.

She had placed the jade Buddha,
    as small as a thimble,
    into his hand.
    Its coolness against his skin
    felt like a prayer.
    This is for good luck, his maa-maa had said.
    So you won't be lonely
    when you're alone.

There is a moment in everyone's life
    when the whole world seems to
    shift beneath one's feet
    and you fall through.
    Like a time bomb,
    you can almost count down the seconds
    until it happens: three, two, one . . .
    Boom.
    Joshua finished his cigarette
    as Hong Kong became enveloped in darkness.
    He sat and gazed at the city
    until all the stars came out.

TOMMY AND EVA

Silence has become Tommy's enemy.

Whenever it visits, his life falls apart, even more than it already has. Whenever he stays too still, too stagnant, it comes. Even when he tells himself he's got over everything he has to get over.

And so he distracts himself—with trips to the past to see Peggy, with video games, with his old friends from football, the ones who don't ask him questions. Who pretend he's the same Tommy as the Tommy of before. They sit in parks, hiding cigarettes and cans of beer in their jackets. Laugh. Jostle and mock. Chase each other around the city, wild and uninhibited, children on the brink of fancying themselves adults.

It is easier when he doesn't have to talk about It. Easier when things are happening all around him, mindless distractions pulling him in every direction. A sip of something strong that numbs him. A shout. A kiss. A thrill of not feeling anything. How fun. This emptiness.

But then the silence comes in the still hours before sleep. When he's alone, hearing his thoughts rattling around in his brain like a bird trapped inside a room.

His father sits beside him.

This is a memory, he knows.

But a memory is never just a memory.

"Sit up straight, Tommy," Joshua says, not even looking at his son, his eyes trained on the mobile phone in his hand. They are at Wong Kei, the famous Chinese restaurant in Chinatown, with plates of barbecued pork and rice before them. Tommy stares at his food, unable to eat.

Now they are in his father's office at the university. Joshua at his desk, writing, writing. Sometimes he's on the phone, talking, talking. Someone comes in—a student, a colleague, a friend, whoever. Tommy stares at the book he's been given, unable to tell the words apart.

Now they are walking by the river, Joshua's strides long and purposeful, Tommy almost skipping to keep up, his eyes on the ground. His father says to his mother even with him close by: "Why is my son so quiet, eh? The boy never speaks."

Tommy's whole body trembles. "Men can't be silent," his father tells him. "You have to speak up. You can't let people walk all over you. Why are you so afraid? Why are you always so afraid?"

This is the scene Tommy finds when he knocks and enters his sister's bedroom:

Eva lying on the floor, her hair spread out in every direction. Next to her is a record player. Their father's. She must have taken it down from the attic. Joshua wasn't a music head, by any means; he only had a few albums from a handful of artists he loved and cherished. But he has played them so often, some of them jump and skip from wear and tear. Both Tommy and Eva would know these tunes in their sleep.

Tommy stands in the doorway for a while. Lets the melody his sister is listening to seep into his skin and stir up childhood memories. But only for a moment.

The singer is Teresa Teng, the Taiwanese crooner who made it big when his parents were teenagers. It is the music they listened to as a family whenever they were in the car together. She is singing softly, sadly, sweetly.

> *Just one soft kiss*
> *has been enough to move my heart.*
> *Since our love ran deep*
> *I have longed for you . . .*

Eva is moving her lips along to the Mandarin lyrics. Then, upon seeing him, she pushes herself up on one elbow.

"I'm working on something," she tells him. "See?"

She shows him the paper lying next to her. On it is a painting of a young woman with short black hair. She is wearing a light jacket and scarf and sitting with a cup of tea and a book in a café. The city is Hong Kong: the skyscrapers behind the woman make it unmistakable. It is drizzling on the streets outside.

Tommy sits down next to his sister. "Who is it?"

"Don't you know?"

He thinks he does. His sister is a good artist, and he's seen black-and-white photographs of this woman before in his father's office. He thinks it might be his father's mother or grandmother. But he realizes he doesn't want to know if he's right. Instead, he asks, "Has Ah-ma talked to you?"

"Yes."

"What did she tell you?"

"Probably the same thing she told you."

"No more?"

"No more."

"And did you listen?"

She fixes him with a look and nods at her painting. "Obviously not."

"When?"

"This one?" She blows air out through her teeth. "Five nights ago."

They lapse into silence for a while. He lies down on the floor next to her and listens to Teresa sing.

"So . . ." she begins quietly. "Where do you go every time?"

He draws in a sharp breath. "I don't ask you where *you* go."

"You *know* where I go. With me, there aren't many places I *can* go."

Their eyes drift to her painting again. To the woman.

Briefly, Tommy wonders what he would do if he had Eva's ability to travel back to the timelines of their immediate family members. He, on the other hand, can only travel solo to London from 1900 to around 1950; it has always been this way ever since his abilities started to develop when he was eight. If he were Eva, would he be able to resist? Could he do what she does, which is simply watch from afar as lost family members move and breathe before her very eyes, without trying to do something? He likes to imagine that he could—that he possesses that amount of self-control. But the way his insides twist into knots at the sight of the painting makes him afraid.

"So?" Eva prompts.

Trapped, Tommy finds himself squirming a little. "Maybe I'll tell you one day," he says.

She scoffs. "When?"

"One day."

"You're being a prick. *I* tell you everything."

"I don't ask you to."

"Yes, but that's not the point. We're supposed to share things. You don't share things anymore."

The song changes. Tommy feels his sister's gaze on the side of his face.

> *As sweet as honey,*
> *your smile is as sweet as honey.*
> *Just like the way flowers bloom*
> *in the spring breeze.*

"Do you want to?" Eva asks.

He knows instantly what she means. "Go with you?"

"Yes. It can be to where I was last night: when they met for the first time. I sat across the road and watched them watch the fireworks."

He holds his breath. "Eva—"

"It might help. You don't talk about them. Not even to me. And I *need* to talk about them."

"Eva, I'm sorry."

Her gaze makes him want to hide, to disappear in shame.

"Suit yourself," she says, her voice brittle. "But you're not fooling me."

"I don't know what you're talking about."

"You can lie to yourself and to everyone else, Tommy. But you can't lie to me."

I wonder where on earth,
where on earth I've seen you.
Your smile is so familiar to me,
but I still cannot remember where.

She whispers: "I can't stop myself. Sometimes I think . . . I hope . . ."

He nods. "I understand."

"Maybe. I know it's stupid."

"It's really not."

"What do you do with it?"

"With what?"

"The hope."

He turns his head and their eyes meet. "I ignore it," he says.

"Does that work?"

"Most of the time, yes."

She asks: "Do you think they'll ever come back?"

"No."

This is the first time either of them have ever said this out loud.

And for a moment it feels like progress.

Almost.

For a while.

> *Ah . . . in my dreams,*
> *in my dreams,*
> *in my dreams I've met you.*

JOSHUA

1987

This was his first time flying.

He had read all about flying—
    the Wright brothers and how they made
    what seemed like a mishmash pile of steel lift off the ground.
    The science behind it made his heart lift, his mind race.
    The possibility of
    taking off from all you have ever known and
    starting over
    on a blank blue canvas.
    The man on the moon, planting a flag like it's
    a monument. A revelation.

He gripped his passport tightly in his hand.

His first passport.
It seemed strange . . . that this one little thing had
the power
to change his life
so irrevocably.

He was sitting at the gate, waiting.
    The flight attendant began telling
    passengers to start boarding, her voice magnifying
    over the speaker, first in Cantonese, then in Mandarin, and
in English.
    People shuffling to their feet—white tourists in shorts,
    souvenir T-shirts, and sunglasses; and locals in cardigans,
    turtlenecks, and light jackets. The rustling
    of newspapers as they were put down. The sound
    of luggage being wheeled toward the queue.
    There was a song he recognized
    playing softly through the airport speakers:

> *Just one soft kiss*
> *has been enough to move my heart.*
> *Since our love ran deep . . .*

He remained in his seat.
    Outside he saw the plane that would
    bear him across oceans and continents to
    a new life, a new him, and somehow that metal contrap-
tion seemed
    too small, too constraining, incapable of holding up
    all this life around him. The sky, too,

looked so vast and unpredictable.
It covered the entire world while he
was merely a speck of dust below it.

His father was not there this morning to say goodbye.

His mother had delivered the news to him
in a quiet, strained voice: Your father has gone away.
He needs to pick up some delivery for the restaurant.
Oh, right, Joshua replied,
as though this made complete sense.
Never mind the fact that his father
got everything he needed for his dishes
from within the Walled City itself.

Boxes of their things were piled into almost every corner
of every room, all ready (or as ready as they could ever be)
for the
relocation; he moved a couple of them out of the way so
he could
embrace his mother, let her kiss his cheeks, cry on his shoulder.
Come home soon, she said.
Like "home" was ever a place he could
return to so easily.

His sister, Dorothy, was on her way out.
She simply looked over her shoulder and
gave him a nod. Don't die out there, she said.
And with the briefest of smiles and a wink,
she was gone.

His maa-maa's flat was the last place he visited before
　　he caught the bus to the airport. The old woman's health
　　had been deteriorating fast in the last year, ever since the
demolition
　　was announced. His mother had packed some of her old
clothes
　　into boxes. Wrapped her fine china in newspapers.
　　But many things at Maa-maa's remained unchanged from
his childhood:
　　the Chinese calendar on the front door,
　　the dining table that her husband had made for her so
long ago,
　　her stove, her books, her embroidery.
　　Even the pale-yellow blanket that was draped over her sofa
　　whenever he came to visit.

You'll do great things,
　　she told him when she embraced him for the last time.
　　She did not cry,
　　but patted his cheek, the top of his head.

And you will see me again.

You will see me again, as he took the bus to the airport.
　　You will see me again, as they put a stamp on his passport.
　　You will see me again, as the passengers around him began
　　to get up from their seats and take their places in the queue.
　　You will see me again, she had said.
　　But it will not be the same.
　　Nothing will ever be the same again.

His hand went inside his pocket: the coldness of the jade Buddha
    that his maa-maa had given him a year ago. He thought of
his father at his stove,
        the sound of the steel spatula clanging against the wok.
        His mother's tears. His sister's smile.
        They were all
        slipping away.

This was what he wanted, right?

In the back of his mind, the smallest of voices:
        I could get up and leave. Right now.
        Go back. Resume my old life, my old self,
        as comfortably as lying back on a
        patch of grass in a park and closing my eyes.
        Wouldn't that be simple and
        fitting?

He could not move,
        even when the flight attendant made another announce-
ment.
        He was
        every emotion under the sun.
        But he could not move.

The song continued to play:

> *You ask me how deep my love for you is,*
> *how much I really love you . . .*

A young Chinese man sat down beside him and said:
     Are you going to London? No place like it.

The sound of another person addressing him
     sent a jolt through him.
     He stared, forgetting to even speak.
     The stranger looked about the same age as him, but taller.
     A square jaw. Longish hair fell into his eyes,
     eyes that were friendly and twinkling
     but with an indescribable edge.

The stranger asked: Are you prepared for the rain?
     Joshua forced a thin smile. Yes. I think I am. Are you?
     Of course. The man's Cantonese was heavily accented. West-
ernised. He crossed his legs.
     I was born there, said the stranger. I go back and forth often.
Is this your first time?
     Yes.
     Ah. University?
     Yes.
     You'll hate the rain, the young man said. But everything
else . . . Oh, I think you'll love everything else.
     This is my first time leaving Hong Kong, Joshua confessed.
Doing so felt like a relief.
     Oh, I know. The stranger laughed and quickly said: I mean,
I can tell. You look a bit nervous.
     Well, it's a big change, Joshua said. And change can be
unpredictable.
     The stranger grinned. I know. Isn't that amazing?

Joshua wanted to ask questions—

about the city he was heading to and

everything else that awaited him there. About where he could

find jobs or eat food that would remind him of the home he was leaving behind.

About how it would feel always to have the burden

of English on your tongue instead of Cantonese.

And whether this feeling of being torn in two would ever subside.

But more passengers around them got to their feet,

grabbing their luggage, their passports.

Joshua started to stand up too, slight panic rising in his chest.

But the young stranger quickly said: It's okay.

He put a hand out and the gesture drew Joshua back into his seat.

Look. The man pointed at the long line of passengers,

starting from the gate and snaking all the way to the back of the room.

You're good, he said. We still have time.

So the two young men sat and talked and laughed.

And by the time the plane took off and Hong Kong became

a maze of twinkling lights below him,

Joshua's resolve had transformed into a solid part of his beating heart,

steely, true, and winged.

Like hope itself.

PART TWO

一寸光阴一寸金
寸金难买寸光阴

AN INCH OF TIME IS WORTH AN INCH OF GOLD, BUT AN INCH OF GOLD MAY NOT BUY AN INCH OF TIME

TOMMY AND CHRISTELLE

2010

When Tommy and Eva were as young as seven, their father, Joshua, sat them down in the living room for their first lesson on "How to Use Our Abilities in a Responsible and Productive Way."

Their mother, Lily, sat perched on the arm of the sofa, sipping tea from a giant ceramic mug that she had made herself. Her job was to make sure that the children stayed focused. But with their father in such a mood—serious and forbidding—the twins were already too terrified to do anything but sit very still and try not to upset him.

Joshua had brought out the blackboard from his office and on it, he drew one long, straight line with the help of a ruler.

"Time," he told his children, "is a line very much like this one. The line does not bend or break or come back around in a circle or any of that stupid nonsense. You can't erase it. No matter what you do with your abilities, you must not try and change events that have already happened. It will not work. You can't change time."

"But you can play with it, maybe," said their mother, her eyes twinkling at their father. "But only if you're an adult, which neither of you are."

"You can't *play* with time," said their father in the same level tone, as though he had not heard his wife's teasing. "But you can duck in and out of it, which means that sometimes time can seem to go by very quickly. Or sometimes very slowly. Like this." He drew a much longer line underneath the original one. "Do you understand?"

The children nodded.

"Do you have any questions?"

They both shook their heads.

"It is our responsibility to always remember that this is how time works." Joshua pointed at what he had just drawn. "So whatever you do with your abilities, you must not mess with this. Do you understand?"

The children nodded again. Their father gave a nod in return, his brows still furrowed. He drew another, shorter line underneath the previous two.

"This is how time moves when you're in the past," he said. Then he pointed to the original line, the longer one. "And this is how it moves when we're together in the present. So again—"

"You can't change time," said their mother.

"You can't change time," agreed their father, nodding, "but you can learn to move with it."

Tommy has found himself thinking about that memory quite often since The Experiment.

In the months following November 2004, he would sometimes lie awake in the middle of the night, staring at the ceiling and imagining how his life felt very much like that very long, very straight line his father drew. Perhaps there is no end to the line, he thought. His father ran out of space with the blackboard, so in reality, it could go on forever and he was doomed to keep following it until he dropped dead.

Years later, when he is eighteen, he tells Peggy about what his father had said. They are sitting by the docks, him smoking and her scribbling in her notebook. It is a sunny day in London. The mist has lifted over the Thames so he can see Greenwich across the way. Flocks of seagulls swoop over the water, squawking and weaving between the funnels of the ships.

"That's one of the reasons why I like being here," Tommy tells her. "Time feels shorter when I'm with you."

But Peggy simply rolls her eyes. "That's your problem, Tommy," she says. "You can never stay in one place for too long. You want time to feel shorter everywhere."

———

In 2010, both Tommy and Eva start their respective university careers having spent their entire adolescence feeling as though the line is both short and long—short, of course, when they're off to the past, and long when school or life in general must be endured.

By the time Eva begins her course in fine arts at a semi-respectable London university, she has resigned herself somewhat to the fact that time will always be long. To her, anyway.

By the time Tommy follows in his mother's footsteps and begins his course in history at a semi-respectable London university, he has resigned himself to the fact that he will never be content with time being slow. Ever.

But it is here, at this semi-respectable London university, that he meets Christelle.

Christelle spots Tommy first. It is during their orientation: he is sitting in front of her, laughing and joking with friends he only just made an hour ago. She, on the other hand, is hungover from the night before. In front of her is a cup of tea from Tesco, a bag of salt-and-vinegar chips, one of her dad's chocolate croissants, and the pair of sunglasses a lecturer had told her she must remove.

Aside from them being the only two East Asian students in the room, she doesn't know why he grabs her attention, especially when she's in such a disorientated state. It is not because of his tall physique and striking features—he is definitely not her type—and it is certainly not because of his loud, overly friendly personality, which she finds annoying. All she knows is that she spends almost the entire hour observing him.

She notices how he smiles often and easily—to the new friends around him, to the girl in the row behind him, to the lecturer behind the podium—but the smile doesn't quite reach the rest of his face. He excuses himself to go to the bathroom and comes back with his eyes a little bloodshot, his hair rumpled, and his skin a shade paler. During the break, he slips outside with his new mates to smoke. He makes them laugh like he's known them for years. But he has this tick, this fidget; he is constantly looking around, tapping his left hand against his thigh or rubbing his right thumb across the bridge of his nose. Even the way he smokes—casually, effortlessly, almost like an afterthought—says something to her. He fidgets the same way, too, throughout the entire orientation.

But more importantly, the energy changes in the air around him, as though he is tugging along a shadow on an invisible string.

When you come across something you've seen before, Christelle thinks, you recognize it, despite yourself. Or at least it taps you on the shoulder, beckoning you to come closer and find out whether you're right.

And so, during their first class together the next day, Christelle sets her bag and her cup of tea down on the empty table right next to Tommy's. Her sunglasses are perched on top of her head, her hair hangs down to the small of her back in one thick braid, and she has on her favorite pair of jeans and boots. No longer hungover, she finally has the energy to explore her suspicions about him.

"Hey," she says. "This seat taken?"

He is sleeping with his head resting on his arm and he looks up, startled. There. Dark circles under his eyes. Something acute and thorny in his pupils tells her, yes, she's right: she's seen this before.

"Hi," he mutters, surprised. "No, no one's—"

But she's already pulling out the chair and sitting down. "I'm Christelle," she says.

"I'm Tommy."

"Yeah, I know who you are."

Christelle decides to take it slow. After just one conversation with him, it is obvious that Tommy knows himself just as well as the average eighteen-year-old boy does, which is to say, not very well at all.

They study together in the university library or at cafés. Sometimes they go for drinks or for nights out at cheap uni bars where the boys like to get a little bit too rowdy on the dance floor and where white girls either stare at her up and down or try to get her to dance with them.

Tommy is popular, she is not. But she doesn't mind it, really. Her mother had told her once: "As long as you know who you are, and you don't betray that, then you're doing well."

"You're Tommy's friend, aren't you?" the girls like to ask. "Can you introduce us?"

"You're fit!" the boys like to crow. "I wish my mates looked like you."

And she always rolls her eyes and brushes past them all like they're nothing but dust.

She tells Tommy about them afterward, sometimes when she's waiting for him to finish a cigarette between classes. Other times while they are outside a club on a chilly night. When he's drunk, he laughs about them. Says his twin sister, Eva, someone Christelle's never met, would think all of this—the parties, the popularity, this university scene—was just pointless.

But there are times when he would put an arm around her

shoulder to steady himself and say, "I'm fucking exhausted, Chris. Let's get out of here," and she would laugh in his face, relieved, and go with him to search for fish and chips, leaving everyone else behind in the suffocating room filled with flashing lights. One night, in the biting coldness of early December, outside a pub in South London, he puts his arm around her and says, "Chris, I think you're my best mate."

And so the days go on like this: they bend toward each other in friendship and she continues to notice all the signs that he is different—different yet so very similar. Everything she saw on the first day they met, but multiplied. She is reminded of something her dad once told her a long time ago: "Some people are a car crash waiting to happen, and sometimes there is nothing you can do to stop them."

———

They are supposed to do a group project together before they go on their Christmas break, and Christelle arrives at a café near his house exactly on time: eleven o'clock on a Saturday morning.

She ends up waiting for him for three hours. After noon, she begins texting him ferociously, wanting to know if he's okay but receiving no reply except for one very rushed, very apologetic "Running late, I'm sooo soooo sorry" at around one-thirty.

It is a little past two in the afternoon when he shows up looking like he hasn't slept for days and with a cigarette hanging from the corner of his mouth. It is not the first time. Usually, she would let it slide. But today, for inexplicable reasons, a switch flicks inside her mind. She can see the crash happening. She would be wise to leave it alone, she knows, but she has never been one for standing still.

She waits until he has taken his seat before asking, "Who do you think you are, Tommy? James fucking Dean? I couldn't get in touch with you at all and now you show up like this! A little bit inconsiderate, don't you think?"

Tommy winces. "Chris, don't yell." He puts the cigarette out in the ashtray and takes a large gulp of her tea. "I went out last night and I'm barely hanging on."

"Went out? Where?"

"Just out."

She rolls her eyes. "Do you think I'm stupid, Tommy?"

"Of course I don't, Chris."

"Then why are you lying to me?"

"I'm not lying," he says, but his eyes drop from hers a little. "Look, I'm sorry I'm late. Can you please drop it? I'm just hungover, that's all." He attempts a laugh. "It's not the first time."

"No, it's not," she says with annoyance. She studies his expression for a moment and then snaps her textbook shut. She's made up her mind: she is done with pretending. "Come on," she tells him. "We're going for a walk."

They end up at a nearby park. There are children playing football, one team in white uniforms, the other in red. Parents are pitchside, cheering, waving at the referee or engaging in jovial discussion with the coaches, one of them a tall, athletic man in his thirties in a slick black-and-gold Adidas tracksuit. A goal is scored, and everyone watches as the goalscorer performs a cartwheel and receives his congratulatory high five from the coach on the touchline.

Tommy and Christelle sit down on a bench some distance

away from the action. She doesn't know that Tommy feels something sharp tugging at his heart, that he doesn't quite know how to tell her that this is where he used to come to play football before It happened, that the coach over there in the cool tracksuit had showed up at his house three months afterward, asking Ah-ma if he might want to come back to training. In the end he didn't, of course. Obviously.

"I had an uncle and an aunt," begins Christelle.

Tommy cuts in: "Chris, we all have uncles and aunts."

"You're not listening. Shut the fuck up and let me finish."

He lets out a long breath. "So, your uncle and aunt?"

"Yes. The aunt was on my mum's side, the uncle on my dad's."

"And?"

"And they were just like you."

"Just like me?" He laughs humorlessly. "What do you mean?"

She sighs. "The same look in your eyes. The same energy. The same . . ." She sucks her teeth, searching for the right word. "The same patterns."

He laughs again, but this time the sound rings even more hollow. "What are you on about?"

"Tommy, what happened to your parents?"

"I told you. They died in a car accident."

She shakes her head, frowning. "I'm so tired of you pretending that everything's fine when we both know it's not. You're a fun person to be friends with, everyone loves hanging out with you. But no one knows you. Not really. And that's really fucking sad."

"Don't talk rubbish, Chris, you know loads about me!"

She groaned. "Don't play dumb, Tom. You tell me things,

sure, but not many things that really matter, and I'm sick of it, I really am, because that's not how I am with you. If you're not going to be real with me, then why are we even friends?"

"It's not like that—"

"Tommy, answer me this then. What happened to your parents?"

"Chris, leave this alone, I've told you—"

"I've been wanting to tell you something—"

"Whatever it is, I don't want to hear it." He starts to stand up, but she holds firm to his arm. "Nothing is wrong, everything is fine. For the last time, Chris. I. Am. Fine."

"I've been waiting for the right moment," she repeats, shaking her head. "And I've tried to be patient, Tommy, I really have. But you can be so in denial—"

"How many times do I have to tell you that I don't want to have this conversation?"

But Christelle continues like she hasn't heard him. "Ever since we met," she says, "I've been waiting to tell you." She looks him straight in the eye. "Tommy, you're not the only one."

Later, but not much later, Tommy takes Christelle down to the South Bank, to his and Eva's spot, where his parents sometimes took them for walks by the Thames. It is too cold to just sit, so they stroll around, looking at the lights and browsing the Christmas markets.

At first, the full extent of Christelle's revelation leaves Tommy speechless. For a while, he stands still, taking in the scenery with narrowed eyes and a thumping in his chest. Surely not, he thinks. It can't be possible. It's supposed to be just us. He didn't realize before how heavily the secret had weighed on him, like a constant black hole in the pit of his being. For one fleeting moment, he thinks of his sister, wondering what she would say.

Christelle tugs at his sleeve. "Do you have any questions, Tom? I'm willing to answer them."

He nods. "Yeah," he replies. "Let's talk."

As they walk on, Tommy starts bombarding Christelle with questions about her aunt and uncle, and his own tales about the travels he and his family have been on begin pouring out. But the more he talks, the more Christelle listens with a blank expression, her eyes mostly on the path ahead, and offering no reply.

Eventually, Tommy draws her to a halt as they reach Millennium Bridge. "What's wrong?" he asks her, flashing a playful grin. "Are you still angry with me?"

Christelle sighs. "No, not anymore."

"Then what?"

She is silent for a moment, thoughtful. Then she looks at him square in the face.

"I loved my aunt and uncle," Christelle tells Tommy. "We were very close to them. My father, especially, did not want to give up on his brother. But I see in your eyes what I used to see in theirs. We knew what they could do, but it was so obvious that it came at a price. We could all see it."

"See what?" he asks, bristling a little.

"That even when they were here, you felt they were somewhere else." She pauses to pluck his cigarette from his mouth; she has always disapproved and has never been afraid of letting him know. "Sometimes they would disappear somewhere for a

long period of time. I could hear my parents talking about it—
about how they couldn't bear to stay in one place or how they
were going to get themselves hurt. My father tried to beg my
uncle to stop. Or sometimes I would get to see them, but they
would just be . . . silent. Not there. Lost. I was a little girl and I
didn't understand. Where did they go when they disappeared?
And could I go there too?"

"But you couldn't."

"No, I couldn't." She gives him a sad look. "Sometimes it's
like that with you, too. I could see it in you the very first day we
met, although I wanted to be sure. But now, the more I know
you, the more obvious it becomes. You might have gotten away
with it with someone else, Tommy, but not with me. Not with
someone who's lived around it before."

For a moment, Tommy considers denying everything—calling her crazy or simply walking away, refusing even to entertain
the idea that there is a cost to his gift. But one look from her
changes all that. She looks at him the way his sister, Eva, does
sometimes—so surgical but completely genuine—and he feels
ashamed. So he tells her about what his father had said about
the lines.

Afterward she is silent for a very long time, before saying,
"Your dad is wrong, though."

He scoffs. Rubs the bridge of his nose with his thumb. "I
don't think that's possible. Whatever he was, the man was always
right. He had to be."

She shakes her head. She thinks it is tragic that he does not
know this. Does not seem capable of understanding. "The line
doesn't have to feel long here, Tommy," she says. "Not always."

JOSHUA

1987

September in London did not make Joshua miss home.

In many ways it should have, really, because everything was so very different: the weather, the people, the language, the food, the feeling, anything and everything.

He had been told that the gray skies and constant rain clouds would be a problem. But instead they had seeped inside his skin and made a home there, not very unlike the English he had been taught in school and was now trying to perfect. He got accustomed to the buses and the Tube relatively quickly. Learned how to navigate his way from his very small, very cramped and windowless one-bedroom flat in Chinatown to his university. The landlady, Madam Rose, was a friend of a cousin of his father's, someone his immediate family members in Hong Kong had never really met but knew of because she had married an Englishman and was now "living the good life in London."

The "good life" in question included running a decent-sized restaurant in Chinatown, where Joshua now worked four days a week, waiting tables and washing dishes in exchange for his extremely cheap rent. The other two days in the week, when he was not at university or in his room, traveling through the past and documenting his experiences, he was at the Chinese supermarket, working behind the till.

His mother called every once in a while, ringing the phone Madam Rose had installed at the bottom of the stairs that led up to the three stories above. She always asked him the same questions: Are you eating enough? When will we see you again? Are you paying attention in school and doing your homework? He talked to his maa-maa only once; she was becoming too frail, her hearing suffering as a result. He did not get to talk to his father or his sister, Dorothy, at all.

Madam Rose had two sons, both half-white and hand-some. She would brag often that, had they lived in Hong Kong, her sons would be celebrities by now. The eldest, Jonathan, had already finished university and had his own flat and a high-paying job in Central London. The youngest, Kevin, was around Joshua's age and occupied the bedroom directly below his. Kevin's room was significantly larger, with two windows and enough space for a bookcase, a desk, and a television of his own. Madam's husband, Gary, had another business (Joshua never quite knew what) and was gone for long periods of time, traveling to countries in Asia and coming home only at random hours of the night.

Joshua remembered the only thing his father had told him

after they had put him in contact with Madam Rose and her family: You are smarter than these people and you know how to work harder than them. So you must do better.

October in London.

At university, he was good. No, not just good. He was brilliant.

After he solved a particularly difficult math problem in front of the whole class, his lecturer leaned back against his desk and said, quite in awe, Well, Mr. Wang, whatever we've been expecting from you, it's certainly not *this*.

Something in the man's tone made Joshua feel like he should be offended. But he was getting quite good at the game now—as good as one ever could be in this situation, anyway. And so he plastered a humble smile on his face and said, Oh, it's really nothing. Anyone could do it. Math is the same everywhere.

But it wasn't, of course. Not really. At least not for someone like him.

While they were studying in the cafeteria between classes, one of his course mates, an Englishman by the name of Jamie, asked him: Which school did you go to? When Joshua hesitated, the man pressed on: I'd have guessed Eton, but that was my school and you weren't there. It must have been one of the other top ones or you wouldn't be *this* good. Although your accent . . . your accent makes me think maybe not.

Joshua did not even look up from his notebook. My school was in Hong Kong, he told Jamie. You wouldn't know it. All of us were taught to speak in this accent because we were too poor to learn the Queen's English.

Jamie looked stunned, unsure whether Joshua was joking. But Joshua did not care to elaborate.

Remarks like Jamie's, he came to discover very quickly, were not unusual. Not only did his Chinese features draw double takes, but whenever he spoke in his thick Hong Kong accent, people would have something to say. Like how good his English was, questions about where he came from, or tales about their last visit to either Hong Kong or China. A white customer at the Chinese supermarket, while paying for a bottle of soy sauce and a bag of rice, insisted on speaking with him in broken Mandarin, to "practice his fifth language." Sometimes, while walking down the road, teenagers would jump into his path and yell at him in mock Chinese—Ni hao, ni hao!—or pull their eyes back and laugh in his face.

He had to remind himself that he was not here to make friends. He was here to make a life. These were incidents he could live with. What was the alternative? If there was one, he could not imagine it. What was the use of being frustrated about things he could not change when he could ignore and navigate his way around them instead? Life, he reasoned, should not have to be harder than it already was.

———

November in London.

He explored the city by himself on a Sunday, walking all the way from Leicester Square down to Trafalgar Square, then to Buckingham Palace and back again. By dusk he was on the other side of the river, past the London Eye and along the South Bank.

He stood by the water where he could see St Paul's Cathedral across the way and lit a cigarette. A short distance from him there was a busker strumming on a guitar and crooning softly. A family walked past, husband and wife arm in arm, watching their little boy chase a football around. He felt the breeze toying with his hair, which was beginning to grow too long, and its touch, too, felt different.

He didn't miss home, Joshua realized, as he watched all the lights blinking across the river and the dome of the cathedral touching the pink sky. He could close his eyes and be home in a second. But this place, with all its unfamiliar, quaint habits, this place could be something.

December in London.

His very first Christmas.

When everything was shut down and the city was a ghost town, he did not leave the house. After he finished the leftovers he had saved from his shift the day before and worked on some of his assignments, he lay down on the floor, squeezed in between the bed and the door, and closed his eyes.

He remembered. And remembered.

But nothing happened.

After a while he got up and began pacing around the room. He took out a book from underneath his bed, flipped quickly through it and stopped at a photograph: Hong Kong in 1897. He stared at the photograph for nearly twenty minutes and then lay back down again.

He closed his eyes once more. Still . . . nothing happened.

A knock on the door. Then more knocks. He opened it and saw Kevin standing there in his cool, expensive jeans and Arsenal top. Mate, sorry to interrupt, Kevin said, making it sound like they were more mates than they really were. But your dad is on the phone.

His father told him down the line: Maa-maa slipped in the shower yesterday.

And that was enough. He knew.

The morning of New Year's Eve.

It had rained in the night, and he woke up to find frost gathering on his windowpane.

He had managed to attach a string to his grandmother's jade Buddha so he could wear it around his neck, hidden underneath his shirt. She was right, his maa-maa. She could be gone but not really be gone. He could see her any time he wished. How permanent can death be when you can bend time? Or so he told himself.

He dreamed about her sometimes. Or he thought he did. At least he thought they were dreams, for there was snow in them, delicate flakes drifting around his face and hers, but it had not yet snowed in London.

On that last day of December, he worked the entire day in the restaurant, starting in the front room and ending it in the kitchen, washing a mountain of dishes with two new waiters who had just recently come over.

When they were finishing up, Kevin strolled in. He was in his flashy clothes—blue jeans, combat boots, a white T-shirt, and a denim jacket—and his hair was neatly oiled back; a cigarette protruded from his thin mouth. His Cantonese was clumsily accented, like a shirt that fits your style perfectly but is a few sizes too small. Josh, mate, you doing anything tonight for New Year's?

No, not really, Joshua replied. I have assignments to finish.

I'm going to a party, Kevin said. Mum says I should ask if you wanted to come. To take your mind off your maa-maa. Sorry about that, by the way.

Joshua shrugged, picked up a cloth, and began wiping the kitchen counter. Thanks, he said. The jade burned a hole into his skin.

Well. . . Kevin avoided his eyes. Me and some mates from uni are going to this flat in Islington. You should come along.

It was so simple, that phrase: *You should come along.* There was really not much meaning behind it and, coming from someone like Kevin, it was imbued with little true sentiment. But years later Joshua would still replay it over and over in his mind as the moment his life truly started to change.

Two hours later, Joshua was standing outside a stranger's flat, in a strange part of town, smoking a stranger's cigarette while 1988 arrived in sips of vodka and clouds of marijuana smoke, the sky splitting open with fireworks.

And there was a girl.

A beautiful girl who was cold yet warm. Who was just as lost as he was, but in different ways. Who would be the reason why, from then on, the path ahead that he had thought was straight and narrow would become an open field, with yellow flowers swaying in the tall grass, an ocean of sun as far as the eye could see.

But first.

A little about the girl.

LILY

Lily Yu was born in 1969, the year of the rooster.

She came a few weeks early, while her father, Henry, was away from London working on an important case. Her mother, Carol, had been in a state of deep worry for the entire pregnancy.

Having gotten married at such a young age to a much older man, Carol already viewed sex as merely a mysterious and necessary endeavor. Sometimes pleasurable—particularly when her husband would say things to her as they lay entangled in bed that he would never say out of it—but ultimately a territory in which she was lost, as though she were stumbling around in the dark, trying to find the light switch. Therefore, the result of it—another human being coming out of her—felt like nothing more than an added embarrassment.

Carol lay awake for nights on end, trying to imagine

the baby's head emerging from her body. The blood. The screams. The excruciating pain that could go on for days. When Henry noticed how stressed she looked as the pregnancy progressed, he suggested that she rest more. But rest did nothing. For how could she get that frightening image out of her mind?

Yet for all Carol's worrying, when the time came, her daughter entered the world so easily and so unexpectedly. She could scarcely believe it. It was a miracle, she would later tell her friends. An auspicious sign of prosperity and luck.

It was a rare snow day in London. Almost all public transportation was shut down, and a thin layer of frost obscured every window in the house. Carol and her mother, Mary, were on the sofa in the living room when the contractions began. Carol started to panic, despairing at the fact that neither of them could drive and there was no way for them to make it to the hospital in time. It's too early, Mum, Carol kept muttering. Too early. We have to . . . call Henry . . . it's too early . . .

But Mary was an old hand at babies. When Carol was young, and mother and daughter had lived in Liverpool, many women in Chinatown would call for Mary when their time came. Carol would often accompany her and watch as her mother lay a gentle hand on these women's foreheads or grip their arm with a terrible firmness and urge them to push.

Now, when it was Carol's turn, her mother displayed the same calm as she took Carol's clammy hand in her own and laid her down on the bed. In a shrill voice, the older woman called for the maid to bring in fresh towels and hot water.

Breathe, my child, said Mary. Breathe. You're doing well.

It's too early, Carol said again. Mum, it's too early. Please . . .

Be brave, my dear, said Mary, kissing her daughter's forehead. This child is coming right when it's supposed to.

And sure enough, a while later, Mary caught her granddaughter as she slipped out from between Carol's legs, a fish finding water, gasping for air with fresh lungs. The baby's cries were sharper than anything Carol had ever heard.

Mary cut the umbilical cord, washed and dried the baby with the same extreme, calculated precision she had done everything else in her life. A girl, Mary said, like one would say, Oh, it's a nice day today, then placed the little bundle in her daughter's arms and retreated to the hallway to call her son-in-law. Your wife gave birth tonight, she told him down the line. A girl. She's small, but loud.

As though she had heard her grandmother, Lily began to scream once more. But this time she did not stop. Not even when Carol held her close to her chest, shushing her through exhausted but grateful tears.

———————

Growing up, Lily's father, Henry, paid for her ballet lessons, piano lessons, art lessons, and tennis lessons. Her bedroom, in their refurbished townhouse in Primrose Hill, was painted powder blue, and later, when she was a teenager, rosy pink.

At eight months old, Lily learned how to walk. At one year old, she learned how to use chopsticks. She could recite the entire English alphabet in crisp, beautifully enunciated Queen's English a few months before her second birthday. As a reward, her parents gave her a collection of children's chapter books with only a few illustrations and stored them in a brand-new mahogany bookshelf bought in Mayfair.

At five years old, she gave a piano recital in a grand hall with paintings of cherubs and angels on the ceiling.

At six, the painting she had done of the park from the top of Primrose Hill was hung up in her father's office.

At seven, she sat, straight-backed and serious, at the Ritz, indulging in afternoon tea with her parents and her father's colleagues and their wives.

You have such a charming little girl, Mr. Yu, one of those wives simpered to Lily's father, leaning forward to pinch Lily's cheek. My, what a little wonder you are. An absolute marvel.

A marvel: a china cup that never chipped. Polished and cold. Elegant. That's what they raised her to be.

But being a marvel was boring for little girls. This was what Lily learned so early on.

Her parents, too, were boring: immovable, detached, separated from reality. On rare occasion, the three of them would sit down for dinner as a family. Her mother was always chatty and insistent, trying, trying. Her father, jovial when he wanted to be, attempted to put on a show, but inside he was flailing.

Their house, too, was boring, big, and empty, despite all the expensively decorated rooms.

Her father was hardly ever there. Her mother sometimes was, but she was never the right kind of company. It was empty, too, on days when there was a tutor or a nanny. Grown-ups who looked serious and kept insisting on filling the empty spaces with cajoling sweetness: Lily, let's read! Lily, let's paint! Lily, let's sing and dance! Let's go outside and play with the other children!

The house was even boring and empty on those rare Sundays

when both of her parents were present, and they would walk Lily across the park to the London Zoo. She would stand between the two adults in pristine, expensive clothes, her shoes perfectly shining, and say hello to the bear in the cage.

And so, as the years dragged on, she wandered alone from room to room, trailing stardust in her wake—grown-up stardust, not the kind you've heard of in picture books and fairy tales—and learned how to make friends with the emptiness and morph it into something else. A dark seed, perhaps, or a stone that she hid in the crevices of her heart, like a time bomb.

Her father kept bringing Chinese paintings home and hanging them up next to hers for when company came. Look at the brushstrokes, he told her, pointing. Beautiful. You should learn to paint like this. You'd get far.

Her mother would remark often: You should pay for more lessons then.

And Lily would watch from outside herself, a hawk circling high up in the sky, looking down at its prey. How could there be so many things in the world for a little girl to do?

At eight, the little girl learned to shut her eyes to the big, empty house and float away.

There was a date
    scribbled on the back of a black-and-white photograph—
    January 14, 1950—
    in her ah-ma Mary's flowing handwriting.
    She found it hidden in the bottom of her mother's trunk.

The photograph was of Mary, holding her mother, Carol,
by the hand,
     a little girl with pigtails and a stern expression.

Lily stared at the date. Committed it to her childish memory.
     On a whim, she closed her eyes and made a wish . . .

Liverpool. By the River Mersey.
     A rare sunny day, the golden rays
     shining through the few clouds dotted in the sky.

She took a step forward.
     Breathed in the air, thick with fumes, sweat, something
bitter,
     and life, life, life.

And for the very first time in her very young existence,
     she tasted what the world could hold
     for someone like her,
     someone with such a largeness in her chest that,
     even when silenced,
     she could never stop screaming.

Around the time Lily began studying history at a university in
London, Ah-ma Mary moved in with her parents, who were
still living in the house in Primrose Hill.

     It was upon Carol and Henry's insistence. Ma, it is no longer
safe for you to live alone, Carol had said. Let us take care of you.

It's the way it should be. And so, just as the old lady moved into the guest bedroom down the hall from hers, Lily moved out.

Her father had bought a house on Kennington Road for Lily, close to the Thames. An old Georgian terrace with a tall tree in the front garden. In spring, the fresh green leaves fanned out like a canopy and Lily would lie on the grass beneath it, dreaming of far-flung places she had read about in books or visited back in time. In autumn, she crunched her way through the orange and brown leaves, as warm and earthy as a hearth fire on a cold day. In winter, she would look out from her window to see frost or snow gathering on the naked branches.

A home. At last. Even though it was not entirely hers, it was something that was her own.

More importantly, it was the perfect place for her to do what she did best: close her eyes, plunge briefly into darkness, and see history appear, bringing with it the feeling that all was right with the world.

Lily could go anywhere in England in the twentieth century as long as she had a specific place and a date in mind, and so she did. She wrote page after page of description, drew picture after picture, of British cities, people, and time periods—all that she had seen after the turn of the twentieth century. She heard what words were thrown out from policemen and bystanders when she walked from Hyde Park to Trafalgar Square during London's very first Gay Pride parade. She stood on the shores of Ramsgate, her feet sinking into the sand, as she watched the Little Ships return from Dunkirk. Her sharp eyes caught a small boy trying and failing to toss his hat onto the *Titanic* as he waited on the docks with his mother the morning that doomed luxury liner started its voyage from Southampton. During these trips, history became a real person to her—a lover who knocked on her door every night, begging to be let into her bed. She never refused him.

But at university, history was bland, stifled, her experience there made no better by the various men—young, middle-aged, old, it did not matter—making up excuses to put their hands on the small of her back, complimenting her eyes or telling her how gorgeous her skin was, how exotic. Or the white girls giggling behind their hands or regarding her with smug looks on their faces, their lips pressed firmly together in self-righteousness.

There were friendly girls too, but she'd find herself being fawned over, told incessantly how beautiful she was by girls trying to take her under their wing, include her in their clique. No matter how hard Lily tried (and she could never quite figure out why she tried), there was always a sheet of glass between them.

It was these friends who told her often: I think it's marvelous how different you are from all these other Asians. You really are special, do you know that? Your parents raised you right.

These remarks gave Lily a heady, indescribable feeling. Like when one has consumed too much sugar. Oh, I'm glad you think so! She always replied with a strained smile. I don't know about the others, but I'm just trying to be myself.

Yet afterward, when she was alone, her cheeks would flush with . . . excitement? Shame? Worry? Whatever it was, the feeling made her breath quicken and her skin crawl, as though something was always chasing after her and she was running out of time.

New Year's Eve. 1987.

Her first year at university.

Her friend from school, Pauline, called her up and invited her to a party at a flat in Islington. Daniel will be there, Pauline informed her giddily. He's been asking about you. The one from July, do you remember?

Of course Lily remembered. The blonde. A year or so older than her. A rower. Future MP. Pauline's boyfriend's friend. He and Lily had shared a kiss once, at another party. She had let him pull on her hair, bite the nape of her neck and, when they got back to his dorm, pull off her dress and guide himself into her mouth. She didn't fully enjoy the act itself, but when it was over, it gave her a deep, heavy satisfaction. They lay in his bed for a while afterward, smoking, and she thought of the bear at the zoo, the one from her childhood, and her parents standing behind her, telling her to read the information on the sign out loud.

Daniel had said that they would see each other again when he kissed her goodbye. That he would call her. But he never did.

She went back a few times to sit outside his window on that night and watch herself make him moan. She was powerful, was she not? Reckless? Free? A woman who knew herself and what she wanted? Her parents would be scandalized. The little girl she once was would be too. Somehow that felt right. And just.

And so she said to Pauline on the phone on that last day of December: Alright, I'll be there.

A few hours before 1988 arrived, Lily put on bright red lipstick and a long red dress with a plunging neckline. She arrived half an hour before midnight and, look, there he was: Daniel, with his megawatt smile, perfect hair, and startling blue eyes, basking in the adoration of his friends. Yet his arms were wrapped around a girl whose curly brunette locks were touching the bottom of his chin.

Immediately Lily recognized the girl as someone from her course—one of the ones with the plastic smiles and, like Daniel, the perfect hair. Nicola-something. Or Jane.

Pauline shot Lily a look from across the room: Sorry, I didn't know.

It should hurt more. And in many ways it did sting. But the relief was just as sweet.

Lily knocked down one glass of champagne, grabbed another and downed that one too, pulled her coat back on, and went outside.

The moon was high.

She stood by Pauline's dying rose bushes and lit a cigarette.

The music from inside the house pulsed in her ears, beating down on old promises.

Then there was a boy.

JOSHUA AND LILY

1987–1988

Can I have a cigarette?
　　The boy asked. I've somehow lost mine.

He spoke in Cantonese.
　　That, and the sight of him—
　　someone who was like her, even if not completely—
　　rendered her a little speechless.

He stared at her, confused. Then recognition dawned on his face
　　and he shifted to English: Don't you speak Cantonese?

I understand a little, she said. My parents and grandmother
speak Teochew.
　　But I don't know it that well either.

She handed him one of her cigarettes—the most natural thing she had ever done in her life.

She lit it for him. Watched his cheeks hollow as he breathed in.

He has a serious face, she thought, as he stepped forward and then back again.

Stern. A little unreachable. But determined. She liked it, she decided.

It made her feel safe.

She asked, Where are you from? Even though she could already guess.

He replied: Hong Kong.

What are you studying?

Maths. You?

History. Why math?

I'm good at it. And I enjoy it. Why history?

I understand it.

Doesn't everyone?

Oh, you'd be surprised. There are layers to it.

What sort of layers?

Aren't there layers to math?

Not to me.

She laughed. I would call you arrogant, but you said that as though it were a simple fact. Like, the earth is round or the sun rises in the east.

One plus one equals two, you know.

Ah. Absolute truths.

Aren't there absolute truths in history?

I don't know. You tell me.

Their eyes met for a few seconds and both looked away at the same time.

He cleared his throat. And you were—
    I was born here.
    Oh.

A brief silence. Not an uncomfortable one.
    Just light and glittering with possibilities.

She brought her cigarette to her lips once more and asked:
    Do you know anyone at this party?
    Kevin. Do you know Kevin?
    No. But I've heard of him.
    Really? From where?
    White friends who keep asking me if I know this other Chinese person they know.

He laughed. The sound was guarded and contained, like someone who did not laugh often and carefully dispensed his precious joy. She noticed how his clothes—jeans and an ordinary collared shirt—were a bit rumpled, as though he did not bother to make any effort. His leather shoes, too, were old and worn, peeling a little around the insoles. His hands were long and quick as he rolled the cigarette between his fingers, smoked it, pulled it away, flicked the ash onto the dirt, and took another drag.

Have I met you before? She asked, the question surprising her as it touched the air.

He considered it for a few seconds. No, I don't think you have. I would have remembered.

A teasing smile. Are we related?

He groaned. Oh, please don't say that.

Well, our friends here would say that that was a very good joke—

I don't really have *friends* here . . .

She pretended to study the rose bushes intently. Well, I hope you have at least *one*.

That drew another smile. I hope so too, he said. And you might be right. We might have met before.

Have you ever had those dreams when you—

Feel like something that's happening has already happened? She jumped in.

Yes. His breath caught in his throat. They locked eyes.

I have those dreams all the time, she said.

Me too. There was a playful quality to the shape of his mouth. Maybe this is one of those times.

She chuckled. Or this might just be two very lonely Asians at a very terrible party.

Or maybe that.

Then, from inside the flat, jubilant shouts: Twenty, nineteen, eighteen . . .

Their eyes snapped away from each other's.

She took a side step, reducing the space between them.

It's a nice night, he said. I like your dress.

She felt a sliver of a smile touch her lips. I'm surprised you can see it when I have this coat on.

He shrugged. I saw you through the window.

Ten, nine, eight, seven . . .

She decided to be bold: Do you want to dance? She asked, without looking at him. I mean, a little later?

Sorry, he said, I don't dance.

Three, two, one . . . *Happy New Year!!!*

Fireworks burst into life before them, illuminating the cars and houses lining the street in a shower of gold. Next an explosion of violet and orange and green starbursts. She felt the heat creeping up her cheeks, stinging unbearably.

She dropped her cigarette into the rose bush. Alright then, she said. And went back inside, leaving him there.

He stood alone for a few minutes, watching the fireworks. Then he shook his head, cast a brief glance in the direction she had gone, and started back home.

PEGGY

1937

Peggy's first ever memory was when she was a little girl and her father took her down to the quay one summer evening while the gulls were swooping over the water and the ships were coming in to dock. He had lifted her up and put her on his shoulders. She must have been only four or five years old—she could not remember for sure. All she knew was that she felt as free as a bird and thought that her father was the strongest, most amazing man in the world. Look, my little pea, he told her in Cantonese, pointing out over the waves. Look at how blue the sky is. And she had laughed her childish little laugh, waved her hands about, and tried to drag down the clouds with her pudgy little fingers. It's you and me now, her father said. You'll never have to feel alone as long as I'm here.

Her mother was not in the memory.

She was never in any of them.

Peggy first had a conversation with her father about her mother when she was six or seven. She had come home crying after a boy from Nanking Street called her names. At dinner time she sat sullenly at the table, ignoring the plates of dim sum and fried chicken that her father had prepared. He was spooning rice out of his bowl with chopsticks when he raised an eyebrow at her. What's wrong? He asked sharply. Why aren't you eating? She rubbed her eyes with her sleeve. Pa, what's a whore? She asked. Her father put down his bowl and scowled. Where did you hear that word? He demanded. A boy, she mumbled, looking down. What boy? His face was like thunder. Just a boy, she said. We are not really friends. But he told me that my mother was a whore. Is that true? I . . . I don't know what that means. Her father remained silent for the longest time. Then he shook his head, picked up his chopsticks, and continued eating. Your mother was a good woman, he said abruptly. So don't you believe what other people say. But what happened to her? Peggy asked. Another long silence. Then, without looking at her, her father said, No more questions about your mother. She's not coming back. That's all you need to know.

She's not coming back, he had said.

But she must be alive, Peggy thought.

Just out there somewhere. Waiting.

Now, her father is no longer the strongest man in the world. His left knee is damaged, the result of an accident by the docks when he was moving a shipment. He has to lean on a walking stick to get from place to place, and after a particularly harsh winter, he carries around a terrible cough that shakes his entire body and often renders him breathless. But he told her when his condition started to worsen: the café stays open. No matter what. And so, he limps around the place—barren, cold, old, with paint peeling off the walls—making tea, dim sum, greeting customers with a loud cackle and a warm smile. She chides him for exerting himself too much and does her best to do everything for him. You should be out there living your life, he tells her. Find a husband. Make me a grandfather. But she always laughs and says, You want the café to stay open, don't you? Who else can keep it running, old man, if not me? You? You can't even lace your boots without my help!

Mother, she finds herself thinking,
    if there was ever a time for you to come back,
    this is it.

Tommy smiles and laughs easily with her, but he comes and goes like the tide. Some days he arrives and he's a bit younger, other days he is there but a bit older. Every time it happens her world spins a little and, when their lips touch, she can feel a sharp needle piercing into her heart. She thinks of her father hunched over the stove, wiping sweat from his brow, then hobbling over to grab a tray, a fork, a kettle, anything. She thinks of the café door swinging shut in winter, but not before the snowflakes drift in, landing lightly on their wooden floor. Don't you ever think, she asks Tommy once, that we can't go on like this for much longer? He pauses, his fingers on her wrist jerking away. What do you mean? He asks. I mean, she tells him, I am tied to my world and you are not. So how can I be real to you? He stares at her, his eyes sharp as flint, and says, You're more real to me than anything in my world. Am I not real to you? She looks away. Mother, help me, she begs to the sky.

I don't know what to do.

———————

Peggy's father has never met Tommy. But Tommy catches sight of him sometimes and must feel like he knows him because Peggy has talked about him so much. She also tells Tommy all the dreams she has for them—all the things she longs to do so her father never has to work again. One day, after she has told him more of this, he becomes unusually quiet. What are you thinking? She asks. He hesitates. But he then says: I can make sure that everything you dream of is safe. She frowns: What do you mean? He gives her a look and she knows. No, she says immediately. No, Tommy, you can't. Panic steals into his expression. Peg, you don't understand, he says. Some things are coming. Where I come from, everyone knows. The entire world will change. You and your dad . . . you need to be ready because I want the two of you to be safe. I can't . . . I can't just let you go on and—Tommy, no. She repeats herself like a broken record.

I've thought about this and I can't let you. No matter what's about to happen, how dangerous or difficult it might be, you can't tell me. That's not how it's supposed to work. The future is the future. I don't ever want to know. Especially not about mine. Promise me. He tries again: Peg, if you would just listen. What's about to happen to the world is big—But she silences him with a look. If you care about me like you say you do, she tells him, you'll promise me this. Tommy, promise me. Please. He has no other choice: he cannot bear losing her. And so he promises.

Mother, she thinks while looking at him sleep,
       would you have asked the same?

Peggy reckons she is in love with Tommy. A young, foolish, hopeless kind of love, she knows. But love all the same. As for whether he is in love with her too, he has never said. But at this point, he doesn't really need to: their bond has become an unspoken pact. Still . . . Peggy thinks often of leaving everything behind. Just taking her father by the hand and escaping this place forever, never to come back. She will never see Tommy again, but when she thinks of what she wants—that cottage by the sea, her father healthy and whole, a different life—she wonders if it might be a price she is willing to pay. But what follows is a guilt so intense, she has to bite down on her lip to stop herself from crying out. Tommy will never leave her, she knows. So why would she ever contemplate leaving him? And then there is the dream: her mother, returned. The door of the café swinging open one morning, and in walks a woman. In this dream, their eyes meet across the crowded space and Peggy just knows . . . this is it. Her life has finally begun. Her mother has returned.

So, Mother, she thinks, how would you find me
    if I were to leave?

TOMMY, CHRISTELLE, AND MAY

2011

For Tommy, having someone who knows even just a little about who he is, is something precious.

Christelle is different from his parents and even from his twin sister. Yes, there are certain things she can never understand—the feeling of time-traveling itself or the way his mind can keep pivoting between the past and the present—but he can tell her things that he cannot tell his ah-ma or his sister.

Things like:

I think about my parents sometimes and I don't miss them.

I think about my parents sometimes and I miss them too much so I don't think about them at all.

I feel like I have to be strong for Eva.

I don't think I have the space for Eva.

It is easier in the past. In the past I am always moving.

I keep trying to stay here.

I keep wanting to go back.

I'm fine, really, I just need a minute.

Christelle tells Tommy she does not know why so many girls fancy him. He throws his head back and laughs. "I don't fucking know either," he says. "I have my charms, I suppose."

And Christelle rolls her eyes and asks if he fancies any of these girls in return. "Siobhan is nice, you know," she says, her eyes twinkling mischievously. "I did a group project with her once. She's smart. And she's fit."

Tommy shrugs. "I'm not really looking for a girlfriend."

Christelle scoffs. "Who said anything about a girlfriend? Asking a girl out on a date doesn't mean you're in a relationship with her."

"Don't let Diana hear you say that."

"Di knows what we're about—don't try to deflect." Diana is a girl Christelle recently just started seeing: a sweet, dimpled brunette who has a habit of saying whatever comes to mind, whether random or awkward. Unlike other girls Christelle has been involved with, Tommy has a soft spot for Diana and secretly hopes this relationship sticks.

Christelle steals Tommy's beer from him and takes a sip. They are sitting in a park and the sun is shining, the first stirrings of spring. "Go on then, out with it."

"Out with what?"

"Whatever else you haven't told me."

Tommy shakes his head, exasperated. But he does tell her, in the end.

He tells her things about Peggy—things he has never been able to tell anyone else.

Things like:

how beautiful she is,

her writing, her wit,

how he can spend time in her company in complete silence and still feel as though they have both uttered a thousand words,

how everything feels different with her, how it all feels right.

She is not like any other girl he has ever met.

"Not even me?" Christelle asks jokingly.

"You're a mate," he says, grinning. "It's not the same."

Christelle shakes her head, laughing a little. "It is very you, though."

"What is very me?"

"Being in love with a girl from the past."

Tommy corrects her quickly: "I'm not in love with her."

"Isn't obsession an aspect of love?"

"I'm not obsessed with her either."

She gives a wry smile. "Whatever you say." She takes another sip of his beer. "I wonder if she's still alive. How old would she be now?"

Tommy's expression shifts. "I've thought about that."

"And?"

"And . . ." He scratches his jaw absentmindedly, steals the beer back from Christelle, and takes a swig. "I've decided I don't want to know."

"Why?"

"I just don't."

"Tommy, have you thought about how this is ever going to work?"

"No," he says, very honestly. "That's why I said I don't want to know."

Tommy keeps expecting Christelle to ask if he can try and take her along on one of his trips.

To his surprise, she never does. And he has learned to stop asking about her aunt and uncle who were like him. There are certain things that his best friend doesn't want to share with him, and this is one of them. But he is too proud to acknowledge that he's hurt by it, so he pretends that it is just one of those "Christelle quirks," like how she holds her chopsticks like a pencil or how she never posts pictures of herself on social media.

His father, again, had been right: even when they try, it is impossible for other people to fully understand the time traveler's life. Their gift can be a lonely burden. "But it is imperative," Joshua had said, "that they never lose sight of the fact that it is also a blessing."

May arrives in Tommy's life a few weeks after he tells Christelle about Peggy.

His ah-ma Carol is the one who tells him about her: "I have a friend from my book club who moved back to Hong Kong. Her granddaughter is coming over to study English. I told her that you can help the girl settle in. Find time to go meet her. Take her somewhere nice. Buy her dinner. Show her around for the day. We have to look out for each other."

And so, like most things in their household, his ah-ma's words become law, and Tommy finds himself sitting in a café in Central London one day with a young woman who keeps blushing and avoiding his eyes.

May arrives in London alone at nineteen, a large sum of money newly deposited into her bank account by her parents.

She arrives with a reasonable grasp of English, two suitcases, a duffel bag—containing six pairs of shoes and three handbags—and ambitions to make something of herself in a country she has been obsessed with since she was a teenager.

May has never been a very social girl. Growing up, books were her best friends—stories that would take her far away from the very ordinary life she lived with her parents and her over-achieving, protective older sister. All the best stories, she has long since concluded, are set in England. Everything about the country fascinates her. Even the climate, the history, the unique idioms people use in the books she reads or the movies and television shows she watches.

After May finished secondary school, her mother suggested a gap year learning English in London, and it felt like destiny. She planned her itinerary to a T, packed her bags, and told her family that she would be seeing them in a year's time and there was no need to worry.

Her older sister, Anne, who had recently gained an MBA

diploma and a lucrative job offer, gathered her into a tight embrace at the airport and said, "I hope you have the best time, May, and that when you come back, you'll finally be ready to start life as an adult."

Their parents had nodded fervently in agreement, and so May decided to let her sister's comment slide. Her family would never understand if she told them that "life as an adult" is the last thing she wants. Her sister's path is already set in stone: impressive degrees, a high-paying job, a wealthy husband, and children. But May's future, ever since she opened those books and began dreaming of uncharted waters, lies elsewhere. She is sure of it.

May meets the boy Tommy out of respect for her grandmother. And a little out of loneliness.

A few days after she lands, he finds her on Facebook, sends her a friend request, and messages her immediately. She clicks on his profile picture: he's handsome, she thinks. There's no denying it. The knowledge scares her. More than a little. But something makes her type back a reply, saying yes, of course, she's so grateful for his help, and, yes, maybe they should meet.

She arrives at the café a few minutes late on purpose so she can peer in from outside.

He sits at a table, fidgeting, his gaze darting from his phone to the menu, to his watch, to something in the corner of the room that she cannot see. He is even better looking than in his pictures.

She pushes the door open and goes in, her head bowed.

She is pretty, Tommy decides. Soft features, slim, angular cheek-bones. Her long black hair is parted very squarely in the middle and falls to her waist, shiny and untangled. Her hands, one resting on her lap while the other plays with the spoon in her teacup, look soft. She can hold a conversation reasonably well. She is not Peggy; Peggy is full of intentions and straight-talking determination. But May has a quiet and gentle sensibility to her that he finds endearing.

From the very first moment they meet, she flusters around him, and her awkward, shy laughter sounds like tinkling bells.

"Your English is already so good," he tells her.

She blushes, and he feels a sudden urge to be as kind to her as he possibly can. The feeling surprises him.

Avoiding his eyes and smiling with embarrassment, she mutters, "You're very nice, but . . . but . . . I don't think I'm that good."

"Were you nervous about moving here?"

"A little," she admits. "It's scary because I don't know anyone."

"Try not to worry too much," he tells her gently. "You'll make lots of friends. You've made one already."

"One . . . ?"

"Me, of course!"

His eyes twinkle at her and he turns away to spoon more sugar into his tea. She steals a glance at him as he does; she finds she can only look at him when he doesn't see. A shining man, she thinks. Someone whom all the planets revolve around. Out of reach for her. Again.

"So." His eyes snap back to hers and she drops her gaze to her hands. "Where in London have you been to so far?"

"I saw Big Ben and Buckingham Palace."

"Ah. The essentials." Every time he smiles it brightens up

his face. Makes him appear even more dashing. "Have you been to Covent Garden yet? Or Oxford Street? You look like a girl who knows how to shop."

A warmth erupts inside her chest. "Really? What makes you say that?"

"Your whole look." He gestures at her outfit with teacup in hand: a suede spring coat, black ankle boots, fuchsia-colored dress, and tights. "You dress with style—I really like your boots. Are you excited about the shops here? Most people who come over usually are."

"Of course I am!" Her face breaks into a lovely smile. "I just . . . prefer going shopping with friends, that's all."

"Oh, well . . ." He looks thoughtful for a moment. "What are you doing next Saturday?"

"Nothing."

"I'll take you shopping next Saturday then."

"You don't have to—"

"Oh, come on! It'll be fun! And have you been to the London Eye?"

May shakes her head, speechless.

The thought of Peggy flickers in the back of Tommy's mind, but something daring takes hold of him; he cannot explain why. As he looks at May—at her pretty, unjaded smiles, her adorable bashful expression—he can feel loneliness rolling off him like raindrops. The last thing he wants to do right now is make his way back to his ah-ma and his silent bedroom. So he makes a choice.

"Well . . ." He grins. "How about we go now?"

He takes her on the bus and they arrive at the London Eye in the late afternoon. The area is packed with tourists, but he urges her to pose for pictures. He buys her an ice cream and points out all the interesting museums in the area. He teases her and makes her laugh. She thinks this is the best day she's had in London, while he marvels at how peaceful it is to know that this day—along with all its little moments that have made him feel alive—need not be rushed. He finds his gaze lingering on May as she gasps at a street busker who's twisting his limbs into impossible angles, the way her entire face opens up with awe.

When they get tired from strolling aimlessly, they sit down on a bench a little way from the Eye. He begins asking her questions about her life—what her interests are, what her friends are like back home, and even what she dreams about when she is alone.

She tells him about the plan: finish her language course in London, find a job, and build a life here in the UK. What she leaves out, however, is her secret hope of finding love. That is a detail she does not dare utter. What if she says it out loud and jinxes it? Especially when his eyes are fixed on hers so intensely.

Before he can stop himself, he has asked her, with a playful smile, whether she has a boyfriend. She blushes and tells him of the only boy she has ever loved. Unrequited, from afar, for six long years. A family friend she has known since she was very little.

Tommy looks surprised. "Six years. Wow," he says in awe. "Do you guys still talk?"

She shakes her head. "No, I'm . . . I'm over that."

"Good."

He gives her a firm nod, and she glows under his approval. She tells him more about things from home she misses—mainly the food and speaking in Cantonese. But she also shares with him a belief that she has held since she first wanted to come to England, a belief that feels almost like longing: that by being here, she will, for the first time in her life, become visible, herself.

"I'm sorry," she stammers, blushing and looking away. "I must sound crazy. I don't . . . You must think I'm crazy."

"Oh, don't be sorry," says Tommy, laughing easily. "It's not crazy. I completely understand what you mean."

"You do?"

"Oh, absolutely!"

"I thought you'd make fun of me! Or think I'm being . . . 'unrealistic.'"

"Oh, no, not at all! Why, do others think that?"

"Some of my friends. My sister."

"Well, they just don't understand. There are some things"— for a second he has a faraway look in his eyes—"let's say, some things only a few people will understand about you."

She beams. "This is the most I've spoken to anyone in more than a week."

"That makes me happy," he replies, mirroring her grin. "If you ever need anything, you can always call me. I'll be there."

He is surprised to find that this is a promise he wants, more than anything, to keep.

———

May makes her way back to her place that evening with a smile on her face.

She was right: this is where everything will start for her.

She considers calling and telling her big sister about it,

just so there's someone she can share this moment with.

But she already knows the questions Anne will ask:

What job does he have? What kind of family does he come from?

Is he the sort of guy that'll marry you, or will he just date you for fun?

So, instead, May chooses to dwell on the twinkle in Tommy's eyes, his smile.

Replaying every single detail of the day they have just shared.

Imagining what it would feel like if his smile were one day to touch hers.

Maybe. Just maybe, she thinks. You never know.

Tommy texts May the minute he gets home: "It was nice meeting you! I had fun today, let's do it again sometime."

Then he tosses his phone onto the bed and makes his way downstairs to rummage for food in the kitchen.

Later that night, he checks to see her reply: "Thank you for showing me London! I had fun today too. I would love to hang out again."

He finds himself staring at her text with a mixture of emotions he cannot quite name.

A split-second longing for Peggy, so intense it feels like sadness.

Yet an unspeakable thrill at the memory of the day by the London Eye.

His fingers hover over the keys as he contemplates: is there a point to this?

But before he can come up with a definite answer, he is already composing a reply.

She reads it only a few seconds after it is sent. An invitation. Then . . . more typing.

Maybe. Just maybe, he thinks. It'll be nice to have a new friend. You never know.

Christelle tells him straight to his face once: "I don't envy any girl who fancies you."

EVA

2011 / 1994

Eva loves in colors:
    warm gold, light blue, and red like a sunrise.
    Dark green, neon pink. Yellow, bright like a sunflower.

Her mother had told her ever since she could hold a brush:

"Choose colors that make your heart burst, my dear," and so,
    after that November, most of what Eva paints is
    black-and-white. Sometimes dark blue and gray to match
    the rain falling outside, the rain drizzling inside.
    She misses the other colors occasionally, when the heaviness in her head
    becomes almost unbearable. But at least, she tells herself,
she is still

drawing and drawing and drawing. What else is there for her to do?

Her ah-ma Carol tells her repeatedly:

"Your mother would not want you to draw all the time."

Her classmates at university throw her curious glances and ask:

"Do you want to come out with us sometime?" But she always declines.

Her professor looks at her portfolio through narrowed eyes:

"You have a very unique style. But I don't feel the intention behind your art."

And she bites her bottom lip, keeps quiet, comes home, and lies down on the floor in the middle of her bedroom, dreaming, listening to voices from the past that keep whispering, whispering,

until she shuts her eyes to her life and wakes again when the world and its colors are slightly different from her own.

Her ah-lao-ma Mary, standing by the sea, wishing.

Her mother, Lily, sitting on Primrose Hill, dreaming.

Monsters, sometimes. A stag with three eyes, a gaping mouth.

A unicorn with two horns. A stone griffin. A bear with claws for eyes.

"I think you should get out more," Tommy says. But she shakes her head,

closes her eyes, hears the voices in the back of her mind calling her name,

and there are faces again: a young Chinese man in a boat, rowing for his life.

Another young man out at sea, staring into the eye of a storm.

An old woman lying in bed, gasping for breath, dying.

And she picks up her pencils and brushes and—Goddammit, why won't the colors return? But at least she is drawing, drawing, drawing.

"How do you cope with it?" she asks Tommy on one of those rare nights

she sneaks into his room and hides under the duvet to talk.

"Cope with what?" he asks.

She gives him a look and he shrugs.

"Oh," he says. "It's different for you, I suppose. I don't hear all these voices."

"Why do you think I'm the only one who can?"

"Probably because you're mental."

She rolls her eyes. "Is now really the time for jokes?"

"Oh, I wasn't joking when I said you're mental."

She hits him in the arm. "Can't you be serious for just one minute?"

"I don't know, Ev." He shakes his head. "Everyone is different when it comes to this thing. You, me, Mum. Dad. I've stopped trying to understand why."

"Mum always said that there's something important for you to discover in your travels. That's why you keep returning to the same time period. Do you think that's true?"

Her brother shrugs. "I don't know. Mum gave me too much credit sometimes. Dad thought it's just because I'm not good enough to go anywhere else."

"That's not true."

"Well . . . who knows? At this rate I think Dad might be right."

"You don't know that. Maybe you just . . ." She scrunches up her face and adjusts her large-framed glasses. "Maybe whatever it is you're supposed to find, you haven't found yet."

His expression becomes more solemn. She has never seen him like this before. Almost frozen, like he is carved in stone.

"I don't know," he says again. "I might have . . . I just . . . I don't know."

She decides to leave it. After all, there isn't much for either of them to know anymore.

Sometimes, she thinks, as she puts pencil to paper and begins drafting a thorny rose,

she has already known the darkest secrets life has to offer. There is now nothing new in the world.

It is getting harder to leave the house, even her room.

University is no longer the fresh and exciting adventure she had dreamed of as a child;

how can she go into an art studio with strangers and expect to splash colors onto a blank canvas?

How can she possibly make gold feel warm again? Or make red vibrant? Make black

dark and bold? Even by herself, in her room, the lines she draws are starting to blend into

the scenes and the faces she keeps seeing in her dreams.

She hears her ah-ma calling from downstairs: "Eva, don't you have to go to class?"

But she ignores it. Pulls the duvet over her head and, with the light from her bedside lamp,

begins to trace the outline of her mother's face.

Sometime later, there's a knock.

Tommy appears in the doorway. She peeks out at him from under the covers.

"Did Ah-ma send you?" she asks.

Tommy nods. "You're making her angry," he says. "You're scaring me too. A bit. Just"—he scratches the back of his head—"pull it together."

"What do you mean?"

"Just pretend." He shrugs. "Ev, it's not that hard."

She thinks she has already said this before, but she says it again: "Tommy, I'm not you."

After the portrait of her mother is done, she drifts off into darkness.

Someone is calling her. This time it is someone new; she can feel her heart beating out of her chest.

Warm air. A sharp scent in the breeze. Metal, perhaps. Or rain. Something cooking over a fire.

She hears Cantonese. She opens her eyes, looks straight up at the sky, and sees the sun.

To her left and right are restaurants and shops with signs written in curving Chinese;

she is on a crowded Hong Kong street in the middle of the day.

She moves off the road and into an empty alley, waiting,

looking down at herself as she begins to appear. There is light shining somewhere.

A light that does not come from the sun, but from deep within.

She turns, and there, at the other end of the tiny street, a young woman.

She looks to be around the same age as Eva, a little older.

A round face framed by a stylish bob and a warm look in her eyes

that makes the breath catch in Eva's throat.

She stops as she spots Eva. Hesitant, but curious.

There is something stirring in the air and both can feel it.

Who are you? The woman asks in Cantonese.

The question sounds like: I've been waiting for this moment all my life.

Eva takes a step forward and gives the woman her name.

A look of recognition passes across the stranger's expression.

Do you know me? Eva asks. Her Cantonese is clumsy, but for the first time, it feels right dropping from her lips.

I might, says the woman. She, too, steps forward. You look so much like him.

Eva's head spins. Like who?

My big brother, the woman replies.

Later, much later.

They walk beside each other down the road, talking.

There is so much to talk about. So many things to explain.

Too many impossible things, too many clues to be solved.

They stop at a restaurant and sit at a table outside,

the humidity making sweat gather on Eva's brow and neck.

Aunt Dorothy orders her char siu with rice and an iced tea with lemon.

How are you not more surprised? Eva asks.

Your father has always thought that he's so clever, Aunt Dorothy says. But I have always been good at discovering his secrets. It's what little sisters do. I knew something might happen. I've had an inkling. I just thought it'd be him who comes back.

Eva's eyes drop to her plate. Maybe he still will.

How is he whenever or wherever you are? Asks Aunt Dorothy. We don't hear from him much. You must be—what?—two or three years old right now. But the only photograph I've seen of you was when you were just born. Mum keeps wanting him to call more often. We don't know anything about how he's doing. Nothing about you and your brother, his wife . . .

He's . . . The truth sticks in Eva's throat. Aunt Dorothy, there is still so much I have to tell you.

Later, much later.

After the tears and the disbelief and the shock,

with the grief still fresh in her aunt's eyes and in every line of her young face,

Eva asks: How did you find me?

The other woman gives a sad smile. I think you were the one who found me.

But why haven't I found you before now? I've been traveling for years.

I don't know how all of this works, my dear. But maybe . . . Aunt Dorothy reaches out and tucks a lock of Eva's hair behind her ear. Maybe you need me right now. Maybe we need each other.

Their hands meet across the table and Eva realizes,

Oh, this is how it feels to have someone to cry with.

Warm white. Light brown. Gold, crackling like Christmas lights.

Dark gray. Bright orange. Silver, like her mother's earrings.

JOSHUA AND LILY

1988

Timing is imperative when it comes to love. Lily had always believed this. Meeting the right person does not matter if the circumstances are not aligned, if both of you are in different stages of your lives. You might be entangled for a while—sometimes even for longer than a while—but eventually the wires will always get crisscrossed or severed. It is inevitable. Timing, Lily always said, gives love wings.

If timing had not cooperated, she would not have decided to go to that New Year's Eve party at Islington on the last day of 1987. She would never have stood outside, smoking by Pauline's rose bushes, and met Joshua. A month or so later, if timing had not been on her side, Pauline would not have suggested going for Chinese after class one evening, and they would not have ended up in the restaurant where Joshua worked, exactly when he was working. Lily would not have worn her yellow dress, her turquoise earrings, sat down at the table with her friends, and almost gasped when he walked briskly over, a notepad and pencil in hand, ready to take their order. His eyes swept over her face and then he said . . . he said . . .

Just one small change—she and her friends could have gone somewhere else, he could have been assigned a different shift, her mother could have birthed her a week later, she could have taken a wrong turn down a road once—and their love would never have materialized.

But Joshua would disagree.

Love, Joshua said, does not hinge upon timing. Instead, the opposite is true. Why fear time when fundamentally it is what you make of it? If he had not agreed to go with Kevin to that party in Islington, if Lily and her friends had not shown up at his restaurant a month or so later, love would find other ways to bend time to its shape, to its design. Other things would have fallen into place. On a different day, perhaps, under a different sky. They would eventually meet, their lives intertwining and molding into one; fate makes it inevitable. She might even be in the same yellow dress, with turquoise in her ears, her face lighting up in surprise as their eyes meet, and she would say . . . she would say . . .

Oh. It's you.

He arched an eyebrow, paused on her face for a second, and then it was over. Are you guys ready to order? He asked Lily's friends.

Lily recalled how their last conversation had ended and

wished nothing more than to sink into the floor. Pauline narrowed her eyes. Do you guys know each other? She asked, her gaze shifting from Lily to Joshua.

Lily shrugged. We met at the New Year's Eve party.

Oh, said Pauline's boyfriend, Harry. I thought you might be related.

Joshua frowned; Lily could sense him tensing up. Why did you think that? Asked Joshua. The look he gave Harry was one of insolence.

Harry looked alarmed. I meant nothing by it! He said.

Joshua smiled thinly. Clearly you meant—

Oh, for fuck's sake, said Sam, one of Harry's uni friends who had invited himself along. His fingers brushed against Lily's knee under the table. Can we just order and be done with it?

Joshua took their order in a clipped but efficient manner. His gaze did not linger on Lily again as far as she was aware, for she made a point not to look either. But she could feel her cheeks heating up under the yellow fluorescent lights.

After Joshua went away, Sam turned to Harry, shaking his head. The service here is horrendous, he said. We should have gone somewhere outside Chinatown.

Lily recommended this place, said Pauline, almost apologetically.

Oh, you did? Sam turned to Lily. I'm sure it has its perks. I can see why you like it. But personally, I prefer a more . . . relaxing dining experience. He gestured at their surroundings—Asian customers chatting and eating, the sounds of chopsticks against porcelain, waiters shouting in Cantonese—and she felt something akin to humiliation tugging at her insides. But I suppose you know best, Sam said. Flippantly. Indulgently.

Harry squeezed Pauline's hand. You're right, he said. It's a bit chaotic in here.

Pauline gave an assenting nod. Well, hopefully the food won't take ages to arrive.

Lily took a sip of her tea.

A little later, Joshua arrived with their food. He carried four plates—two in his hands, two balancing expertly on his fore-arms. He recited the dishes to them in a bored, robotic tone: Peking duck, sweet and sour chicken, egg fried rice, stir-fried beef in black pepper sauce.

More tea, said Harry, lifting his half-empty cup.

I'll get you more tea, said Joshua.

This duck shouldn't have taken this long, said Sam, pick-ing up his chopsticks. "It's supposed to be an appetizer. If you want us to tip you . . .

Lily's face burned. Sam, it doesn't matter—

Of course it matters, said Sam. We're paying customers and—

The duck is a main dish, Joshua cut in. And you don't have to tip me if you don't want to.

Can I also get more tea? Asked Pauline.

For Lily, that dinner seemed to last an eternity. Later, she would not be able to recall what she said to her friends or what the food tasted like. She spent the entire time wishing she were somewhere else, and that Joshua was not moving around the room, judging her for her friends' terrible behavior.

When it was time to pay, she breathed a sigh of relief that it was another waiter who brought them the bill. She cast her eyes briefly around the restaurant and spotted Joshua at another table, taking orders. His back was turned to her, but she noticed his tense shoulders, his curt nods. How intently he scribbled orders on the notepad, flicking the pencil between his fingers and then lodging it behind his ear. She ripped her eyes away from him when Sam brushed his fingers against her hand. Let's get out of here, Sam said. Anyone fancy a drink?

Lily stood up and said she needed to use the bathroom.

She ran into Joshua on her way back to her friends, at the junction in the corridor leading to the dining room in one direction and the kitchen in the other. He was heading toward the latter, balancing empty plates and cups.

I'm sorry, she said immediately, not quite knowing why.

He shrugged. For what?

She felt the need to explain: They're not all my friends.

He shrugged again. I meet these kinds of people all the time. It doesn't bother me.

It doesn't? she said dubiously. Don't feel you have to be polite. You can be honest.

I am being honest. I just didn't think you would be friends with them, that's all. But it also makes sense.

She was not sure if he was simply being playful. But the jab put her on the defensive. You could have at least tried, she said.

I'm their waiter. Not their friend.

She chuckled dryly. You could have tried in general.

Something flickered in his expression. What do you mean?

At the party, I asked you if you wanted to dance.

I don't really dance.

But like I said: you could at least try.

His eyes dropped away from hers. I need to get back to work.

Yes, I'm sure you're very busy. Then the question slipped out before she could stop herself: But how are you?

He looked caught off guard, as though he had not been asked that question in a while. I'm . . . alright, I suppose, he replied. Work. School. Nothing special. You?

Classes are boring.

History, was it?

Yes. Math?

Yes. He smiled a little, and the gesture tugged at the corner of her own lips, as persuasive as sunshine. But I should . . . I really should get back to work.

She blushed. Oh. Right.

Their bodies began angling away from each other, cleaving apart. I'll . . . She paused, her right hand drifting to her left elbow, caressing it. I'll see you around.

He nodded and then was gone.

The cold bit into Lily's skin as she stepped outside the restaurant minutes later. She pulled on her coat and adjusted her maroon scarf. She felt unsteady on the cobblestones, even though she wasn't in high heels. Sam offered his arm, but she pretended not to see it.

Lily, said Pauline, looping her arm through her boyfriend's, Sam's taking us to this bar he knows in Soho. Come with us.

Thanks, but it's late, Lily heard herself say. I think I'm going to head home.

There was a dripping pipe jutting out from the side of the building. On his break, Joshua leaned against the wall near it, smoking, and watched as the water dripped, dripped, dripped onto the stone. The moon was half hidden by clouds, winter stretching itself across the sky. He had the coat he'd found among Kevin's old things wrapped tightly around him, and his breath mingled with the smoke, curling and twisting in the air before him like some crazed puppet show.

It had been hours, but he could not shake the feeling. It was a new one: like a hook sinking into his heart, and then pulling. He could not explain it nor comprehend what it was. He was a rational man, but unlike the time-traveling trips and the theories he had written down in his notebook, there were no hypotheses for him to turn to with this. No logic. He only knew that it was a complication of sorts. A discovery.

He sighed, giving up. The toes of his left sneaker dipped into a small pool of water. His cigarette butt followed. He turned, about to head back inside, when a movement out of the corner of his eye stopped him in his tracks.

Oh, he said. It's you.

It should not have made any sense, but of course it did. They were always going to meet again whether here, the past, or their future: what else was there to do?

She stepped closer, her expression as still but as open as he remembered from earlier in the evening. But she was not wearing the same yellow dress; she was in jeans, thigh-high boots, and a long brown coat over a deep maroon sweater. She had silver in her ears, and her hair, which she had put up in a high ponytail, was now cut shorter, brushing against her shoulder blades. Her eyes—older, wiser—shone in a way he somehow recognized.

The hook in his heart sank in deeper. They considered each

other for a moment, and he realized the truth—that they were the same—and his entire world shifted.

She smiled. Go after me, Lily said.

And so he did.

EVA

1994 / 2012

Eva talks in colors:
> green, rich, and vibrant; melancholy blue; red, like flames.
> She talks the way she paints:
> messy but precise, uninhibited, real.
> And her aunt Dorothy listens the way her mother used to.
> The way her father never did.
> And perhaps that is why Eva keeps on talking and talking,
> and the questions keep on coming:
> Aunt, what has Dad told you about us?
> What is your mother, my maa-maa Jiayi, like?
> What are you like? What was Dad like, as a child?
> Am I anything like him?

Most of the time Dorothy answers.

She tells stories the way she loves the people in her life:
warmly, meticulously, wisely, with liveliness.
The way her own mother was afraid to.
The way her father never knew how to.
And the more stories she tells,
the more her heart opens
and memories come pouring out,
both the happy ones and the ones she thought
she had forgotten or shelved away.

But there are some questions that cannot be answered.

Territories that cannot yet be crossed.

Not when Dorothy is still grieving a brother who,

in her world, has not yet died—events Eva was forced to relay

with tears in her eyes. Dorothy's mother, Jiayi, will be heartbroken,

even though she has already been heartbroken since the day
Joshua left all those years ago.

Dorothy does not know how one can ever be prepared for heartbreak.

She cannot decide if it is worse to not know or to know and not be able to do anything about it.

Why is it that time is always running out?

Eva's voice is laced with guilt: I didn't think . . . I didn't want to cause you any more pain.

I'm so sorry, I think I've messed everything up.

And Dorothy has to shake her head and comfort her niece by saying,

You didn't mess anything up. Some things are meant to be.

We just have to learn to live with it.

One day, while they are talking over cups of fragrant tea,
    Dorothy asks Eva: How is your brother doing?
    Eva is surprised. They have not talked about Tommy much,
if at all.
    Mostly their conversations are centered around Joshua, Lily,
    and their childhood years, which Dorothy considers unim-
portant but mean everything to Eva.
    Tommy's the same, Eva says, shrugging. He goes to uni.
Hangs out with his friends. I don't see him very often.
    Does he still travel?
    Of course he does.
    As often as you?
    Eva grows quiet. Thinks about the question for a few
seconds, then: I don't know. With him . . . sometimes it's hard
to tell. He hides it very well . . . when he wants to.
    I wish I could meet him.
    I wish you could too. But Tommy . . . Eva frowns. Tommy
is . . . complicated.
    Everyone is complicated, Aunt Dorothy replies. That's just
how people are. Is Ah-ma Carol still angry with the two of you?
    Ah-ma is always angry.
    They both sit for a while in the comfortable silence, sorrow
that hasn't yet sunk in
    pooling around them like an overflowing river.
    Aunt, says Eva, I don't know what I'd do if I hadn't found
you. You were right. I needed you.
    A change in Aunt Dorothy's expression, like a light being
flicked on.

Maybe I'll need you, too. She takes her niece's hand. When the time comes for me. Will you be there? Will you come to me?

Eva tells Tommy her decision at their spot by the river, outside the Globe Theatre, overlooking the ivory-colored dome of St Paul's Cathedral. It is evening, and the South Bank is buzzing with people: tourists, office workers on their way home, buskers, and street performers.

A group of children are nearby, blowing giant bubbles that expand and then pop softly in the spring breeze. Tommy leans against the railing and lights a cigarette. He smokes it while she explains. Then his eyes narrow. He stands in silence for a very long moment and then says, "Ah-ma Carol will not like this."

Eva has the answer ready: "I'm not doing it to please her. And when it comes down to it, she cannot stop me. This is my life."

"And what about uni? Are you sure you want to quit?"

"If I want to come back, I'll come back. She casts her eyes to the Thames. "But I can't paint here. Not like I used to. Not right now."

His gaze can't seem to settle on hers; it keeps drifting off to the Globe, the Millennium Bridge, and the London skyline. She looks at him and suddenly thinks: *Oh . . . maybe . . . is there something new he wants to tell me?* But then his eyes find hers again.

"You should go," he says. There is a broken layer underneath his words that she has not been expecting.

"Tommy—"

"I've seen how hard it's been for you. You should go."

She wants so badly to grab his hand. "Will you be okay? Without me, I mean?"

He gives a dry laugh. "I've been waiting for this moment all my life. You're fucking annoying, do you know that? It'll be nice to not have you around for a bit."

And so the moment passes. She punches him playfully in the arm. "You'll miss me when I'm gone."

He wraps an arm around her shoulders and pulls her into an embrace. "Oh, come off it," he says. "Don't go thinking you're all grown up now just because you're traveling to the other side of the world. In my eyes, you'll always be my little sister."

But Ah-ma Carol stares through Eva with unseeing eyes.

"You are making a mistake," the old woman says. "There is nothing for you there. Everything you have is here. One day you will see that."

Eva does not have the heart to tell her how wrong she is.

Instead, she goes over and kisses the old woman on the cheek, feeling her grandmother's incredibly soft skin against her lips for a brief second.

"I'll miss you, Ah-ma," she says.

A tiny movement: the old woman's hand lifting to touch Eva's arm and dropping away.

"Take care of yourself," Ah-ma whispers.

It is only Tommy who comes to see her off at the airport and hug her goodbye. Hours later, she won't be able to recall any of their parting words. Only the safety of her brother's embrace and the sudden surge of emotion that rises within her, making her doubt, for the very first time, whether she should be leaving.

She turns around to get one last look at him: he lingers near the long line of passengers clutching their passports and boarding passes, his hands in his pockets, teetering uncertainly on his toes. When he spots her looking, he raises a hand in farewell and smiles. The smile she can conjure in her mind's eye in an instant at any time. But then the line moves and he is gone.

She sleeps for almost the entire flight, with the airplane blanket covering her face and body like a cocoon. When she is awake, she draws in her sketchbook places in London that she loves and knows she will miss: their house on Kennington Road, her and Tommy's spot by the river, Camden Town, the skateboarding park near the National Theatre.

As her hand moves and the places come alive at the tip of her pencil, she feels an odd pang in her chest, as though she is already remembering a scene from another life—a life lived by a completely different person. Another Eva, who is younger, brighter. Who paints pictures with colors from the biggest palettes she can find.

Nostalgia is tricky like that, she thinks, as she accentuates the ripples in the River Thames. Sometimes it even makes you miss things you haven't truly lost.

The plane begins to descend . . .

She pushes up her window shade and is greeted by the clouds.

She looks down and, oh my,
her breath falters.
The sun is shining over Hong Kong,
and she has never seen the sea so blue.

Everything is glistening below her:

a new day.

She smiles.

This, she has a feeling, is going to be a very good trip.

TOMMY, CHRISTELLE, AND MAY

2012

Christelle's mother, Chanice, is a primary school teacher. Her father, Roger, is a pastry chef. She has two older sisters, both of whom have already left home, and a younger brother who is currently studying for his GCSEs. They live in North London in a three-bedroom house, and when Tommy arrives there for Christmas, dinner is already on the table.

He gets hugs immediately. Kisses on both cheeks. Exclamations of excitement at the fact that Christelle's best friend, the one she's been going on about for months, is finally here. Laughter. Shouts. He is seated beside Christelle, with her brother to his left and her father across the table. Food—so much food—from crispy Peking duck wrapped in pancakes to steaming dim sum buns in bamboo baskets. And then they are talking.

Christelle's father, a big, jolly man with an infectious smile, throws Tommy questions as though they are playing tennis. "Where do you live?" "What kind of music do you listen to?" "Are you a football fan?" "Ah. Which team?"

"Liverpool," replies Tommy.

"Liverpool?" Roger scoffs, shaking his head and laughing. "Mate, it's Arsenal for me. Only Arsenal."

Christelle's brother fist pumps the air in agreement and the sisters hoot. Christelle's mum snaps her fingers and hushes everyone. "Don't scare the poor boy away," she chides her husband. But Roger continues to laugh, a rich, warm laugh from deep within his belly.

After the meal, Christelle and her sisters go into the kitchen and return with a giant chocolate cake, with sprinkles and caramel drizzled on top. They eat the cake over tea and talk some more. Tommy asks them about the photographs on the walls. So many photographs: Christelle and her siblings as children; Christelle's parents on their wedding day and on their twentieth wedding anniversary; the five of them on holiday in China; the grandparents with their grandchildren; the grandparents as young people, pictured in black-and-white. Cousins. Nephews and nieces. Aunts and uncles. Just family.

Tommy finishes his slice of cake, sips his tea, and listens to the stories. Christelle's mother is an animated storyteller and she, like her daughter, relishes having a captivated audience. Every family member is brought vividly to life by her words, her gestures, and the high-pitched nature of her voice.

Her husband cuts in sometimes, offering a joke or an anecdote that she has miraculously forgotten. Christelle and her siblings must have heard these stories a hundred times already, but they keep requesting them; Christelle, especially, is eager for Tommy not to miss anything. She keeps elbowing him in the side. "Wait for this bit," she keeps saying. "You'll love this."

Tommy is good company, he always has been, but especially since he started uni. He asks the right questions, laughs in all the right places, claps Christelle's dad on the back in return whenever they arrive at a particularly hilarious segment. He is enjoying himself, Christelle knows him well enough to tell. But she knows it is costing him; it is easy for her to see that.

After the cake has been eaten and they have helped clear away all the plates, Christelle's mum asks Tommy whether he wants another cup of tea. Her father, winking, asks if he wants something stronger. "It is Christmas, after all," says Roger.

But Christelle can spot the exact moment the decision arrives in Tommy's expression: he is ready to leave. And sure enough, Tommy shakes his head at her father. "You're very kind, Mr. Chan. But I'm going to be a good boy today."

Catching Christelle's eye, Tommy excuses himself to go outside for a smoke. On his way out, he graciously thanks Chanice for the dinner and makes sure to clap Christelle's brother on the back before he puts on his jacket and slips outside.

Christelle follows him, zipping up her winter coat. It is the coldest December for over a hundred years; they keep being told that on the news. Snow is settling on the streets and the cars, gathering on rooftops, turning the world white and still. Every time Christelle inhales, she can feel the cold stinging her lungs and chilling her insides.

She holds back from making a sarcastic comment as Tommy rolls his cigarette and begins smoking it. His posture is stiff, remarkably different from the way it was with her family. The buoyant smile, too, has disappeared.

"You alright?" she asks.

He gives a strained smile. "Yeah, I'm grand," he replies.

"'Grand' is a bit of a stretch," she remarks.

"What else do you want me to say, Chris? I love your family. They're amazing. You have a really good thing going here."

"Tommy—"

"You're right, after all, Chris," he says, staring straight ahead. "Time can still feel shorter here."

"Have you talked to your sister much since she left?"

"We've texted a bit. I just made sure she's settled in okay. But we're both bad at keeping in touch."

"You shouldn't be alone at Christmas, Tommy."

She does not know what to say, or what he needs her to say, and so she says nothing. They stand together in silence until he finishes his cigarette.

"Tell your mum and dad I had a good time, yeah?" he says. "I'm going to head home."

"You don't have to."

"No, I need to. Ah-ma will be waiting. I do have"—he fidgets and avoids her eye—"my own family to get back to."

She watches him until he disappears down the road in the blurring whiteness.

A little while later, the door opens behind her and her dad appears, wrapped up in his coat, scarf, and beanie. "Your mum told me to get you," he says. "Is he gone?"

"Yes, I'm afraid so."

He comes to stand next to her and she links her arm through his, feeling like a little girl again.

"Poor boy," her dad says, following her gaze down the empty road. "Reminds me of my brother."

Christelle does not have to ask which one: she already knows. If she had a suspicion the very first day she met Tommy, her dad probably does too. He tells her quietly: "Baby girl, you can't always save people from themselves."

"I'm not trying to save him," she says.

Her dad chuckles. "Whatever you say, my dear." He tugs on her wrist. "Come on. Let's get back inside. It's freezing out here." And he kisses the top of her head.

Ah-ma Carol is reading in the living room when Tommy gets back.

She looks up and gives him a little smile. "Ah. You're home," she says. "About time. Did you enjoy yourself?"

"It was nice." The warmth inside his chest is fading. So, too, are all the stories that he heard in that dining room. "Merry Christmas, Ah-ma."

"Merry Christmas, Thomas." She looks back down at her book. "If you're still hungry, I left some food for you on the stove. You can heat it up."

He mumbles his thanks and makes his way upstairs to his room. He crashes on his bed and lies still for a while, contemplating the silence. His phone vibrates and he picks it up to see a Christmas message from May flash across his screen. He feels a slight pang of guilt. It has been ages since he last checked up on her. He had promised her dinner and a movie, just as friends, but then completely forgot to follow it up.

Briefly he wonders what his sister is doing right now in Hong Kong. Probably sleeping. He considers calling her up;

aside from a few messages here and there, it's been a long time since they've properly spoken. But where would their conversation lead to? Knowing Eva, probably down roads he'd rather avoid altogether. So all he does is text her a quick *Merry Christmas* and leaves it at that.

His mind drifts to Christelle's parents, to the warmth in their eyes and in their embraces. He wishes he had accepted her dad's offer of something stronger . . .

There is a patch of faded paint in the corner of his ceiling. It reminds him of Peggy's bedroom and a very old memory of Christmas carols ringing from the street below . . .

He picks up his phone and writes a reply to May.

———

Boxing Day. The chilly wind is snapping at his face. But the lights from the Christmas market are shining so warmly, the scents of chocolate and chestnuts swirling so richly in the air. He finds the cold more than bearable.

May is bundled up in a giant fluffy coat that somehow still manages to be stylish. A thick yellow scarf winds around her neck in elegant twirls. Her long tresses are left loose and flowing in the wind. He teases her about how unprepared she is for the British winter, and she, blushing and giggling, tries to mock his lack of flair.

"At least my jacket isn't a boring color," she says, rolling her eyes at his dark-green ensemble. "My shoes aren't cheap. And I have these lovely earrings on."

"Exactly. Earrings." His fingers brush the strands of silver dangling from her ears, grazing lightly against her cheek. "Who prioritizes earrings over a hat in this weather?"

"You wouldn't understand," she says coyly, sipping the hot chocolate he'd just bought her. Her eyes are shining adorably with mischief. "A girl has to make sacrifices for the sake of fashion."

He chuckles. "Ah. Fashion. Okay." Smiling with her, he realizes with surprise, is so incredibly easy.

They continue strolling around the market, stopping at a few stalls, looking at key chains, rings, and postcards. The conversation begins to flow more naturally, full of little jokes and mindless chatter. She buys him a hot dog and he insists on getting her a woolen hat. Blossom pink. To match her lipstick, he says. She puts it on, feeling exceptionally giddy, and asks him to snap some pictures. She checks them afterward: golden lights are twinkling behind her, the cup of hot chocolate is in her hand, and she has her legs crossed a little, with a bright, cute smile on her face. She can barely recognize herself.

They sit down for a while by the river so they can share a small bucket of popcorn.

"I think this is the best Christmas I've ever had," she admits, shocking herself with her own bravery.

"Is it the company?" he jokes.

She laughs, looks away, her heart quickening a little. "No, it's just the city," she says, biting her lip to stop herself from grinning too widely. "It's like a postcard. Or something out of a movie."

"Trust me, it doesn't feel like that when you're actually *living* here."

There is a note in his voice that piques her interest. "How was your Christmas yesterday? You never said."

"Oh, it was . . . nice," he replies casually. "I spent it with a friend and her family. What about you?"

She wants to ask questions about that friend but doesn't

want him to think she's the jealous type. So she fishes another piece of popcorn from the bucket and says, "I just stayed inside and watched a movie."

"Oh, I'm sorry."

"No, it's okay, it wasn't bad." She takes a sip of her drink, her leather-gloved hands seeking its warmth. A pause. Then nearly as a whisper: "But thank you for inviting me here."

A little of the weight that he's been feeling lifts off his chest. He looks sideways at her; she is intent on not meeting his gaze. "Do you like ice-skating?" he asks.

She squeals with excitement. "Oh, yes!"

"Are you free tomorrow?"

"What do you think?"

He laughs. "Alright, I'll send you the details later."

Another pause. This one laden with unspoken hopes. He can feel himself veering down an unexpected path, and with it comes a falling sensation—small and inconspicuous, yet undeniable, like when you miss the step off a curb. But he shakes it away and gets to his feet.

"Come on," he tells her, extending a hand. "We have to get some pictures of you in front of that tree."

JOSHUA AND LILY

1988–1991

They were not falling in love.

At least that was what they told themselves.

Both of them thought love was nothing but devotion. For Joshua it was his mother at the dining table, using her chopsticks to place the best morsels of beef in his father's bowl. It was her at the sink, scrubbing the bottom of a pan, the sponge coming away stuck with charred bits of iron. For Lily it was her parents in the front seat of their car; her father on the phone, and her mother placing a delicate hand on his knee. Love was nothing but a stifled thing. Ancient and boring and regimental.

So they told themselves that what they had was simply attraction, affection, and their shared ability to travel back in time. The exhilarating joy that they were no longer the only ones.

They spent hours and hours in her house on Kennington

Road, drawing and recalling places that each of them had visited and loved. He told her of the Hong Kong of his past, sharing the notes he'd taken on every trip he had been on and his every attempt to bend the course of time, while she painted pictures of the many Englands she'd seen before they morphed into the one of today.

One night they held hands while warm yellow lights beamed down from above, casting a glowing tint over their skin, an unforgettable brightness. They closed their eyes as one, and for the first time, she saw Hong Kong. The sun peeking from behind skyscrapers. A young boy sitting on a rooftop, dreaming.

A few days later, their hands met again as their eyes fluttered shut together. That familiar darkness overwhelmed them for a moment, and then they found themselves standing on the bank of the Thames, looking across the water at a London unlike the one Joshua knew. Lily turned to him, their fingers still interlocked, and asked, Can you spot the differences?

The world, they both reckoned, had never seemed more vast or real than when they were together.

Once, when he had fallen asleep in her living room, lying on cushions strewn all over the floor, she lay on her side and traced the outlines of his features with light fingers, wondering whether her future was already written in the details of his face. Would this future look like her parents' lives? Her childhood in Primrose Hill and her nursery with the light blue walls and the tutors and those trips to the London Zoo? The barrier between three people who are simply sitting down for dinner?

He turned in his sleep, mumbling something indecipherable under his breath, and her hand shrank away. She thought to herself, *Oh. Here it is. The beginning of everything. I hope I'll make it through.*

They were not falling in love.

A few weeks later. On top of Primrose Hill, the twilight winter sky was deep purple with slashes of red. Below them, down in the park, the little girl Lily was walking between her parents, each of them holding her by the hand. She'd forgotten how young her father had looked. How even younger her mother was.

She felt Joshua's hand encircling her own. She turned to him, surprised, because they had never held hands just because; there had always been a purpose.

Is this the moment? she asked. He had told her about the Lily from the future, the one outside the Chinese restaurant that February, the one who had told him to go after her, and she had wondered ever since when she would become that woman. Is this when it all starts?

I told you everything I know, he said. I don't know anything else.

Fear tugged at her heart. I don't want that to be us, she said, nodding to her ghosts, wandering through the park.

He gave a daring smile. He rarely smiled. But when he did, it filled her world with colors. We could never be that predictable, he said.

I don't think I'll ever grow tired of you, she told him. I will always miss you.

Miss me? His smile slid off his face, his eyes narrowing in confusion. Why would you miss me? I'm right here.

She lifted her other hand to cup his cheek and pull him to her. And they sank into each other, helplessly, hopelessly, in the only way that new lovers can.

They were not falling in love. But it became his things in her house, her room. His silence in her kitchen in the mornings and evenings. His notes and diagrams on her walls, next to her paintings and sketches. Fewer visits from university friends, whose faces were colorless compared to their own. Phone calls from Hong Kong and London that went largely ignored. Late nights spent tracing each other's skin, whispering, dreaming, planning, planning.

The questions they shared felt endless: What if we did this again? What if we go there one more time? What if we go somewhere new? What if time could stand still? What if we could make it stand still? What if? What if? What if? And the months flowed into a year, then two, then three. The natural order of things.

Want to know a secret? she asked one night, lying cradled in his arms. I think we might be the only ones.

He kissed the top of her head. Want to know mine?

Go on.

I like that we might be.

They were not falling in love. But then one night he came home from a university fundraiser and found her sitting on the floor in her bathrobe, her back pressed against the side of their bed. He joined her there, sitting down cross-legged, undoing his tie with long, lanky fingers.

How was it? she asked, staring down at her feet.

The same, he answered. Half of them were fawning, the other half stupid. The usual.

She pulled off his tie and draped it around her own neck. I have something to tell you, she said. You won't like it. She could not meet his eye, instead toying with the end of the tie.

Is this something to do with your parents? he asked. They did not know about him and, frankly, he did not care.

She shook her head. Do you remember that day I took you to Primrose Hill, when we first started seeing each other?

Yes. He frowned. Why?

Do you remember what I said?

Which part?

You said we could never be that predictable. She gave a broken little smile. I have to ask you to keep that promise now.

She pressed the test into his hand and the plus sign stared up at him, unblinking.

What if, she whispered, we won't be the only ones?

After the initial shock had subsided, he laid the test on the ground beside them, took her face in his hands, and kissed her until she smiled. I'll take care of us, he whispered.

She lay her head on his chest and felt the beating of his heart while fear gripped hers. She pressed her lips to the warmth of his skin. I love you, she said.

He let out a breath. I love you too.

EVA

2012

Eva arrives in colors:
    cream, light blue. Purple, calm, and luscious.
    Brown, earthy and deep, the soil itself.
    Orange, like a resplendent sunrise.

From the moment she steps off the plane,
    stumbling into the arms of her aunt Dorothy,
    all the remnants of both their pasts mingling together,
    life feels purposeful again.
    "Do you remember me?" Eva asks.
    Because for her aunt it has been eighteen years.

The older woman's smile quiets all doubts.
    Grief rests in her aunt's eyes now, clouding the sparks Eva

had noticed during her travels.

Age has made her body thicker, painted more lines on her face, but her voice is just how Eva remembers it from the past and down the phone.

"Of course I remember you," Dorothy says. "In all these years, you have not changed for me."

Her embrace—now tangible and firm in a way it could never be in the past—tells Eva what she has always longed to hear:

Welcome home.

Her father's mother, Maa-maa Jiayi, stands in the open doorway to welcome Eva when Dorothy brings her home—a small two-bedroom flat in a high-rise building, squeezed into a very tiny corner of a grand metropolis.

Jiayi greets Eva in Cantonese: "Welcome, my dear heart."

When they embrace, the old woman's body feels so fragile. Eva thinks she might disintegrate into thin air as she holds her.

"You've grown so much," Maa-maa Jiayi says. "Your father sent me pictures. But you were a baby in most of them. Now you're a young woman."

"A beautiful young woman," says Aunt Dorothy, smiling. "Come inside, Eva. Come see where we live."

There is a small sitting room adjoining the kitchen; inside is a coffee table, a beige-colored leather sofa, a decent-sized TV, and a fishbowl with two goldfish.

The Walled City where Eva's father grew up might as well have existed in a fantasy.

Beside the TV, she sees framed photographs of family members. Faces. So many faces. Eva thinks she can recall some of them from her past; the sound of their voices stirs in the back of her mind. And there, that must have been her father when he was young. She drifts to the photograph and holds it up, looking into his unsmiling, childish face. The downward curve of his mouth.

A pang in her chest.

Did she know him? At all?

And there, standing beside him . . . "Your je-je," says Aunt Dorothy. She takes the photograph from Eva. It is of Zhang Wei and Jiayi and their children, all dressed up; her father and Dorothy can't be more than ten.

"My brother looks like him," says Eva, a little in awe. She has heard her je-je's voice before, but has never found him in her travels. His voice always comes as a whisper, low and mumbling, saying things she can never decipher, only filtering through when other urgent voices are not calling her name so loudly.

"I don't remember where we were going," says Dorothy, eyes transfixed on the photograph with a sad expression on her face. "We must have been going somewhere important. Otherwise, we wouldn't have looked so nice."

Jiayi steps forward, takes the photograph out of her daughter's hand, and stares at it for a moment. Unlike Ah-ma Carol, Jiayi's every movement is soft, slow, reminding Eva of her ah-lao-ma Mary, who calls to her often from beyond time.

"We went to the cinema that day," says Jiayi. Her voice, too, is soft. "It was on my birthday. Your father said it was a treat for our whole family."

"Ah," says Aunt Dorothy. "I cried the entire way on the bus, I remember now."

Jiayi's eyes rest on Eva. "Did your father ever talk about your je-je?"

The lie slips out very easily then. "Yes," Eva says, forcing herself to smile. "All the time."

Later that evening, after Maa-maa Jiayi has gone to sleep, Aunt Dorothy brings Eva a blanket and a pillow so she can make a bed on the sofa.

"Thank you," her aunt says, "for lying to your maa-maa about your dad. My brother was many things, but never sentimental."

"It's not like that," Eva says quickly, defensively.

Dorothy arches an eyebrow. "What is it like then?"

Eva finds herself unable to find the right words. "I don't know," she eventually says. "Dad was . . . I've seen . . . what I mean to say is . . . he wasn't always that cold."

Dorothy gives a sad smile. "Sometimes I feel like the man we knew must have been two completely different people." She sits down on the sofa and pats the spot next to her. "Come here."

Eva joins her there and rests her head on her aunt's shoulder as if that is the most natural thing to do in the world.

They sit in silence for a while as Dorothy gently strokes Eva's hair.

Eventually Eva says, "I wish Tommy were here."

But there is a semblance of direction to Eva's life now, from that moment onward.

TOMMY

In celebration of Tommy's graduation, Ah-ma Carol prepares a feast: xiaolongbao dumplings that melt in the mouth, the soup inside bursting with minced pork and Chinese herbs; Peking duck, crisp and juicy, wrapped in pancakes with fresh spring onions and sweet sauce; morning glory stir-fried with garlic, small chilis, thinly sliced ginger and mushrooms; egg fried rice, fragrant and fluffy, with diced barbecued pork and green peas.

She pours oolong tea from a black ceramic kettle into two tiny cups with bamboos and red flowers daintily painted on them. The brushstrokes are as fine and precise as the knives she sharpens and stores in a special cabinet.

She makes him sit down at the table at noon, telling him that he cannot leave until they have had this meal. "It's your graduation, after all, Thomas," she says. "And you're the only grandchild I have left."

"Eva will come back," Tommy tells her, feeling annoyed at the way she has phrased her sentence. "Ah-ma, you still have two grandchildren."

"I meant you're the only one who is still here." She sits down at the head of the table like she always does and gestures to the seat opposite hers with her chopsticks. "Sit down, Thomas."

Tommy picks up the chopsticks she has set out for him: black and plain, the ones his father always used. "Thank you, Ah-ma," he says.

She inclines her head, satisfied. "Enjoy your food before it gets cold."

They share the meal in silence, savoring the food and the lack of conversation. He can hear the clock above the fridge ticking away the time. To his surprise, he finds himself rather enjoying this muted celebration.

"The duck is really good, Ah-ma," he remarks. "The best we've had in a long time. Really, really good."

And he makes sure not to interrupt as his grandmother begins to explain, step-by-step, how she prepared every dish.

Christelle's mother, Chanice, gives her a small sum of money in a red envelope as a graduation present. Her father, on the other hand, is determined to go big. As an Arsenal ticket holder, Roger decides to take his daughter to Selhurst Park to watch his beloved Arsenal play Crystal Palace. Upon Christelle's insistence, Tommy is invited along. It is his first live Premier League match.

It is autumn. Late October. A tense affair, with Arsenal hanging on to a one–nil lead after going down to ten men against a Crystal Palace side with no manager. Tommy and Christelle sit on either side of Roger, feeling the sway of the crowd, the songs, the chants, the cheers, even the half-cheers when chances are squandered and moments missed. Tommy snaps picture after picture, elated at the experience, and decides to send some to May in reply to her texts about her recent excursion to Borough Market.

It is a new experience for Tommy having Roger by his side, whooping at a particularly nice piece of play, complaining under his breath, and gesturing with frustration at a loose pass or a missed tackle. When the Arsenal penalty goes in, the older man embraces both him and Christelle so fiercely, Tommy feels a sharp pain in his side. When Oliver Giroud rises up and heads in the winner toward the end of stoppage time, Tommy almost falls to the ground as Roger wrangles him into a headlock, shouting at the top of his lungs: "We're top of the league!" He kisses his daughter on the cheek, then thumps Tommy on the back. "Top of the league! Top of the fucking league!"

Tommy cannot help but laugh along at the older man's joy. "Wait until you play us at Anfield in February." He beams. "Will you still be top of the league then?"

Roger wags a finger at him. "You're doing well this year. So far. But trust me, we're going for more than fourth place this time."

Tommy grins. "Why do you think this year's going to be any different?"

Roger laughs. "'Cause my baby girl just graduated!" He swings an arm around Christelle's shoulders and kisses her on the top of her head. "This girl is good luck for the Gunners. The day she was born—"

"Oh, here we go again. Dad, please don't," Christelle says, rolling her eyes. But her smile is bright.

"On the day she was born, it was the last game of the season. Highbury. Five-one against Southampton. I'll never forget it. I saw the goals in the hospital. Ian Wright—"

"—breaking Gary Lineker's record, yes, I've heard this story a thousand times."

"But Tommy hasn't!"

Tommy laughs. "I don't think I need to hear a story about Ian Wright scoring goals for Arsenal."

As Tommy's eyes stray to the pitch where the players are walking around, shaking each other's hands and applauding the fans, one of the memories he has been trying to push away all day creeps into the forefront of his mind.

In the memory he has a ball at his feet, the goal in front of him, the entire pitch opening up. He can see the exact spot where he is going to slot the ball. A turn of the head—one momentary break in concentration—and, there, out of the corner of his eye, standing pitchside, his parents: his father, arms crossed, fixing him with a steady stare, his mother with both hands on her head in tense anticipation. Then his gaze snaps back to the goal again. So very neat. Just perfect. He shoots.

Christelle is staring at him. "You alright there, Tom?" Concern steals into her expression. Her father, too, is looking at him carefully.

Tommy forces himself to deliver a bright smile. "Yeah, why wouldn't I be?"

Not much later, the three of them are strolling through

South London, sharing fries and gravy and sipping beer, and chatting about Tommy and Christelle's plans now that they have their degrees.

Christelle and her girlfriend, Diana, are going to travel for a bit, maybe to Asia or South America, and then she will try and find job in a museum. "Or," says Roger, his eyes twinkling, "if you want to do a master's . . ."

"Dad, why would I want to do a master's?"

"You like studying! And then . . . I don't know . . . maybe a PhD? Doctor Christelle . . ."

Christelle tsks, shaking her head. "Dad, don't."

Roger laughs. "Maybe one day, Chris, don't rule it out. Tommy, what about you?"

Tommy takes a deep breath and considers the question for a moment. The answer, when it comes, surprises even him. "I've thought about working for the university my dad used to work at," he says. "I still have my dad's contacts, and the research projects he and my mum were working on . . . they're still unfinished, so . . . I don't know."

"Wow, Tommy," says Christelle, "I don't think I've heard you mention that before." The fact that he almost never talks about his parents hovers in the air between them, unspoken.

Roger gives him an empathetic smile and claps him on the shoulder. "That sounds like a really good idea, son."

They hug Tommy goodbye at his bus stop. After he and Christelle break apart, she lingers for a moment, searching for something in his face. "I'll see you around, yeah?"

Tommy nods and kisses her on the cheek. "I'll call you."

She gives him a pointed look. "No, you won't."

"Come on, Chris." He winks. "Have a little faith in me."

The bus arrives and he squeezes on with a crowd of football fans. When they pull away, he turns around for one last look. Roger has his arm around Christelle and both of them raise their hands in farewell, smiling.

As he journeys across London, he cannot help but sense that there is something different about today. After jumping off the bus, he thinks of heading straight home, but for some reason, his feet take him in another direction. Before he knows it, he is at the park, the one he went to with Christelle when she first asked about his parents. The one he came to play football at as a child. His thoughts turn to his sister, and he suddenly remembers that he hasn't yet replied to her short message congratulating him on his graduation.

He sits down on a bench and lights a cigarette. He thinks of the adrenaline rush at the match, the roar of the crowd after the goals went in. Christelle's father pulling him into a tight embrace. But for some reason it is his father's face that keeps coming to mind.

It has been so many years, he's not sure whether he has all the details correct. What did it look like when his father smiled or laughed? Was his haircut just so? What about the curve of his mouth? The shape of his face? The look in his eyes? If Tommy stood up now, would he be taller than his father? And what of his voice? Sometimes, when Tommy closes his eyes and concentrates very hard, he thinks he might be able to recall the answers to a few of these questions. Yet all the little things keep slipping.

A wave of sadness washes over him, almost collapsing him. The grief renders his throat dry and causes a growing panic in his chest, as though a terrible darkness is bursting to tear its way out of his body, shredding his every sinew, every vein.

He grips the bench and forces himself to take a deep inhale. When he breathes out, he closes his eyes. There are good memories, too; there must be. But even recalling those feels as torturous as drawing another breath.

So he sits for a long time, smoking. He does not cry; he thinks he is physically incapable of it now. Only when darkness arrives does he get up and start heading home.

The house is completely silent when he enters—no sounds from the kitchen or the TV in the living room. The lights, however, are all switched on. He pauses at the front door, his jacket halfway off. "Ah-ma?" he calls. But there is no answer.

He takes a step forward, and then another. All the while a voice deep inside him is telling him to stay rooted, never to take another step ever again. Because isn't there something unexpected and terrible waiting for us beyond every turn in life?

He reaches the middle of their hallway. The living room is to his right. This is the turn he needs to make. "Ah-ma," he calls again. Still, no answer.

He wishes he could retreat out the front door. Retrace his steps all the way to the park and then onto the bus until he was back with Christelle and Roger at Selhurst Park and this entire day could start all over again, and he wouldn't ever have to go into the room at all.

But of course, no matter how much he wished it did, that is not the way life works. So Tommy makes the turn and steps inside.

JOSHUA AND LILY

1991

Lily chose white lilies for her bouquet—five long-stemmed ones tied together with a golden string—and a simple, cream-colored dress, with her hair put up in a chic bun. Silver sparkled in her ears and the cheap engagement ring on her finger winked dully in the fluorescent light. Joshua wore the only suit he owned, the one he bought secondhand in Chinatown for an event at the university in his second year.

This moment was, like their initial meeting, inevitable; there was really no other choice.

Joshua had called his mother two days before and told her what would be happening. He was greeted with stunned silence and then happy tears, while Lily had no choice but to visit her parents in person a month earlier to deliver the news.

Carol had cried when Lily revealed her condition. Henry,

on the other hand, simply stared at his daughter as though she had grown an extra head. When he finally spoke, his voice, usually jovial and pleasing to others, was grave. Who is this boy? he'd asked.

The more Lily told him about Joshua, the more Henry's frown deepened. After she finished, he simply said, I know men like him. This is not the way to get our attention, Lilian. We raised you to be better than this.

She had stood up and walked out.

Yet Carol and Henry still insisted on coming to the town hall for the wedding. Henry arrived in a suit that was obviously much more expensive than Joshua's; Carol was by his side, a disapproving figure in a deep green dress.

Joshua shook their hands and said, Thank you for coming. They offered no reply and could barely meet his eye. Henry turned instead to his daughter.

Lilian, said Henry. Your mother and I would like a word.

Lily's eyes flashed in anger. Dad. Not here. Not now.

Carol took her daughter by the elbow. Yes. Now. You owe us this much.

Lily looked at Joshua; he gave a slight nod. It's alright, he mouthed.

Lily let herself be led out of the door and back onto the street outside. While they were gone, Joshua sat down on a wooden bench, fidgeting with his cufflinks. He did not know what he'd been expecting, but he did not feel any joy, elation, or even excitement. This was something he must do—he'd realized that when Lily handed him the pregnancy test. Just another task he needed to complete. The simplicity—even the logic of it—gave him a steady kind of comfort.

When Lily and her parents returned, Carol's eyes were red, her lips pressed tightly together in an angry line, while Henry simply looked weary. But at least the couple kept their distance and gave Lily and Joshua space for final preparations. The chamber was to their right and very soon it would be their turn to enter.

Is everything alright? Joshua asked Lily when she came to stand next to him, looping her arm through his. Her eyes, too, were swimming with tears, her mouth quivering with anger.

I wish they hadn't come, said Lily. I want it to be just us.

Ignore them. They don't understand.

She wanted to tell him that she was scared. But she did not think he had ever felt scared in his life. And so she said, You need to know that what they think of you is not what I think of you.

I know that, he replied.

No, I meant—her breath caught in panic, her heart pouring out again at the sight of him—I love you. No matter what. If you're sure about us, then I'm sure, too. But I need you to be sure.

There was a pause. Then he nodded. I'm sure, he said. I will never find anyone else like you.

She stepped into the room with him, feeling as though she had wings.

Much later—after her parents had gone home without even offering congratulations, after they had briefly stopped at a nearby pub to accept the good wishes of her university friends—they were back in her house on Kennington Road.

She was standing before the mirror to take off her silver earrings when he came up behind her and circled an arm around her waist. She looked at their reflection in the glass—him towering over her by just a little, the black of their hair inter-mingling as he lay the side of his head against the crown of hers—and thought: What a fine couple we make.

She felt the warmth of his lips on her shoulder.

Where do you want to go this time? he asked.

She smiled. Surprise me.

TOMMY AND EVA

2013

Tommy feels as though he is spending too much of this week just sitting and waiting.

He is on the floor in the living room, cradling his ah-ma's still body while he waits for the ambulance to arrive. She is breathing, he thinks. She must be. A woman like her cannot be taken down so easily by whatever this is. A heart attack? A stroke? A fall?

A little fainting spell, surely.

The paramedics tell him to let her go so they can attend to her. "We'll have to take her to the hospital," they tell him, tone efficient, as though that will somehow calm him down.

"Are there any other family members who should know?" they ask him. "Your parents? You should call them right away."

But he does not have the heart to tell them that the only

family he has left is halfway around the world. "Eva," he says, "Eva." And that is all he can say.

Ah-ma is in the emergency room. Tommy is sitting on a plastic chair with other patients and their relatives, waiting.

His father. He wonders what his father would do in this situation. And his mother . . .

He remembers, vaguely, when his great-grandmother Mary had passed away. His parents did not bring him and Eva to the funeral, and his memories of his ah-lao-ma were minimal, to say the least. But the day his mother told him the news . . . That day he remembers very well. There was a change in the air, a different energy in the house. A hardness in his mother's eyes that he rarely saw. His sister, however, was calm; she had known already, somehow, from her travels.

"We might be able to see her again in the past," his mother had said. "But to us, now, she is no longer here. She's gone."

He thinks of the simplicity of that last word. Gone. The final time he saw his ah-ma Carol was just this morning before he left the house. She did not even bother to spare him a glance as he breezed out the door. All she did was raise her voice and say, "Don't come home too late. If you don't make it for dinner, I'll keep some in the fridge for you."

With a sinking, empty feeling, he realizes he does not know whether she did or not. His mind conjures up a scene of returning home to an empty house and opening the fridge to find a container filled with his ah-ma's rice and fried garlic pork and chili. His face feels numb. His head is filled with fog.

Gone. What a simple word.

He thinks fleetingly of Peggy. Maybe if he can close his eyes right here in the waiting room and . . . No. That is not a good idea. Not even for him. There will be a time for that later.

His sister is probably asleep in Hong Kong right now. They still haven't spoken on the phone since she left, and he still hasn't replied to her message. The Eva he knows has never been much of a sleeper, but don't people change once they are away from you?

He finds her number on his phone and starts the call. It rings for a while . . .

"Hello?" Her voice, a little crackled through the line, but still clear.

"Eva." He is surprised by how much weight sticks to that one word alone.

"Tommy?" Her tone is instantly alert. "What's wrong?"

"I think . . . I think you should come home."

Ah-ma Carol is pronounced dead at the hospital from an unexpected stroke.

She is buried next to her husband, Henry, in the plot they had bought for themselves ten years after they got married. On her other side is her mother, Mary.

Tommy and Eva have never met most of the distant relatives and friends of Carol's who come to the funeral. Yet all of them seem to know who the twins are. They come up to them with solemn faces, offering their condolences and feedback on the burial: "Oh, what a beautiful headstone"; "It is fitting that she is buried next to Henry and her mother"; "It's a shame your mother is not buried with them"; "There should be more flowers." So on and so forth.

The only people Tommy knows are Christelle, Christelle's parents and, to his surprise, May, who comes with a bouquet of roses she artfully arranges on the grave. They were supposed to meet a couple of days ago, but he completely forgot. When she rang him up to ask if he was okay, he had to tell her what had happened. Her sympathy on the phone made him recoil—he didn't know why—but he couldn't lie when she asked for details about the funeral. He just didn't expect her to actually show up.

After the burial, May stops briefly to address Tommy and Eva. "I'm very sorry for your loss," she tells them softly, her eyes downcast. "If there is anything I can do, please let me know."

Tommy swallows and thanks her for coming in a strained voice.

May lifts her eyes to catch his for a moment, hers swimming with tears. But he quickly looks away. "I'll . . . I'll see you around," he mutters.

May's cheeks burn red. She drops her gaze, repeats Tommy's statement, and shuffles away. He does not watch her leave.

"Who is that?" Eva whispers.

But before Tommy can answer, Christelle, Roger, and Chanice are there. They take turns giving Tommy and Eva hugs.

"We're here for you," Chanice says, gripping Tommy's hand. "For whatever you need. You can always reach out."

Roger nods in agreement. "Because of Christelle, you're family now." He lays a strong hand on Tommy's shoulder. "Don't hesitate to ask. You can even come and stay with us for as long as you want."

Tommy mutters: "Thank you. Thank you so much." But he cannot look them in the face. Their kindness overwhelms him to the point that it makes him uncomfortable.

Roger and Chanice seem to understand. They smile at him kindly and announce that they will be on their way. But while her parents head toward the cemetery gate, Christelle lingers behind. "Do you need me to stay?" she asks Tommy.

He shakes his head. "Chris, I'm fine. Really."

Christelle casts a brief glance at Eva, who shakes her head. "Tommy, you're not fine," says Christelle. "I can stay if you want me to."

"No, Chris, it's . . . it's okay." He gestures weakly at her parents. "Go with your mum and dad. I have my sister, I'll be alright."

Christelle looks unsure, but Eva gives her a reassuring nod. So she kisses Tommy on the cheek once more and follows her parents.

After everyone is gone, Tommy and Eva sit down on the bench a short distance away from the graves. Orange and yellow leaves are falling from above, draping the cemetery in a picturesque autumn blanket. The chill in the air makes him think of Peggy's East London. He wonders, not very briefly at all, what she would be doing if he were to go back and see her now.

"At least she and Ah-lao-ma are together now," says Eva.

Tommy does not know if he agrees with that. But there is no use in saying anything else; Eva would only win the argument.

His sister flew in just a few days ago and hasn't had much sleep. But even now, sitting together in the quietness of the cemetery, Tommy finds himself amazed by how different she seems. She looks the same—the same thick-rimmed glasses, black hair edged with purple highlights, her feet clad in her old pair of Converse sneakers—but she does not carry herself in the same way. He cannot quite put his finger on what it is that has changed.

"So . . ." he begins, "how is life in Hong Kong with Aunt Dorothy and Maa-maa Jiayi?"

His sister gives a small smile. "Things are . . . good, I suppose. I'm still adjusting to being there and getting to know everyone."

"What is Aunt Dorothy like?"

"She's wonderful. She wants to meet you one day, Tommy. Maybe you should come visit." Eva's eyes are fixed on the newly erected headstone. "Especially with what's happened . . . You need a break. What is even keeping you here? Is it that girl?"

Tommy bristles. "What girl?"

"The girl who came to the funeral today. What's her name?"

"May." Tommy sighed. "No, she's just a friend."

Eva has the feeling that there is something else her brother is not telling her. But maybe now's not the time for her to press. "So why stay?" she asks.

"I want to continue Mum and Dad's projects." He trots out the line he's told Christelle and her father. "And I've been thinking of doing some research work at Dad's old uni."

"That sounds like a terrible idea."

A prick of annoyance. "Oh, wow, Ev, thanks for that. Your support means a lot."

"No, I just meant . . ." Eva sighs. "You've seen what it did to Mum and Dad. It takes a toll."

"Easy for you to say," he snaps. "You're not here."

"Oh, Tommy." She grabs his hand, and they are twelve years old again. The two of them against the world. "I wish you would come with me."

"I wish you would stay."

She pauses and her expression softens in the dying evening light. "Tommy, I would stay if I could. But it's lonely for me here."

"It's lonely everywhere."

"Not in the same way. I don't know how to explain it." She scowls and Tommy is acutely reminded of how their mother looked whenever she was faced with a tricky situation. "Maybe it has something to do with this country. Or maybe it's just the memories. But sometimes . . . sometimes it feels like I can't breathe here. Do you feel that way?"

He stares for a while at the curve of the tree nearby, the way some of the branches dip down toward the earth. "No," he says.

Eva sees her old bedroom as part of another life, the girl she used to be as another person entirely. Someone she wants to scoop up in her arms and carry away.

She tears down all the sketches, all the drawings on the walls; she will take them home to Hong Kong with her.

She goes back to the cemetery by herself on another day and lays flowers—bright bouquets of sunflowers—at the three graves. Her mother, she thinks, would have approved.

She only sheds a tear or two there, but missing them feels like a rising tide of grief.

She and Tommy take a walk along the South Bank, lingering by their favorite spot in front of the Globe Theatre, joking and talking about nothing, sipping tea in paper cups bought from a street vendor nearby.

My time with him is running out, she thinks, looking at her brother. But her aunt is right: you can try and help someone out of the woods, but they must take the first steps themselves.

Tommy hugs her goodbye, again, at the airport.

Their embrace lasts for a while, everything they cannot say to each other packed into it.

"Don't be a stranger," she tells him. "And take care of yourself."

He grins his affable, charming grin that works so well on others, but never on her. "When have I not?"

She rolls her eyes. "Oh, for fuck's sake, please don't start."

She wants to tell him: Don't be alone. Don't be scared. I understand how hard it is. So on and so forth. But he kisses her forehead and gives her a playful push. "Go on, then. Walk away."

And, again, the moment is gone.

EVA

Eva wakes in colors.

Clear blue, as soft as cotton candy.

Gray as a stormy sky, then black as an inky night.

The first thing Eva sees is Maa-maa Jiayi's ceiling fan, spinning in a soothing rhythm. She hears the old woman shuffling around in the kitchen, the stove being switched on, the clanging of cutlery on porcelain.

It has been a few days since Eva came back from London, a few days since she put those flowers on Ah-ma Carol's grave, but she still needs a minute to collect herself before getting up.

Her eyes close briefly, shutting out the image of her brother with his head hung low, with an angry twist to his mouth. A deep breath to try and lessen the heaviness in her chest.

Then . . . the light breaks through.

Maa-maa Jiayi teaches her how to mix the flour and roll out the dough on the kitchen counter. The best way to season the prawns and mash all the meat together with a spoon. Soft hands folding the dough into a dumpling.

"Did you do this with your children when they were young?" Eva asks.

"I did this with your aunt Dorothy," her maa-maa replies, "but not with your father."

Eva wants to ask why, but she knows, from the painful glint in the old woman's eyes, that this is a story she'd rather not tell.

The hot oil bubbles away in the pan. Then sizzles as the dumplings are dropped in. Cantonese words exchanged, practiced, as they are turned over until golden brown.

Once in a while, a story is offered, a gift gently and unknowingly given. "When your father was young . . ." Maa-maa would begin, again and again. And in Eva's mind, her father would morph from a stern, unshakable man to the young boy her maa-maa speaks of: independent, extremely intelligent, obedient, and perfect in almost every way.

Aunt Dorothy listens to Eva retelling these stories later with a frown, and says, "We all remember the people we love differently."

And Eva grows quiet, remembering the voices that call to her in her sleep.

Strangely, she does not remember the last time she has traveled.

Her parents, especially her father, would be surprised to hear that.

———————

Little by little, Eva's world begins to expand. The park near the flat, at first, and then markets, malls, restaurants, and cafés. Occasionally, theme parks and museums. But her favorite place in Hong Kong, she is astounded to discover, is the doorway of her maa-maa's flat.

Afternoon, with the sun beating down, she sits in the open doorway with a sketchbook. It has taken some getting used to, but she is now comfortable with the flat being open when someone is at home.

She loves seeing the neighbors stop by to exchange food, gossip, and everyday conversations with her maa-maa. They all acknowledge Jiayi's strange, quiet granddaughter from England with a polite smile or a quick nod.

The only ones who stop for longer than a second are the young children.

Sometimes, as they run past, the sight of her drawing stops them in their tracks and they linger for a while, silently intrigued as she draws a dragon with three heads, a girl floating through the clouds, or a mermaid crying into an ocean of roses.

Other times, the children will sit cross-legged beside her on the ground, eyes fixed on her hand as she brings their features to life on paper.

She gives some of them a pencil or a crayon and a page torn from her sketchbook.

Her Cantonese is not very fluent, but there is no need for it to be.

As the children sit and draw beside her, she learns that there is peace in this kind of silence.

She shows her aunt Dorothy some of the drawings the children have done—some are extraordinarily detailed, some messy and undecipherable, but all beautiful.

Aunt Dorothy's eyes sparkle when she hears of Eva's idea.

"It would matter more," says Eva, "if I could share my art this way. Will you help me?"

"Of course." The smile her aunt gives is one of pride. She pulls Eva in for a long embrace, and for a second, Eva feels tears stinging her eyes.

She wonders, very briefly, what her parents would make of all this. What would her father say, knowing she is now back in Hong Kong with his family? And would her mother agree with what she's doing?

There is so much, Eva thinks, she'd like to tell them.

A few days later, Eva wakes up early to rearrange Maa-maa Jiayi's furniture in the living room. The sofa is pushed up against the wall and the coffee table is moved to Aunt Dorothy's bedroom. There is now space for three or four people to sit on the ground in a wide circle. Jiayi is adamant that the family photos stay in the exact same place, a declaration that Eva herself agrees with.

In the afternoon, Eva is back in her place in the open doorway, coloring a picture of a bee buzzing around a bright yellow sunflower.

This time, when the children from neighboring flats arrive, they have brought their friends with them, some clutching sketchbooks and pencil cases under their arms.

Eva invites them all inside.

And the door, as always, remains open.

TOMMY, PEGGY, AND MAY

1940 / 2013

Tommy stands outside the café, the rain drizzling down in darkness.

  He looks inside through the grimy windows:
  all the chairs are upended, flipped on top of the tables.
  As though the place is abandoned.
  But he catches a movement out of the corner of his eye.

He pushes the door and it budges open a little:
  an unthinking invitation. He steps inside, his boots making marks
  on the dusty floor. A lamp, set on the counter,
  flickering.
  The figure turns.

Peggy has a broom in her hand, an apron tied around her middle.
    An ordinary sight, really, but the second she sees him,
    her breath catches audibly. Tommy? she says,
    the note of disbelief in her voice
    ringing loudly in the vast space between them.

Peg, he says, inexplicably frightened. What's wrong?

She looks more mature than he has ever seen her.
    It is not just the stylishness of her dress and hair, or her
newfound elegance.
    But more the set of her jaw, the confidence in the turn of
her head.
    A cold, hardened look in her eyes that takes him aback.

There are years in those eyes he has not seen.

She pauses for a few seconds and then suddenly
    she is in his arms.
    She holds him tight to her, with a ferocity that stuns him.
    Peg, what's wrong? he asks her again.

It's nothing, she says. I thought I'd never see . . .
    Tommy, why are you here?

———————

They sit together on the edge of her bed, exhausted.
    What remains are the pieces, his words shattered like broken
tiles.

She wants to say, I'm so sorry for your loss, but she knows, more than anyone,

that sympathy cannot dampen the freshness of grief; it can only fuel it.

She asks him where his sister is, about the funeral, what he plans to do next.

He shakes his head. Are you alone? she asks.

I have my friends, says Tommy. I have Christelle and May, and I have you.

That new name, said so tentatively.

For him, an afterthought but not quite.

For her, a time bomb, exploding.

She pulls back and studies his face, every line of his expression.

All the pieces in her mind suddenly click into place,

and an understanding, so alien to him, sparks to life in her gaze.

She thinks of what has already happened, and she knows.

This is when it all begins:

the end.

Peg? He frowns, confused. What's the matter?

She wishes this moment could last for an eternity,

but she is not the kind of person

to shy away from the inevitable.

So, she says, you've already met May.

Yes, but—a sinking feeling in the pit of his stomach—Peg, I don't understand.

How do you know who May is? She's just a friend. I don't understand how . . .

A million questions race around his mind, each more confounding than the last.

And then it clicks. Of course, he should've known.

He's a time traveler, after all. It makes sense.

I've already told you something, haven't I? he says.

Future me. Older me. Something must have happened . . .

She reaches out to take his hand.

Tommy, we've made our promises, she says.

I'm not going to tell you your future,

like I've begged for you not to tell me mine.

All these secrets of yours I've kept from you . . .

I've kept every one of them gladly.

But this time . . . This time it's more than that.

Panic rises in his throat: Peg, what are you saying?

Tommy, you have me, she whispers, but I'm here. Not there, with you.

Fear, laced in every syllable he utters: I don't understand—

I can't tell you anything else, she says, but, Tommy, you're my oldest friend. So let's just be friends.

His heart sinks in a way it has never sunk before.

What do you mean, let's just be friends?

Her eyes are sad, regretful, and filled with hurt. It means, she says,

    let's take our hearts out of this while we still can.

———

Tommy is already drunk by the time May arrives.

She has to let herself into the house. She finds him in the living room, lying on the floor in the spot where he had found his ah-ma. A bottle of whiskey—his mother's, found stashed in her studio—in his right hand.

The first thing he says to her is, "I don't understand." And when she bends down to give him a hug, she notices that his eyes are wet. The sight alarms her. She pries the bottle from his grip and sets it on the coffee table next to her purse.

She attempts a smile. "I'm happy you're not ignoring my messages anymore."

"Well, I've been a bit busy," he says, slurring his words.

She winces, the embarrassment stinging. "I'm sorry if I was texting you too much," she says. "I didn't hear back from you after the funeral and I wanted to make sure you were okay."

"I don't understand," he says again.

She sinks down to the floor beside him. "Tommy, you're tired, you're not making any sense."

"Take our hearts out of this while we still can? I don't understand."

"Tommy, what don't you understand?"

"You."

"What about me?" she asks, watching him as his eyes slowly close. "Tommy? Why did you ask me to come?" But he doesn't speak again as he drifts off to sleep.

She stays beside him until night comes, stealing into the room like an unwanted visitor.

Tommy wakes the next afternoon to a completely lonely house.

May must have left sometime during the night. But before she did, she'd somehow found a way to move him to the sofa. He throws off the blanket she'd covered him with and notes the absence of his mother's whiskey, the beers he'd bought from the off-license, and the empty box of pizza from yesterday evening.

The events of the last few days come crashing back. Confusion. The inescapable waves of loss.

Things could be much worse, he quickly reminds himself as the echoing silence welcomes him. He is still privileged, still taken care of. He has prospects, a place to call home, an education. His sister. His whole life still ahead of him. He has no right to carry such an emptiness. Maybe Peggy was right: they're better off as just friends. It could never work between them. And it will all make sense one day.

His eyes lift to the one item in the house his ah-ma had not moved from its original place: the painting of the stag his mother had done so long ago, with its magnificent antlers, its rich brown fur, its head turned away, as though it were hiding a secret to some deep, fathomless peace.

I miss you, he finds himself thinking.

There should be an answer to that.

PART THREE

守得云开见月明

WAIT TILL THE CLOUDS PART TO SEE MOONLIGHT

TOMMY

It is almost like Tommy is playing at being an adult.

First, it is the job he gets. He walks into his father's university, knocks on the door of his father's old colleague, and pitches the idea of him continuing his father's work. Groundbreaking historical research, he promises them. Beyond anything they could ever imagine. They can trust him.

After all, isn't he, like his father before him, family?

"I remember when my father used to bring me to work," Tommy says. "I remember how much he respected this institution, and how much he valued knowledge. I promise that you'll get the same level of dedication from me."

His father's colleague—a bald, middle-aged English man, eager to appear amenable and "with the times"—does not stand a chance. Halfway into their conversation, he is already enraptured, marveling at how much Tommy has grown.

An image flashes through Tommy's mind: Eva putting multiple bouquets of white roses and orchids into vases, the condolences card still clipped to one of the stems. For weeks after that ill-fated November, the university's logo embossed on it had glared reproachfully at Tommy every time he walked into the kitchen.

"You have your old man's spirit and no mistake," says the professor, with the air of someone who's unexpectedly found gold in his backyard. "Your father was one of the smartest Chinese men I've ever met. If not *the* smartest. It would be an honor for us to work with you. You would be . . . um . . . a remarkable asset to our university."

Tommy forces a grateful smile. "You are too kind, sir. My father always spoke very highly of you. Now I know why."

A handshake. A couple of papers to sign. And that was it. Too easy.

Then, it is off to his father's office, where, for years, Tommy and Eva have hardly spent any time.

After his parents disappeared, the room was left sparse, its ambience even less welcoming than before. Tommy takes on the challenge of redecorating with enthusiasm. He buys a new carpet, new curtains, new lamps. Moves in the dark brown leather sofa from his mother's studio and the bookshelf from Eva's bedroom. His degree is hung up on the wall, next to a picture of his parents on their wedding day. The entire room is scrubbed clean, with not a speck of dust on any wooden surface.

And last but not least, his father's things are unpacked from the boxes Ah-ma Carol had put them in. Tommy runs his hands over every item reverently as he returns them to their rightful places. Stacks of documents and books are neatly arranged on the desk, in the cabinets and on the shelves around the room. His father's giant map of Europe is pinned to one wall, his trusty old blackboard pushed up against another.

When he was eleven years old, prompted by his father, Tommy tried to travel beyond 1950. But after weeks and weeks of study with Joshua, memorizing details from photographs and learning about the history of 1950s London, he did not succeed. He could not even disappear from the present, despite clamping his eyes shut for longer than ten minutes and trying as hard as he could to recite every detail he remembered from his research.

The disappointment in his father's eyes was the first thing he noticed when he finally opened his own, defeated. His mother had complimented him, telling him how brave he was for trying. But his father had sat him down and told him to try again the next day.

"Dad, I don't think I can," Tommy said, on the verge of tears. "It's . . . it's too hard. Maybe I can't do it, maybe I'm . . . I'm not supposed to. Dad, I feel like I'm not—"

His father had cut him off: "There will always be hardships in life, Thomas. But we must not feel sorry for ourselves. We must carry on and keep striving toward our goals. Otherwise . . . we might as well just throw away everything we have."

"But, Dad—"

Joshua shook his head. "No 'buts,' Thomas," he said. "Chin up."

So this is what Tommy is doing now: keeping his chin up. He finally has a purpose.

His parents, he hopes, would approve, and would be proud of his strength.

A year after Ah-ma Carol passes away, Christelle comes to visit. She and her girlfriend, Diana, have returned from traveling around Europe. She turns her nose up at the office.

"Why is it always so ridiculously easy for you?" Christelle says, infuriated. "You just . . . what? Waltzed in there and took your dad's old job?"

Tommy smiles sheepishly. "I'm continuing my parents' legacy."

"They give you money just to do research?"

"Important research."

"Do they know that you're cheating?" Christelle asks, tapping her fingers on one of his books absentmindedly. She picks it up and skims the back cover. "Pretty unfair to other World War II researchers that you can . . . I don't know . . . travel back in time?"

"Of course they don't know any of that." Tommy rolls his eyes. "My dad did some good work for them and I'm . . . what do you call it . . .?"

"A product of nepotism?"

"Legacy. I'm a legacy."

"A product of nepotism." Christelle tosses the book back down on the desk and grins at him mockingly. "It's obscene!"

"In my defense, the work *is* difficult. My dad—"

"If I hear 'my dad' one more time . . ." says Christelle, but not unkindly.

"Oh, come on, Chris, give me a break!"

"I'm just saying . . ." She fixes him with a look. A more serious one this time. "Is this what you really want to do? So much of your time just spent in the past? You know how I feel about that. Sometimes I'm scared for you."

"There's nothing to be scared of."

"Tommy—"

"Look, Chris. My mother always told me that there must be a reason why I keep going back to London before and during the Second World War. I think this might be it. How many other historians can say they stood in Trafalgar Square on VE Day and saw the celebrations with their very own eyes?"

Christelle shakes her head, exasperated. "Yeah, I get all that, but I don't think that's the only reason you're doing what you're doing."

"I don't know what you're on about."

She gives him another pointed look. "Come on. Don't play dumb. Your girl."

"Peggy?"

"Yes, Peggy!" Christelle drops into the chair opposite his and spins around in it, her long legs outstretched. "It sounds to me like you want an excuse to keep being in her life or to find out what happened to her after the war."

"I told you that's not how it is. We've agreed to be just friends. And, besides, I already promised her that I won't tell her about her future. So what's the point of me trying to find out what happened?"

"Tom, I love you. But you're a guy."

"What does that mean?" says Tommy, a little aghast. He sinks back in his chair.

"It means . . ." Christelle shrugs. "Guys make promises all the time. Doesn't mean they keep them."

"Isn't that just people in general?"

Christelle glares at him. "I said what I said."

"It's not like that with Peggy."

"Oh, please."

"It's really not."

"If you say so."

"Chris, I don't need this right now, alright? You don't need to worry about me."

"Someone has to."

"Well"—he gestures at his spacious office—"I feel like I'm doing just fine."

"That is just a veiled criticism of me, when I'm struggling to even find a job at Sainsbury's."

"You'll get something decent soon. Last I heard from Eva, even *she* is working."

"Doing what?"

"Teaching art to kids, I think. We only text once in a while, so please don't interrogate me for details. I hardly know anything."

Christelle rolls her eyes. "A great big brother *you* are."

"Shut up. My point is . . . even Eva is doing something decent, and she doesn't have a degree! You'll get something, just believe in yourself."

"Oh, shut it." She picks up a small book and tosses it across the desk at him. It hits him squarely in the chest and slides down to the floor with a thud. "By the way, you need to come over for dinner soon. Mum and Dad have been going on about how long it's been since they last saw you."

"Oh, I know."

"And I know you don't really talk much about how you *feel*—"

"Oh, Chris, are we on that again?"

"—being the big, strong man that you are," Christelle drawls. "But if you ever need someone . . ."

"I don't need—"

"If you ever need someone, we are here for you."

He scoffs. "Who are we?"

"Me. Diana. Even my parents." She gives a little laugh. "My parents would adopt you if they could."

"That would make you and I siblings." Tommy makes a disgusted face. "A horrifying thought."

She laughs. "Oh, come off it!" She picks up another book and throws it at him. This time he ducks and it hits the wall behind him instead.

"Hey! Stop ruining my office!" he cries.

"I'm doing you a favor, stupid!"

He gets down on his knees in search of the book, still chuckling. But once he locates it and tosses it back onto the table, the mirth has disappeared from Christelle's eyes. Instead, she is watching him with an expression that looks a lot like pity.

"What?" he says, attempting to brush it off. "Do I have something on my face?"

"No." Christelle shakes her head but does not say anything else. He sits back down and begins rearranging some papers. He can feel her gaze searing into his mind.

Christelle's voice softens. "Tommy, I know you say you and this Peggy girl are friends, but how does that even work with what you can do?"

"What do you mean?"

"Are there times when you go back and you see her, but

it's a younger her before she decides you guys should just be friends? Things like that."

"It can be a bit confusing, yes," he admits. "Sometimes I have to withhold certain information. But that's what both of us have always had to do since we were kids."

Christelle sniggers. "Not unhealthy at all."

"It's just necessary. You wouldn't understand."

He hasn't yet told Christelle about Peggy somehow knowing who May is. It can only mean that something will happen in his future involving May. Something that will prompt his future self to share certain information with Peggy. He has his suspicions about what that something might be, but he can't bring himself to share any of this with Christelle. He fears what she would say. She wouldn't understand.

"What if one day," says Christelle, "you go back and you can't find her?"

The moment is so small, she almost misses it: for a fraction of a second, Tommy's put-together expression falters. "It hasn't happened yet," he says.

"But what if—?"

"It's not going to happen."

"Tommy, that's not realistic . . . You don't know that—"

"But I do, Chris, I do. It won't." He looks down at the papers on his desk. "Besides . . . I'm moving on."

TOMMY AND MAY

2014

May thinks of Tommy often. How can she not?

The boy who makes her feel like everything she has ever wanted is about to begin.

She sees him online sometimes. Blurry photos he posts on his profile.

His charming smile occasionally teetering on his lips, a lopsided scale.

After the night he asked her to come over and she found him drunk,

they meet every once in a while to catch up. He buys her tea, a meal.

Listens to her quietly tell little anecdotes of how she has been doing with school,

with London, with new friends, with family back home.

And he just smiles.

He finds comfort in her soft eyes. Her little giggle whenever he pays her a compliment. Her cute smiles. He appreciates the way she hangs on his every word, the time she takes to simply be with him. It is nice, he tells himself, to have something uncomplicated. And maybe, just maybe, this is meant to happen; he is simply putting all the pieces together.

She, however, thinks he is the sun.

———————

May finishes her English course but wants to stay on in London; her dream life cannot possibly end now.

At lunch with Tommy, she sips her oolong, and picks at her food with her chopsticks.

He is distracted, she can tell. He tries to smile often, and the smile is still as radiant, as imprinted in her mind as it has always been, but he fidgets. Squirms. His eyes darting about.

A part of her feels guilty for inviting him to this lunch,

because the last thing she wants to be to him is an inconvenience.

(How humiliating that would be; she doesn't think she could ever live that down.)

"Tommy." She says his name like she is dipping a toe into a stream she hopes won't be freezing cold. "Is something the matter?"

"No, no," he says right away, shaking his head. "Everything's good. I'm good. Why?"

"You just seem . . . a bit distracted and a little tired."

"Oh, sorry!" And he looks it, too. "I've just . . . There's been a lot going on,

and I haven't been sleeping enough, and my work . . ."

"Oh, of course, you are very busy," she says quickly, feeling like an idiot.

"You must have a lot going on right now, Tommy. I shouldn't have asked you to come meet me—"

"May, stop." He smiles again and she falters. "I'm okay. I'm a little tired,

but I always want to see you. Otherwise, I wouldn't have come."

She beams, floating. He leans back in his chair, satisfied; he likes making her smile.

"Now," he says, "what were you saying about finding a job? I might be able to help you."

Her heart, kept for so long in a little glass case, begins to open up, crack by crack.

He gives her books, documents, lists and lists, and more lists.

"My best mate Christelle would have been the one doing this," he tells her,

"but she just got a job at the Imperial War Museum, so—" he shrugs, disappointment written in every line of his face,

"—I need someone else to comb through all these."

May blushes. "Thank you so much for taking a chance on me, but I don't know what I'm doing. This is such important work, especially to you. What if I get it wrong?"

"Oh, nonsense!" He waves away her concern.

"It's mostly just locating information, really. Going through different texts,

writing down dates, times . . . that sort of thing! How about you, uh . . ."

He scratches the back of his head awkwardly.

"How about you come over to mine some day and I'll show you how to get started?

That way you'll know what I want you to do and you'll begin to get the hang of it."

She almost drops the books and files she is carrying.

They are walking into a Tube station and she halts abruptly, unable to look at him,

trying to focus on recapturing the papers that have fluttered to the ground. "Oh . . . that's . . . that's . . ."

"Come on," he says with a teasing smile. "I'll even make you dinner.

If free food is not enough of a draw, then I don't know what is."

"Oh . . . I suppose . . ." Her entire body is radiating heat. "Okay, I'll come."

It is her second winter here, but she is still not used to the loneliness, the silence.

The gray-colored buildings, gray skies, the constant rain.

A small flat surrounded by other gray flats, darkness that descends at four in the evening.

Strangers avoiding your eyes on the streets, everyone avoiding your eyes.

The cold, how it chills and presses down on you until you cannot sit up or see brighter days.

Nights when the silence becomes too unbearable.

Sometimes, she closes her eyes and tries to imagine what it would feel like to be touched,

to be adored by a boy, and what she would look like under his gaze.

Would she glow? Shine? Sometimes, as she touches her lips with her own two fingers,

she thinks she might cry. She tries to conjure up the boy again,

but his face keeps shifting from that of the boy she used to love

to the one she thinks she is starting to love.

Tommy buys her a desk that she sets up in the living room,

squeezed between the sofa and the TV, and it is where she works,

combing through books and documents, highlighting, scribbling, and transcribing.

He tells her she is his database. His own personal Google. His lifeline.

When he tells her this—hovering over her as she flips through a book in his office—

her heart almost hurts from how much it folds into itself.

This is the memory she plays over and over as she sits at her tiny desk, working,

occasionally looking out of the window at the rain falling down.

She knows it will be Christmas soon.

She wonders what she'll do for Christmas this year.

There are moments when she thinks things might be different.

When she goes to give him what she has been working on—

answers to the questions he's been asking, information only she can find.

She is not delusional: she knows he must have someone, or many someones.

Girls who are not like her, who do not talk or look or think in any of the same ways she does.

She does not dare believe that she can ever compare. But when he looks at her, sometimes,

for a few seconds, she thinks she catches a glimmer in his eyes. A pause.

It might be possible. She catches him looking, sometimes. He asks her questions, sometimes—questions that make her think he cares a bit more than he lets on.

How is she holding up? What happened to her friends from the course? Does she have any?

How does she spend her days when she's not working?

Maybe she should do some traveling—it might help with the loneliness.

He understands, he tells her, that sometimes in a city like London, you can get swallowed up.

He makes her a cup of tea, sometimes. Sits her down in his kitchen

and listens to her while she talks, and it might be the most she has talked all week.

She wonders often if the feeling she gets under his gaze is something he can physically see.

Does it manifest itself as tiny balls of light hovering above her head?

She imagines that her heart is probably glowing out of her chest, thumping loudly,

and he sees it just as clearly as he sees her sitting across from him but is too polite to mention it,

as though it is considered rude to direct her to her own humiliation.

So both of them continue sitting there, talking,

while her heart beats on, glaringly bright, like a beacon.

One day, after he puts both of their empty cups in the sink, he watches her as she pulls on her jacket, with the folder filled with the documents he has given her squeezed under her arm.

She does not expect his gaze to linger, but it does, even while she is lacing up her boots.

She feels a smile touching her lips.

"What?" she asks. They have now fallen into a comfortable, friendly dynamic in which they can both pretend that they are just friends and nothing more.

He shrugs, a smile of his own playing around the corners of his mouth. "Nothing," he says.

But a tiny expression: there is something else he wants to say, and he stops himself just in time.

An unfamiliar wave of bravery surges through her. "What?" she prompts.

He shrugs again. "Nothing," he says. "I just . . . never realized how long your hair is now."

"Oh." She blushes, running her fingers through her hair, which has now reached halfway down her back.

"I can't remember the last time I got it cut. It must have

been when I was in Hong Kong."

"It looks nice," he says.

"It does?"

That elusive look in his eyes again, the one she cannot quite place. But then it is gone.

"Yeah, it does." He takes a step closer. "Do you ever wear it in a plait?"

"Sometimes. For bed."

"I reckon it looks nice that way, too." He takes another step closer.

Something is fluttering its wings inside her chest. She forces a laugh. "Don't joke."

He shakes his head. "I'm not. Come on. It's dark. I'll walk you home."

It is raining softly that night,
and there is a freshness in the atmosphere.
They walk side by side, talking of nothing.
She feels the air crackle in the space between them.
That walk could last for an entire lifetime
and she would keep on walking, just to have him
continue looking at her with shining eyes. Always.
Her building looms ahead and she spins around to face him.

"This is me," she says. He cocks his head to the side and appraises her.

"May I?" he asks. The answer is already given, long before.

So she nods, Yes, please, yes, and he moves in and captures her mouth with his.

The kiss is warm, wet brightness. She laughs into him and thinks:

All these years, hoping, and the real thing feels so right.

She opens her eyes to see that he is keeping his shut.

His grip on her is firm, and she glows.

Oh, this is it. "I don't want to go home," he whispers.

And so she draws him even closer, presses her lips to his neck, his chin,

holds his face steady with her careful hands, and invites him in.

Later, the way he moves has the power to transform her space.

It almost feels like a dream: he in her little flat, moving through it, and in her bed.

His mouth is fervent, heady, so desperate, she lies back and just knows:

Oh, this is how my life begins.

Much later, when he is sleeping soundly,

she slips out and sits on the floor of her bathroom in her robe.

She leans against the tub, pressing the cold side against the base of her neck.

Her body feels new, but oh so breakable, and happiness tastes a bit like shattered glass;

when she lays a finger on her tongue, it comes away bloody.

She thinks of him in her bed and smiles, because how can she not?

Yet it is still raining outside. She can hear the sound it makes tinkling against the glass.

Tommy wakes and for a while all he sees is darkness.

He feels the heat of her body pressed against him and, for
a second,

he thinks he is with Peggy and the sound of the rain hitting
the windowpane

is the rain he hears so often falling upon the streets of Limehouse.

But no. She stirs, her face turning over on the pillow,
and . . . no,

those are not Peggy's eyes, and that is not her face, her hair,
the shape of her nose or mouth.

He is not that stupid, not that careless. He knew what he
was doing:

Peggy wants them to be nothing more than friends, so he
has to move on.

And, besides, she knows about May. This night is meant
to happen.

At least he is doing *something* right.

He sits up and the light from outside slants in through the
window,

illuminating the curves of May's face, her body. She is smiling a little in her sleep,

and he wonders what it would take for him to look that
peaceful when asleep.

His head is filled with scissors. For a moment he considers
lying down again,

curling around her, pulling her close to him, maybe kissing

her temple, the blade of her shoulder,

telling her . . . What can he tell her? He slips out quietly, but not quietly enough.

She opens her eyes and her hand winds through his. "Are you okay?" she whispers.

"Yeah," he mumbles, his voice sounding scratchy and raw to his ears. "Go back to sleep."

But she sits up. "Do you need anything?" she asks. She always asks.

The dissimilarity makes him want to choke. "No, no, you're good," he says.

In the half-light her expression falters. "I'm sorry if . . . I didn't know . . . I was . . ."

"May, it's okay—"

"All the things I said. If it was too much. I'm sorry . . . I don't want you to . . . think anything and . . ."

"It's fine." And it is. It is not her fault. "Trust me. Everything is okay."

Her eyes are huge in the darkness. "Really?"

"Yes." And to make her believe it, he leans forward and kisses her forehead, her lips.

She still looks so scared, so in awe of him, that he makes a decision.

He kisses her again, more intensely this time.

"May, you're good," he whispers against her mouth. "Trust me."

They fall back into the bed together and he tells himself:

This is for the best.

He can build something different from this.

Maybe all of it, he reasons, has led up to her.

EVA

2014

Slowly, day by day, Eva's art classes start to grow.

At first, there were less than five children sitting with her in Maa-maa Jiayi's living room.

Then, as word spread, more and more children joined, until the entire room is packed and Maa-maa has to retreat into the kitchen until lessons are over.

Eva teaches the kids to create whatever they fancy: rough sketches, with every line flowing softly, boldly; watercolor and oil paintings, with as many shades as possible; drawings of anything and everything, from animals, cartoon characters, and landscapes to monsters and magic.

Eva's Cantonese isn't what she wants it to be, but she tries her hardest to make sure the children have a good time.

She remembers what her mother had told her: "I want this, always, to be fun for you."

The searing memory of her mother's smile, so bright, so beautiful, the moment Eva turned the canvas around to reveal her very first painting: a swirling lavender ocean filled with magical sea creatures. "You have such freedom to express your creativity," her mother had said. "Cherish it." And a little sadly: "I never had that growing up."

So Eva tells her students: "This is a space where you can be yourself, completely." And then, just as her mother had said: "I want this, always, to be fun for you."

Eva talks to Maa-maa Jiayi and Aunt Dorothy one day after classes are over.

"I feel like I'm doing what I'm meant to be doing," she says. "This is the first time since—" she still can't say it out loud "—since I was twelve that I feel like I have something to look forward to each day."

"I have a feeling this is just the beginning," says Aunt Dorothy. "Right now, it's just children from the neighborhood, but pretty soon there'll be others. You should think about getting a proper teaching space. Start charging for lessons."

Eva thinks about it for a few seconds. "If it's kids from around here . . . I really don't want to do that."

Aunt Dorothy shrugs. "Why not? I understand that you love spending time with the kids, so you don't think of it as a job, as such. But it's not wrong for you to make money from it."

"I know it's not wrong," says Eva. "But . . ."

"But?"

"I don't think it's something my mother would do."

Maa-maa Jiayi looks curious; they've not discussed Eva's mother much, if at all. And Eva begins to wonder what her father told his family about the girl he fell in love with and started a family with halfway around the world.

Aunt Dorothy's smile is a knowing one. "But it's something your father would do," she says.

And Eva thinks she might be right.

They are having this discussion over three bowls of noodles with pork spareribs, dim sum, and cabbage stir-fried in fish sauce.

Maa-maa Jiayi sips her tea and, in between bites of food, asks the question Eva has been anticipating.

"I hope you don't mind, my dear, but I want to hear more about your mother. Joshua never told us much about her. What was she like?"

That night, after Maa-maa Jiayi has gone to bed, Aunt Dorothy comes and sits with Eva while she prepares for tomorrow's lessons. The dining table is filled with paper of different colors that Eva is cutting into various shapes.

"I'm sorry if that was difficult today," says Aunt Dorothy. "Having to talk about your mother."

Eva folds a pink sheet of paper into a rectangle and then into a square. "It's okay," she replies quietly. "I've always assumed Maa-maa would be curious."

"She is right, though. We don't know much about your mother. Hardly at all, thanks to your father."

When Eva doesn't say anything, she continues: "From what you've told us, she sounds like a wonderful woman."

Eva picks up a pair of scissors and begins cutting the square in half. After the square, a green sheet of paper is turned into a circle and two triangles.

"She would be very proud of you," says Aunt Dorothy.

Eva tries to think of an adequate reply but cannot come up with one. Tommy would know what to say, she suddenly thinks. Something that would appease the other person yet reveal nothing of what she's really feeling. But she's not Tommy.

Aunt Dorothy sighs and takes Eva's hand. "I know I might not always say the right things," she says, "and I might never understand completely how you feel. But I am here. If you need me."

Later that night, for the first time in a very long while, Eva closes her eyes and opens them to find herself outside her mother's childhood home in Primrose Hill.

It must be around noon, with the sun high in the sky. She stands on the pavement on the opposite side of the road and looks through the downstairs window to find her mother as a little girl, paintbrush in hand, sitting in front of an easel. The canvas shows the beginnings of a dark green field.

Hovering over her mother is a man who looks to be in his early fifties, with dark brown hair and a sandy beard. He is wearing glasses and an air of extreme impatience. Her teacher, Eva guesses.

For a long time, Eva watches as the man painstakingly guides her mother through the process of drawing a typical English country landscape. A few trees, dotted here and there. The sea in the distance. A small cottage.

Her mother fidgets in her seat. Every brush stroke she applies betrays her lack of confidence.

The teacher crosses his arms, his shoulders hunched up in frustration. Eva cannot hear what is being said, but she can see little Lily flinching as he speaks. He motions for her to keep painting. Lily dips her brush into the color palette and cautiously presses it to the canvas. She is trying to paint clouds in the sky, but every movement of her wrist looks even more forced than before. More restrained.

Eva feels a sudden urge to storm into the house and throw that canvas to the ground.

She hears herself say out loud, "Mum, I miss you. I promise I'll do it all differently. Don't you worry."

TOMMY AND MAY

2015

Tommy started planting the seeds for May to gravitate toward him
  from the day they first met. Carefully and subtly.

A small part of him admits this in moments when he chooses
  to look at the situation with as much honesty as he dares.

He decides to be as direct with her as possible when it
comes to

what he can do. Like with Peggy, he shows her how it's
done—

closes his eyes and slowly disappears and then reappears
again out of thin air.

When he returns, he sees her at the edge of his bed,
her eyes wide, one hand clasped over her mouth.

"Oh my God," she says, and then curses under her breath
in Cantonese. "Oh my God."

He beams, and she rushes to him, throws her arms around his neck

and kisses him until both of them are breathless. "Oh my God, oh my God."

Despite himself, he is enraptured by her faith in him; there is no jadedness or skepticism in her.

She believes in him so completely, he sometimes thinks that if he told her he could hold up the moon, she would not question it.

Adoration, he fails to see, is an addiction of sorts.

"Didn't you think I was crazy when I first told you?" he asks her.

It has been a few months and they lie entangled in his bed in the middle of the night,

she with her head on his chest.

She lets out a small gasp. "No, I could never. I would never think you're crazy.

I've always believed you were special. It never occurred to me that you would . . . make it all up."

"Anyone else would have run. Or sent me away."

He thinks of Peggy, her scent on his clothes, how she turns away from him

whenever he wants to talk about the future, her eyes so incredibly sharp and full of pain.

He can feel the shape of May's smile against his skin. "Well," she says, "I'm not just anyone."

"What do you mean?"

There is a long silence. He sees the cliff ahead of them,

but before he can say anything to avoid it, she is already hurtling toward it.

"Unless you have girls tell you that they're in love with you all the time."

There it is. He should have known it was coming.

The way she has told him, too, like she is treading on ice.

"You don't have to say anything," she quickly tells him. "I just want to say it.

I feel like I've spent all my life being afraid. But I don't want to be afraid with you."

He recalls Peggy walking ahead of him by the Thames.

She turns around and smiles, with the sun shining from behind her,

and he feels as though he is floating up into the air.

He kisses May's forehead. "I don't want to hurt you."

"You have never hurt me," she says. "Not once. You're a good man."

The next day, after she has gone back to her flat,

he sits by himself on the floor in the living room,

surrounded by history books and photographs.

In his left hand is a bottle of beer, in his right a cigarette.

Even though he cannot see the face of his mother's stag,

he feels like someone is staring at him, eyes boring straight into the middle of his forehead.

Briefly, he considers calling May and asking her to come back,

but he feels guilty for dragging her into his head. How can she possibly understand?

His eyes do not need to adjust to the darkness this time.

"You look terrible," Christelle tells Tommy.

They are standing outside a pub while he smokes a cigarette.

Inside, Christelle's girlfriend, Diana, is chatting with May and two of Christelle's colleagues.

The weather is becoming warmer, the first few signs of spring.

Tommy shakes his head in amusement, clamps the cigarette between his teeth, and lights it.

He asks, "When have you ever said that I don't look terrible?"

"You look more terrible than usual, is what I mean." Christelle leans back against the wall of the pub, her hands in the pockets of her jacket. "Does she know?"

"Who?"

Christelle cocks her head to the side. "That nice girl you've been sleeping with."

"May."

"Yes, May." Christelle rolls her eyes. "Does she know?"

"About what?"

"I don't know. Take your pick."

"Chris, don't start, alright? We're just . . . seeing how it goes—"

"That girl is half in love with you."

"She's not. Well . . . not half."

"What do you mean?"

He gives her a guilty look. Christelle lets out a groan. "Tommy, I could fucking kill you."

"I didn't say it back."

"Oh, well, at least you're being honest," says Christelle, every word dripping with sarcasm.

"But I could be."

"What do you mean, you *could* be?"

"I could be in love with her. Maybe it's a gradual thing. I care about her a lot. And she's good for me."

"Does she know about what you can do?"

"Yes."

"You told her?"

"Well, I wanted to."

"You fucking narcissist."

Tommy winces. "A bit harsh, Chris."

"Does she know about Peggy?"

A pause. He puts the cigarette to his lips and takes a drag. Gives a quick shake of his head.

Christelle hits him in the arm. "Fucking bastard."

"I will . . . I will tell her. It's just . . . things with Peggy are . . . there's not even a thing anymore."

He feels like he cannot quite breathe. He cannot look at Christelle, so instead

he looks down at his feet, then at the streetlight blinking behind her.

"Peggy and I are friends. Last time I went back we just chatted about nothing. It was nice. But I wasn't quite sure, for her, if it's before or after or . . . You were right. It wouldn't have worked, so I'm . . ." He gestures at May inside the pub. "So now I have this. And it's nice. I want to make it work. I think I'm *supposed* to make it work."

No other words come to him, so he just stops talking.

Christelle watches him as he takes another drag and blows out the smoke. "Oh, Tommy," she says.

"'Oh, Tommy' what? Chris, you don't have to worry about me. I'll be okay."

"We both know that's a lie."

"Chris . . . I mean it."

She sighs. "Oh, Tommy," she says again.

The probability is slim, but it is there, hovering out of the corner of his eye: a different kind of life with Peggy; a new kind of life with May.

Every time he looks into May's eyes, every time he takes her face in his hands and kisses her,

he thinks he can fall in love with her one day, have his feelings for her grow to match those she has for him. They can build a life together in the here and now.

He probably will. Because why else would Peggy know of May?

Peggy can be a friend—someone who'll always be there, but no longer such a mainstay.

As long as he can still see her and talk to her every once in a while, he can learn to let her recede into his past, preserved and perfect.

If you can fall in love with someone, you can fall out of love with them too, right?

Yet there are times when his thoughts briefly stray to his parents, and he wonders:

How were they so sure? How did they know? How can anyone?

It is the second month of spring and the flowers are blooming along his street.

The tree in his front garden is green again, so that when he wakes that morning, he sees the sun shining through its leaves, golden and bright.

His first thought, as usual, is of Peggy.

And then, of course, the familiar ache in his chest that he quickly pushes out of the way,

as usual. Then he thinks about what he plans to do for the day: a paper he needs to finish,

an email he needs to answer, and then a trip he needs to go on again. For him.

He is drinking his first cup of tea in the kitchen when he hears the knock on the door.

He answers it and finds May. He can tell right away she has been crying.

"I couldn't sleep last night," she says, her voice breaking. "Oh, Tommy."

Again, the cliff. He sees it looming, but he cannot run away.

"I don't know how else to tell you this," she says. "But . . . Tommy . . . you're going to be a father."

And the only thing he can think of is his own father, sitting at the dinner table once upon a time.

She sees the look on his face. Hesitates.

This is a good thing . . . right?

JOSHUA AND LILY

1992

Henry Yu died two months before the birth of his grandchildren, Tommy and Eva. It happened very unexpectedly, quicker than anyone—including all the specialist doctors he paid large sums of money to see—could have ever anticipated. By the time the cancer was detected, it had advanced to the final stage, spreading from his colon to his lymph nodes and, before long, to the rest of his body. After years of withstanding so much—of working nonstop through every illness, every sleepless night, every missed opportunity he was not brave enough to label a regret—Henry's body finally succumbed. All it took was two chemo sessions. He passed away in his sleep, alone, in the hospital at five in the morning, while his wife, Carol, was stirring awake in their bedroom in Primrose Hill. He was fifty-nine years old.

The funeral was in the middle of the day, while rain poured

down. Mourners—mostly colleagues in posh suits and distant family members Lily had never met—stood huddled under large black umbrellas. A Christian priest stood over the grave, reading from his Bible. A headstone: just his name, dates, and the words *Beloved Husband and Father*. So simple yet so insufficient to encompass everything Lily felt. She had known this moment would come. Yet she was surprised to find herself wishing that there could have been a loophole. A detour, perhaps. Anything . . .

Lily stood at the back of the procession, hanging on to Joshua's arm. She noticed the stares from cousins, aunts and uncles, and her father's white colleagues: the pregnant young daughter with the husband from Hong Kong, that young man who was always scowling. A math prodigy with a good job at a London university, but still, an outsider. They might as well have wrinkled their noses and turned their shoulders on the two of them; she could feel their disdain crawling on her skin.

After the ceremony, the guests filed out of the cemetery, pausing briefly to offer her their condolences. Some shook Joshua's hand, but they mostly looked past him, as though Lily was leaning against a mannequin. Before long it was just them, Carol, and Mary. The older woman bent down at her son-in-law's grave, her shaking, veined hands planting two incense sticks into the ground before the headstone. Carol joined her mother and lit them herself. The two women stood there for a while, looking down at what remained of the man who had plucked them from their lives in Liverpool so long ago and given them all the riches they could ever hope for.

By the time Carol reached Lily, her face was set: harsh, empty, determined. She did not offer Joshua a glance when she said to her daughter, You are coming home. Your father is gone. There is no one to take care of me and your grandmother.

Lily had her answer ready. Mum, Dad left me the Kennington House. And Joshua and I are starting a family of our own. You can't ask this of me.

Have you no regard for your mother?

Joshua looked away, but Lily did not. You and Ah-ma will be alright, she said. You're still strong and healthy. We'll visit as often as we can.

Carol's face twitched. Your father worked himself to death so you could stand here with everything you have. And now, on the day of his funeral, you disrespect him.

And I am grateful, said Lily, her voice wavering. But—

But nothing! You are *not* grateful. You've become spoiled! Foolish! You forget yourself!

Carol. Enough. It is Ah-ma Mary. The old woman came up to them, her steps faltering a little. We should go home.

Mother, Carol began to protest. But one look from Mary was enough.

Mary turned away from Carol and held a calloused hand to Lily's cheek. The touch alone nearly reduced her granddaughter to tears. You have grown so much, said Mary. I am so proud of you.

Then she turned to Joshua, her gaze making the jade Buddha that his maa-maa had given him another lifetime ago throb against his skin. The old woman spoke to him in Cantonese, in an accent unsoftened by years and continents. Thank you, she told him. For being here.

Two days later, Joshua arrived home from university around midnight to find his wife in the bath. The water was so hot, steam was rising from the tub, with beads of sweat clinging to Lily's back and shoulder blades. Her huge belly was protruding from the water, her hands resting on it tenderly. Tears flowed silently down her cheeks, a steady, still stream of remembrance rather than an outpouring of sadness.

He sat down on the toilet seat, disentangling his tie. No tears, he told her. He hated seeing her cry.

She wiped her face with the back of her hand and said, This is the first time I've cried since it happened.

Your father was a strong man. He wouldn't want you to be sad.

She ignored him. Did you see the notes I put up in the office?

He finished loosening his tie and rested his chin on his hand. Yes. You traveled today. You know how I feel about it.

When they were sure of the pregnancy, she had told him that nothing had to change. She did not want it to. But after discovering that she was carrying twins, the number of trips that she went on began to decrease, especially when it became increasingly obvious that the journeys exhausted her more than usual. Sometimes they would arrive back in the present with her swaying on the spot, her head spinning, and she would have to lie down for a very long time before she was ready to travel again. The feeling, she had tried to describe to him, was more intense than usual. It either felt like her insides were being ripped apart or her entire body was melting into the ground.

Joshua dipped two fingers into the scalding water. I thought you might try and go back to see your father, he said. But instead, you tried to go to France.

I don't want to see him. Lily closed her eyes and let the tears continue to run. And even if I did, what good would it do? Everything has already been written. What difference would it make? There would just be more pain. More . . . complications. But with France . . . with France, I thought . . . if it was somewhere close . . . it might be possible. But, still, no luck.

Maybe it's because of your condition, he said. Maybe we can try again after the twins are born.

Or maybe it can't be done, she said.

He shrugged. When have we ever believed that something can't be done?

She smiled despite herself and found his hand. Thank you for reminding me, she said. Don't ever let me forget.

He kissed her palm. I won't. Now dry your tears and come out of that bath. We can go over your attempt from today. Maybe there's something you missed.

Tommy and Eva arrived ten minutes apart. Tommy came first, silent and still, until the nurse struck him gently and he began to cry. Eva came into the world squalling, fists shaking and railing against everyone and everything in it.

Lily did not call her mother; she had wanted reassurance while she endured the pain of childbirth, but the thought of Carol's stern expression looming over her made her grit her teeth and push through. For a split second her father's face appeared in her mind: him lying on a hospital bed, gaunt, breath rattling through his body, hollowed out by the dreadful disease. But it was just a split second. Then Joshua was beside her, gripping her hand, and then . . . the sound of crying ripping through the air, almost like salvation.

She drifted off to sleep soon after, still feeling yellow lights on her eyelids, the pain thrumming through her body, a constant reminder of change. She dreamed of her ah-ma Mary standing by the docks in Liverpool. Her father when she was a child, strolling through the zoo and sitting at the dinner table, his eyes on the newspaper. Her mother at the funeral two months ago, demanding. Her husband smiling, silent, lost. Then darkness.

As for Joshua, he looked at his children, with their tufts of hair and their tiny hands and feet, and felt a combination of feelings he had never experienced before. He did not know what they were and so he could not name them. Could not even begin to understand where they came from. But there was one feeling he recognized instantly, since he had been living with it ever since he was a child: fear. He held his son's hand, planted a kiss on his daughter's forehead, and felt afraid.

After the nurses had taken the babies away and his wife had fallen asleep, he sat in the chair next to her bed and closed his eyes, counting his breaths, remembering. Before long, he was home in the darkness. His nose caught the scent of damp- ness, rubbish, sweat, and food. He heard the drip, drip of water running down the walls. Footsteps. Children screeching. People shouting in Cantonese. His people.

He opened his eyes and saw a boy crouching at the end of a dimly lit corridor, playing with an old toy car. The boy's hair had been shorn, his sweaty undershirt sticking to his thin body, his flip-flops too big for his feet. Joshua had almost forgotten. Although he still remembered that day.

Much later, he returned to find his wife looking at him from her bed. It was dark in the hospital room, but he could see her eyes shining through the gloom. Where were you? she asked.

He did not tell her. Instead, he pulled over a chair so he could be closer to her and took her hand.

You should get some sleep, he said.

She recognized the smells on his clothes. The faraway look in his eyes. She had seen them before and knew what they meant. But she realized, with a terrifying, cold sensation, that she had never seen him quite like this before. What's wrong? she asked. You can tell me.

He shook his head. Nothing's wrong.

What happened? she asked. Josh, are you alright?

His silence stretched on and on, and when she lifted a hand to trace the lines of his face and call him back to her with her touch, she knew, for the very first time, that no matter how hard she tried or begged, there would always be a part of him that she would never quite reach.

TOMMY, MAY, AND PEGGY

2016 / 1939

May names her daughter Daisy after the flowers that grow in front of the old church on the way from Tommy's house to her flat. Her little girl, she decides, will have a sunny name, an English name. A name that portends nothing but positivity and dreams fulfilled.

She thought that her heart could not expand any more after Tommy. Not after she said those three words to him and felt more than half of herself leave her body. But when her daughter—so vulnerable and so soft—is placed in her arms for the very first time, she finds another compartment within herself that she did not know she had.

This, she thinks, is when her life begins.

And in so many ways, she is right: everything she has

known is falling away, and an entirely new path is being cleared for her.

———————

Tommy is trying to do what is right.

He has failed before, but there are no excuses now.

From the moment his daughter enters the world, her sharp cries piercing the air,

his hand coming into contact with her much smaller and softer one,

he knows what he must try and do.

It does not matter how he feels. Feelings are never to be entirely trusted.

Pay too much attention to them and they can distort your goals

and wreck the established order of your life.

This is something his father would probably have said.

So he plants a kiss on May's forehead, takes the phone from her hand,

and speaks reassuring words to her family down the line:

"Yes, I'm in love with your daughter." "We will get married one day."

"I'm delighted that we are starting a family. I will take care of them, I will provide."

"You don't have to worry. I love your daughter."

These are not lies; he detests men who lie.

In many ways, he has come to appreciate May for who she is.

He likes her and cares about her. And so isn't this love, of a sort?

All the things she does for him, the enormity of her feelings . . . how can he fail to notice?

The least he can give her is a home. There might be things he can never offer

(even he is not foolish enough to believe otherwise),

but at least he can give her something.

That powerful, intense love will come.

And their little family will be even stronger for it.

His daughter feels light as a feather in his arms.

She stirs, moves her mouth, and jerks her little limbs.

He is afraid that if he makes one wrong move

she will slip out of his arms and shatter on the ground like a teacup.

He cannot describe the feeling.

Of course it is love—how can it not be?

Yet it is love weighed down with stones,

making him feel like he is drowning.

He cannot feel anything else.

He puts his lips to the crown of his daughter's head.

He thinks of his parents and wonders . . .

No, he would rather not wonder. What is the point?

May stirs in the hospital bed.

His daughter lets out a small cry.

The moon is huge against the dark sky outside,

an unblinking witness to their new lives.

He takes his daughter back to May's bedside,

sits down next to her and takes her hand.

"We're here," he says. "You're okay."

She opens her eyes, sees them, and smiles.

"I'm so happy," she whispers, tears forming in the corners of her eyes.

"I cannot remember the last time I was this happy. I don't think I've ever been this happy."

He returns her smile and squeezes her hand. "I'm glad," he says.

Yes. This is it. Everything he's been looking for. Finally.

He goes back, and this time Peggy doesn't greet him in the way she used to,

no more kisses, no more touches that linger on his skin
like fire.

So he suspects that, in her timeline,

she must have already told him that they should just be friends.

It is obvious in the way
her eyes look at him with sadness.
The longing in their embrace.

So he sits her down and says:
I have something amazing to tell you.

She puts on a brilliant smile once she hears.
I'm so happy for you, she tells him.

He asks: This is what's supposed to happen, right?

She shrugs. I don't know. You tell me.

I hate how we always have to speak in riddles.

She laughs. You can blame yourself for that.

A strong wave of affection for her
    rushes back to him, and he asks wistfully,
    Do you remember when we first met?

Yes, of course, she replies. So much has changed since then.

This does not have to change. He gestures back and forth
between them.
    Our friendship. Nothing will be different.

Oh, Tommy. She chuckles ruefully, shaking her head.
    The only thing that hasn't changed is how much you can
still amaze me with your—

Charm?

Absolutely not, she scoffs. But you just became a father, so I'm
going to be nice.

He beams. Peg, I miss you already.

They try to build a home:

May moves out of her one-bedroom flat and into Tommy's house.

Everything she brought to England is now kept in his bedroom,

some in his sister's bedroom down the hall. She resists the urge to listen in when he

makes the phone call to Hong Kong and tells his twin that his daughter is finally here.

His family's eyes follow her from portrait to portrait as she moves around the house,

the baby cradled in her arms. The stag in the living room, the one she hates, looms over them both.

She hangs her clothes in his wardrobe, in the space he has made for her,

arranges the baby paraphernalia, finds homes for more of her things,

and slowly, a house that has been solely his begins to transform,

morphing into an altogether different space—

one filled with her scent, her little objects, and the cries of their child.

Her parents in Hong Kong do not understand why she does not come home.

"I love him," she tells them. "And you want us to get married, don't you?

His whole life is here and so we have to stay."

Their anger and disappointment—her mother's tears and

her father's grim silence—

can be felt down the line, but she stands her ground. She has been waiting to do so all her life.

Anne is so furious, she refuses to send her niece any presents.

"Don't you understand what a big mistake this is?" she hisses, the big sister who used to be her best friend. "You're not married.

You're not even twenty-five. Come home right now."

"But this," she tells all of them, "is my family now. We have a good thing going here."

And she is right: the good thing is good. Exhausting, but good.

Those first few weeks and months when her entire world is Daisy and everything Daisy needs.

A new home. A man she loves. A man who bends down to kiss their daughter's forehead,

holds her, and paces around the room with her, trying to lull her to sleep,

his handsome face pressed against her delicate one. She watches them, her heart almost bursting,

and reckons this is the kind of feeling one reads about in books, hears in songs, and sees in movies.

Here it is, right in front of her very eyes. Just for her. Entirely hers.

The only time she ever feels like he is out of reach is when he goes on one of his trips.

Since he first told her what he could do, she has learned that they can never talk to each other about it in depth. She will never be able to fathom what it feels like, what it takes, and so she reasons that she has no right to demand any more time from him.

She is an understanding woman, she tells herself. Supportive. Generous.

There are nights when he comes to bed a few hours before the crack of dawn.

As he lowers himself quietly in beside her, carefully arranging the duvet over himself,

he makes sure to give her a peck on the cheek.

She wishes he would tell her where he goes, or who he sees—

there is a fraction of an idea flickering in the back of her mind—

but he returns every time, does he not?

May does not like to think that there is another woman.

She has grown up around men who have other women.

(She is pretty sure her father was one of these men.)

The way women like her are supposed to respond—

she has learned this from her mother—is to ignore it and rise above it.

At the end of the day, if he comes home and if he provides for their family,

a woman can endure almost anything.

But she does not reckon this is the case for Tommy, she reassures herself.

She thinks: If there is someone he cares about out there somewhere,

what they have can never be like what we have. You can't fake this.

His sweet words. His kindness. Their bond. Daisy.

He catches her looking once, as he balances their daughter on his knees, and he smiles. "You look content," he says.

"Do I?" She pretends to sound surprised and gets up from her chair to plant a soft kiss on his cheek.

"I can't imagine why," she teases.

He whispers: "I know it hasn't been easy . . . I want to thank you . . ."

"Tommy, I know you're trying your best."

She kisses him again, wanting him to know just how much she knows that he's trying.

That it is enough.

"You make me so happy," he says. "I don't deserve you."

No. You can't fake this.

EVA

2016

Progress does not always feel like progress, she has come to learn.

But things fall into place all the same: there is a pattern to the chaos.

A step taken. A new feeling growing. A new window opening.

You never forget, and so nothing changes. Yet everything does.

And one day she sits down and it is on a different sofa, in a different room, in a different flat,

with a different kind of light shining through the curtains, different photographs lining the walls and on the coffee table.

Suddenly a new life. Yet the one she feels she was meant to live all along,

like slipping into a well-worn sweater you have lost and then found in the back of a drawer.

The flat Eva has found is in the same building as Maa-maa Jiayi and Aunt Dorothy's.

It is roughly the same size, with a slightly smaller kitchen. She turns one of the two bedrooms into an art studio, setting up her easel next to the window, which overlooks a tiny playground. Between this room and the living room, she now has enough space to take in more students.

Aunt Dorothy surveys the flat with a wide smile. "I'm very proud of you," she says.

Eva beams. "Thank you for all your help. I couldn't have done any of this without you."

"Oh, you would have. I don't have any doubts." Her aunt extends a hand to touch the corner of the easel. "You're going to do amazing things."

Eva can't help but wonder if that's what her mother would say if she were here.

What she does know, having stood outside that house in Primrose Hill and watched her mother as a little girl put brush to canvas, is that her mother would love her students.

They include: the kids that she teaches for free, those who arrive in secondhand clothes, wearing the brightest smiles and borrowing paint and pencils from her own supply;

kids who arrive in fancy cars, driven by chauffeurs in uniforms and accompanied by mothers dressed in designer clothes and carrying designer handbags;

kids from the neighborhood and from far away—in all of whom Eva is able to find something sweet to nurture, a creative spark to ignite.

She tries to teach the kids the way her mother had taught her.

Gently, with words of encouragement and support.

Enthusiastically, with new activities and ideas at the ready.

She thinks of her father in his study, telling her and Tommy to take down notes from their travels.

His stern demeanor and serious sentiments counteracted with her mother's sweetness and good humor.

Eva shows the children's paintings and drawings to Aunt Dorothy, a sad, thoughtful gleam in her eyes as she confesses: "I used to travel back in time as much as I could, even though I knew I might . . . lose myself along the way. What happened to my parents is proof of that. But I just couldn't stay away."

"What about now?" asks Aunt Dorothy.

"Now I miss my mum and dad the same way," she says, "but I don't need to travel as often anymore." With a bittersweet smile, she picks up the drawings. "Now I have this."

———

One day, after her lessons are done, Eva goes with Maa-maa Jiayi and Aunt Dorothy to the park where the Kowloon Walled City once stood.

Eva's father never talked much about his childhood home. So everything Eva knows about the Walled City, she's learned through the photographs her parents had hung up in her father's office.

"It's very dark in there," was one of the few things her father had said. "You'd have to remember your way around or else you'd get lost very easily."

He'd taken her mother back there once, and Lily had

returned with a faraway look in her eyes.

That night, when she was tucking Eva into bed, she'd said, "I know he doesn't say it very often, but your father loves you very much. Do you know that?"

And Eva, a little confused, simply nodded and let her mother kiss her on the cheek.

Eva thinks of that memory now as she stands at the edge of the lotus pond, looking over the still surface of the water to the lush green trees on the opposite bank. It's hard to imagine that years ago, instead of all this greenery, there had stood an entire city, bursting with life and decay.

Maa-maa Jiayi's eyes are glazed with tears as she looks around. "It's like we were never here," she says. "I'm trying to remember where everything was." She turns to her daughter. "Dorothy, do you remember?"

Eva doesn't say anything while her grandmother and aunt start explaining how everything had once looked: "On that corner was where we used to bring in products for the restaurant," says Maa-maa. "That was where your grandfather used to wait for the delivery vans to arrive." "That was my route to school," says Aunt Dorothy. "I used to wait for the bus right there."

Still Eva doesn't say anything. How can she tell her grandmother that she's seen it all before? That she once walked down one of those long, dark corridors. Once stood on the rooftop and watched her father as a small boy toss pebbles down onto the streets below.

Later, during their ride home in a taxi when Maa-maa is dozing off, Aunt Dorothy takes her hand.

Eva expects her aunt to talk of her father, her grandfather, even her mother. But instead, she asks the question that is on Eva's mind the most.

"Have you talked to Tommy lately?"

Eva crosses her arms. "Not lately. He still hasn't replied to my last messages. He's probably busy with Daisy."

"Your grandmother desperately wants to meet that girl."

"Well, me too."

"Maybe you should go back for a little visit."

"I could. But something tells me that Tommy might not want to see me."

Aunt Dorothy studies Eva's face, frowning. "Dear, what's the matter?"

Eva keeps her eyes fixed on the road ahead. She can hear her grandmother's soft breathing to her left. She tells her aunt quietly: "It is never-ending, isn't it? Even when everything is falling into place."

A look of understanding in Aunt Dorothy's eyes. "What has brought it back this time? The park?"

"A little." Eva breathes in deeply. "The park. The new flat. Teaching. Everything." There is a slight tremor in her voice as she says: "I'm starting to find my footing, but my brother isn't here. Am I losing him too?"

PEGGY

1938

The letter is unexpected.

Peggy never saw it coming.

And after reading it all the way through in one sitting, like a person diving headfirst into murky waters, she wishes she never received it at all.

The photograph that accompanies it shows her that her imagination has not been accurate.

Her mother does not look like her.

Her mother is fuller in the face, with darker, harsher eyes, a button nose, a mouth that droops downward in a broken curve. The hands resting on her knees are much smaller than Peggy's own.

The children surrounding her—the boy and the girl, Peggy's half-siblings—

have her look. Her new husband is not that remarkable, Peggy cannot help but think:

short and stocky, with a grim expression as he stands behind his wife,

his hand resting possessively on her shoulder.

Another family. A newer one, untarnished. Rich, filthy rich.

The words jumble around, slipping off the page, blurring into each other—

words on regret, abandonment, reconciliation, honesty, and bravery.

Peggy lets them all fall to the ground and shatter.

Her father stares at the photograph with unseeing eyes.

I didn't tell you, he says, because there is no need for a little girl to know that.

Know what? says Peggy. That my mother isn't really dead?

Or that she abandoned me and doesn't love me?

Your mother loved you. Her father hangs his head. But she didn't love me. And she missed home. So she went back. I thought you might blame me for her leaving.

Pa, says Peggy, her voice thick with pain, I do not blame you. You are all I have.

He grabs her hand. Will you go? Like she asked? You know that her . . . husband will be able to pay for everything.

Peggy had thought she did not know what to do. But once her father asks the question, the answer rolls off her tongue as easily as if it has been there, waiting. No, she says. There is nothing for me there.

She thinks of burning the photograph,

but instead, she keeps it within the pages of her journal.

She takes it out that night while she is writing by candle-
light,

staring, transfixed, at the face of the woman she has been
dreaming of her entire life.

The words she has written mean nothing to Peggy. They
are empty and hollow.

Like all the years Peggy herself has lived, waiting for love.
No more.

She slides the photograph back in between the pages.

Later, she cannot sleep.

She lies awake, going through every mother she has created
over the years:

the ballerina with yellow ribbons in her hair,

the tragic princess locked in her tower,

the most beautiful woman in the world,

the adventurer.

All gone.

She thinks of Tommy as he once was:

a scared little boy with eager eyes,

his face lighting up with excitement as he helped her weave
together her fantasies.

The thought of him is a knife digging into her ribcage.

She knows now, she realizes, her heart clenching awfully, what
she must do.

She has known it all along; she only believed that she lacked
the strength.

TOMMY AND PEGGY

1941

It happens:
    the time when he goes back and
    does not find her.

It happens
    earlier than he thought it would
    (when he dared to think it would at all).
    Daisy is not yet one,
    his life with May is still straightforward—filled with fun
anecdotes
    about his travels through time that he can go back and
share with her.

He closes his eyes,

expecting fog and rain,
but what he gets
this time
is smoke.
Fire.
Explosions.
Burning, burning.
Sirens.

He stumbles,
and the world spins.
Breaks apart.
Darkness wailing.
And he knows.

He stumbles again.
There is rubble all around.
Charred buildings.
A ball of flames. Another one.
Red fingers grasping for the dark sky.
He cannot see the moon or the stars.
Just smoke.

He should have expected it,
he realizes with a jolt.
His father would have;
even Christelle has.
But, like so much of his life,
he has been too scared
to go there.

Someone is screaming.
  Howling.
  And, for a moment,
  he does not remember where he is.

This cannot be it, can it?

Another explosion.
  Far away
  or close by
  (he cannot tell anymore).
  Sirens. More sirens.
  Wailing.

He recognizes the street.
  The café. The house.
  His knees buckle and he
  falls.

He tastes ash on his tongue,
  on his lips.
  The smoke burns his eyes and everything is
  burning,
  burning,
  burning.
  Gone.

And he does not see her.

He runs.

Or at least he thinks he is running.
It feels more like
stumbling,
falling,
falling.

There should be something
for him to hold on to.
There should be something,
someone,
anyone,
in the rubble.
But he cannot find
anyone.

The sirens keep on wailing.
He thinks he calls out her name.
But his throat, his mouth, his tongue—
all feel like sand.
So how can he?

He should have known.
He should have known.
His father would have.

Someone is trying to drag him up,
yelling in his ear,
something about a shelter,
about bombs raining down from the sky.
But he knows all of this already,

doesn't he? And so he continues to fall.

He speaks her name.
    And closes his eyes.

JOSHUA AND LILY

1992–1999

Lily could travel back in time to Hong Kong when Joshua held her hand and took her with him. She, in turn, could take him anywhere in England after the turn of the twentieth century. They discovered how the body reacts to staying in the past for too long. They learned how to breathe in a certain way so that they would disappear or reappear faster. Joshua even developed Lily's ability to travel back to a specific date and time. But still, despite all their efforts, they could not travel anywhere else.

After Tommy and Eva were brought home from the hospital, keeping the new parents up at night at strange hours, Joshua and Lily decided to move their cots into the office. They took turns carrying the twins, shushing and rocking them, while scribbling new ideas and theories on the wall—ways they might travel to another continent, push the boundaries of time by going back beyond the twentieth century.

Sometimes Lily would stop her pacing and stare down at one of her children, cradled in her arms fast asleep, and say to her husband, Do you think they know what's going on?

Joshua would scrutinize his children for a moment and say, They must. If not, they should. It's in their blood. It's the only sure thing they have.

Joshua said what he said with such certainty. Long before the twins ever started displaying any abilities, Joshua had made up his mind that the only thing—the only permanent, irrevocable thing—that he could ever give his children was what he himself valued the most: his gift. It didn't matter that he and Lily had, to their knowledge, been the first in their families to have it; he was convinced that his children would be time travelers like him.

When the twins were very little, they showed no signs of any extraordinary abilities. They only breathed and wept and slept and learned to crawl in the very room where their parents would disappear, separately, on trips or spend hours on end documenting and discussing their endeavors. Perhaps by being close to it, Joshua told his wife, whatever magic or science it was they had in their veins would be sparked into life.

Joshua even thought that something would happen after he and Lily sat the children down in front of their TV to hear the news of the demolition of the Kowloon Walled City. He himself sat transfixed while the broadcaster, a bald middle-aged Englishman with a wisp of a mustache, was giving out information in a monotonous voice: . . . nearly 10,700 households . . . more than 33,000 residents . . . an enclave outside the jurisdiction of both the Chinese and British governments . . . a haven of drug abuse, prostitution, gambling, and triad activities. He heard the words, but the only thing that seemed to register in his brain was the sound of his maa-maa's quiet laughter. He saw the softness of her smiles.

He did not know why, but he got it into his head that once one of the strongest ties to his home country was severed, there would be an unexplainable shift in the fabric of time. After all, wasn't the Walled City the place where his talents were discovered and nurtured? Surely its destruction would have an effect on his children and their own abilities. Yet it did nothing, and the twins persisted in being ordinary children.

Tommy and Eva learned to walk and then later to form words. They would pull each other's hair and lie curled up asleep together as though they were still in Lily's womb. Then, as they grew older, they learned to string letters together, paint, and draw; Eva, especially, could spend hours doing it. Tommy, on the other hand, had so much energy, he ran up and down the entire house multiple times per day until Lily bought him a football and sent him into the front garden.

When they were six years old, Joshua sat them down in the office in front of the wall covered with notes, diagrams, and charts, and told them, This is what your mother and I are doing. Important work. Something that could change the world. It is special, he said. Not everyone can do it and so we must protect it.

What about us? Eva dared to ask him once, speaking over the silence that he enforced on them. Can me and Tommy do what you and Mum do?

Maybe, said Joshua. There was an excited gleam in his eye.

You should be able to. Your mother and I have discussed this many times. Maybe what we can do is a gift that can be passed down genetically. Do you know what that means?

Tommy nodded mutely. Eva put her hand up as though she were in a classroom and declared brightly, Something you get from your parents!

Tommy. Joshua turned to his son, his eyes whip-sharp. Is your sister correct?

Tommy looked down at his feet, clad in warm blue socks. Yes, Dad, he mumbled.

What's that? asked Joshua. I can't hear you. Speak louder.

Tommy tried to lift up his head. Yes, Dad, Eva's right.

The twins were nearly eight years old when everything began to change.

It started with a tingling sensation that made them feel faint, or as though something heavy was pressing down on their chests. Any normal parent would think it was an illness—a fainting spell, perhaps, or dehydration—but Joshua and Lily were not normal parents.

Once the twins explained what they had experienced, husband and wife stared at each other, wide-eyed, the rest of the world disappearing for just a moment.

It's not just us, breathed Lily. Do you remember what I told you that day?

Yes, I remember. Joshua almost smiled. How could I forget?

Eva said in a trembling voice, Mum. Dad. Does that mean we're special? Like you?

It might, replied Joshua excitedly. Close your eyes, Eva. You too, Tommy.

Close their eyes? said Lily, a bit startled. Right now? Josh, maybe that's not—

He met her gaze with a look that silenced her. Do you remember your first time?

Yes, she said.

Do you remember how it felt?

For a few seconds she stared back at him, unblinking. Then she turned sharply to her children and said, Do as your father said. Close your eyes. Hold our hands. Whatever happens, don't be afraid.

The twins did as they were told, and in a split second, Tommy took them to Trafalgar Square in London.

They were thrust into the middle of a jubilant crowd, with people dancing past, arms linked, songs and shouts ringing in their ears. No one let go! Joshua shouted immediately, panic taking hold of him. He held on to his children—Tommy to his right and Eva to his left—with a viselike grip that caused his son to wince and his daughter to cry out in pain.

Union Jacks were snapping in the wind, bells clanging like a battle cry. Up ahead, two navy officers were in the fountain, splashing water at two blonde women in uniforms that Lily immediately recognized from her travels. She called out her husband's name. Joshua's eyes met hers over Eva's head, and she had to shout at the top of her voice to be heard over the cheers of the crowd. I know where we are! she yelled.

Tuesday, May 8, 1945: VE Day.

When it was Eva's turn, she brought them to the last place and time Joshua ever expected. A rooftop at dusk. Pigeons flapping their wings in a cage. The Hong Kong of his child-hood stretching below him, an ocean of memories he had tried so hard to forget.

Joshua spotted a young couple standing on the other side of the rooftop, oblivious to their presence. The man was tall, much taller than Joshua, his white, collared shirt and cream-colored trousers creased and a little stained. He was handsome, in a restrained, still kind of way, his hand casually running through his longish hair. The woman leaned into him; she was much shorter, her pink floral dress less creased, her hair set and curled at the ends in a very exact way. They were not in conversation, but simply standing with their arms around each other, watching the sunset.

Joshua felt a lump rising in his throat. His daughter's hand in his, slack before, tightened as she squeezed his. Lily turned to him with a confused expression. He shook his head, unable to speak, but his wife understood him nonetheless.

Come on, let's close our eyes, Lily whispered to the children.

They had not even become visible yet, but they all did as they were told.

The moment they were back in their own time, in their own home, Joshua crouched down so that his eyes were level with his daughter's. How did you do that? he asked.

Dad, I don't know who they are, whispered Eva. Are you angry?

No, I'm not angry, he said. But that was your maa-maa Jiayi and your je-je Zhang Wei. My parents. How did you do that?

When you and Mum told us to close our eyes, I heard their voices.

Their voices?

I couldn't hear what they were saying; I just heard people talking. Just voices.

Joshua looked at Lily. His wife was standing behind Tommy, her hands resting protectively on their son's shoulders. There was a thoughtful expression on her face, but he knew her well enough to recognize the shining gleam of excitement in her eyes.

Since it was a special day, Joshua and Lily did the children's bedtime together that night. To Joshua's surprise, Eva threw her arms around him and pulled him close. Dad, please don't be angry with me, she said. I didn't know.

Oh, Eva. Joshua was not used to his children showing him such affection. He was surprised to find that he was not at all opposed to it. He brushed a strand of hair from Eva's forehead. What you did today was a miracle. How could I be angry with you?

Promise?

Promise.

Can you teach me how to do it again?

Joshua found that he could not speak; he could only give her a nod. He kissed her tenderly on the cheek, and Lily flicked off the lights.

Tommy, on the other hand, did not want to talk. The boy pulled the covers up to his chin and stared down at his hands.

You were so brilliant today, Tommy, said Lily. She hugged him tightly and kissed him on the forehead. How about we go over it tomorrow? Do you want to learn more about what you can do?

Tommy muttered, Yes, Mum.

Aren't you excited? Joshua asked, a little incredulously.

Tommy seemed to mull over the words carefully before he delivered them: I think it's cool . . . to do what you and Mum can do.

Joshua's serious expression dissolved into a smile so bright, it took even Lily by surprise. He ruffled his son's hair. I'm very proud of you, Thomas, he said. Well done.

A sparkle in Tommy's eyes. A small smile escaped from the corners of his lips. Thanks, Dad.

When they were by themselves in the hallway, Lily rested a hand on her husband's arm and felt the tension in him right away. I'm sorry for Eva's trip, she said quietly. That was unexpected.

No, don't be sorry. Joshua breathed in deeply, collecting himself. The image of his parents when they were younger flashed through his mind, but he wouldn't even know where to start explaining how he felt. Not even to himself.

Lily took his hand. Are you okay?

Yes. He sighed. What happened was unexpected, but like I said . . . quite a miracle.

How do you think it works?

Honestly? I have no idea. We have to work with her some more to find out.

And Tommy?

What about Tommy?

I saw how happy you looked, said Lily teasingly, when he said it was cool to be like us.

A smile again, so rare for Joshua, as he pulled Lily into an embrace. He remembered all of today's revelations—his children's abilities and their willingness to embrace them—and felt a sense of happiness so great, it scared him a little.

All he could put into words were what he whispered into his wife's ear: I never thought I would ever have this.

They held on to each other for a long while, forgetting time.

TOMMY AND PEGGY

1938

He comes in with the snow.
    Comes into her room, through her window,
    the way he has done so many times before.
    Flurries of white fluttering on her floor,
    flakes clinging to his shoulders, his eyelashes,
    his cheeks red and stinging from the cold.
    When she touches him, she can feel the frost,
    the ice beneath, sending a shiver through her,
    and yet every part of him is on fire, and she knows.
    Oh, she knows.

He refuses to sit down, paces around her room,
    telling her of planes, bombs, fire, and sirens,
    and she shakes her head, yells at him, telling him,

no, no, no, she does not want to hear any of this.
Hasn't he been listening? Hasn't he already promised
that the future is the future and he will respect the fact
that she does not want to know,
does not need to know? No, no,
no, why can't he understand the word?

He falls, but this time she does not catch him.
Don't you understand? He wants to scream.
I don't want anything bad to happen to you, ever.
You're going to get hurt. And his face breaks when he says
that.

I'm walking into this with my eyes open, she says, sinking to
her knees in front of him.
I know that there are risks, but I am walking in anyway.
It is my choice. Don't you dare take my choice away from me.

What about your father? he asks.
And he knows the sentence hits home when her face turns
hard.
It's a bit selfish, isn't it, he presses on,
if I can save your father, but you won't let me?

She gets on her feet and turns away from him.
I think you should go, she says.
He stands up, too, and tries reaching for her.
Peg . . . I'm trying to help, I don't want anything to happen
to you,
and I couldn't . . . I couldn't find you.

Don't ask me to stand by and watch you . . . watch you . . .

Then don't, she says.

What do you mean? he splutters.
    Do you expect me not to do anything?
    If you had been there . . . if you had *seen* . . .
    If your father . . . or me . . .

Tommy. She pulls him to her, suddenly, desperately.
    Holds him so tightly, it takes his breath away.
    Tommy, I know, I know, but this is my choice.
    And my choice is . . . this is not how it's supposed to be.
    I can't let you help. And it breaks my heart that you can't
see that.

Something this dreadful cannot be explained properly:
    no words can do it any kind of justice.

Fundamentally, it is a very simple act:
    the girl tells the boy that this must be the last time that
they see each other.

She tells him this knowing full well that she might yet see him,
    but a younger him, from an earlier time,
    the knowledge of what she is doing to him now absent
from his eyes.
    The thought of that brings her an intense sadness—
    so acute and sharp, she might fall to her knees, howl, and
tear her hair out.

You know, like a crazy woman in love is said to do.
But she tells him just the same.

This is not how it should be, she repeats.

No, he replies, shaking his head, his anger ricocheting all around the room.

No. This . . . this is not how it should be. I thought we were friends.

They circle around each other,

swooping in for blows,

trading tears, words—words they cannot call back after they've been released.

Words they'd thought that they would never utter at all.

Don't make me say it, she pleads.

Say what? he demands. What else can you say that is worse? Is there someone else?

No, she replies, shaking her head, tears streaming down her face. There is only you. There's only ever been you. And maybe that's the problem.

He is stunned to silence. His anger is fading away now.

But what replaces it is more terrible: devastation. Despair.

A person truly without hope is not a person at all.

Is it because I broke my promise? he asks.

She cannot lie. She owes him that much.

Yes, she says. But not only that.

There is no life with you. Not like this.

She kisses him one last time. (Even if it might not be the last time, not really.)

In her bedroom, the scene of their childhood and adolescence.

Kisses him as the rain pours down outside,
with thunder roaring in the distance.
Out of the corner of his eye, beyond her shoulder,
he catches sight of lightning.
A fraction of a second
when the entire sky
splits apart.

The answer, he feels, is staring him right in the face.

It has never been clearer; why has it taken him so long?
Why has he been trying to ignore it?
Peggy, May, all those attempts to move forward—
the answer is clear now.
Everything, he realizes once again as he looks at Peggy,
has led up to her.

And yet, when the object of your love has gone but the love remains,

what then?
How do you say goodbye to more than half of your life?
He believes you can't. You hold on and you don't let go.
She believes you let go, little by little. And you endure.

He dreams of his father, his face silhouetted against the River

Thames;

Tommy is twelve again and it is November and they do not return.

He dreams of his sister, laughing. His mother, smiling.

Peggy by the docks, turning around to look at him, her face lighting up.

There is sunshine through the clouds, seagulls swooping overhead.

She kisses him and laughs into his open mouth. Is this a memory? Or a wish?

He does not know. Does not care. Lets himself linger there. Stay for a moment longer.

A little longer. Oh, how he wishes he could . . . just a moment longer.

But then . . . a piercing cry. His daughter.

And he is wrenched away.

Tommy's first thought when he wakes is of fire.

MAY

2017

Daisy calls her "Mama" and calls Tommy "Papa."

He glows every time she does, even when grief is heavy
in his eyes,

or when he turns away quickly afterward.

Sometimes Tommy picks Daisy up, swings her around,

throws her into the air, and catches her, makes her squeal
and giggle until she is breathless.

On some nights, she sneaks into their bed when he is
there and

curls her little hand around his wrist,

even when he is asleep facing the wall, away from them both.

Daisy's face lights up when May scoops her up in her arms,

reads to her before bed, and cheers her on as she takes her
first steps.

The three of them go to the zoo once, the park a couple of times. The beach once.

He tries to build his daughter sandcastles, with a moat and towers.

But she keeps knocking them over with her tiny hands and feet.

Tommy plants a passing kiss on May's lips, sometimes on her shoulder,

when he comes to their bed in the middle of the night.

But those are the good days. And the good days start to become rare.

It all starts with what first brought them together: his work.

May doesn't realize it at first. Instead, when Tommy asks for her help, she feels a great sense of pride. It is so special, she gushes to herself, to be needed, especially by someone you love.

He hands her a list of books to buy, a list of dates and information he wants checked.

She scans everything, and discovers that all the research he wants is on the Blitz.

How peculiar. She wonders if . . . No. Brushes the niggling feeling aside.

Cracks a teasing smile and says, "This is like old times, isn't it?"

His mouth twitches humorlessly, but he doesn't reply.

She works during the day, through sleep deprivation and exhaustion, whenever she can make time away from Daisy.

But he works all day and all night, mostly in his office, writing, reading, sometimes disappearing.

She wants to ask, What is going on? What are we looking for? as she leafs through page after page of stories and photographs of the disaster.

Whenever she finds the courage to prod him for answers, she can only ask soft ones like, "Is there anything I'm missing?" or "Is there a specific aspect of the research you want me to focus on?" But he always shakes his head and says, "Just bring me everything you can find."

Eventually, he asks for her help less and less, preferring to do the research himself.

And even when she offers to help, he waves away her request, telling her that he doesn't want her to waste her time. That she has done enough and he has got it from here.

Being preoccupied with Daisy, May does not notice it at first: Tommy's absence.

He keeps it to his working hours and so nothing seems out of the ordinary.

She finds herself at the door of his office, peering in. Always looking in from the outside.

He is always slumped over the desk or he is writing, reading, writing, writing.

"I'm busy at the moment," he says without looking at her. "Do you need anything?"

And she finds herself mumbling, "No, just wanted to know if you're okay."

And he says, "Yes, of course I am, why wouldn't I be?"

But then she begins to notice that she cannot find him sometimes when she

wakes in the middle of the night to tend to Daisy.

Or sometimes even in the middle of the day, when he is supposed to be in his office.

He comes back with ash on his clothes, a haunted look in his eyes.

The smell of fire and smoke clinging to every part of him. Even on his lips when he vacantly kisses her. There is a different look in his eyes, as if he is floating, unrooted to her, their child, this house.

And she cannot shake the feeling that he is hiding something from her.

That maybe—despite her not wanting to admit it—she is asking the wrong question:

it is not *what* he is looking for, but *who*.

Still, she does not dare ask. Because he is here, isn't he? Here with her, sometimes.

With their daughter. At least he comes back. And when she reaches for him in the dark he still reaches back, and so why would she ask? Why would she dare ask?

We are supposed to fight for what we love, aren't we?

Fight tooth and nail and not give up on it, even when the object of our love pushes back.

He tries to stay, she can tell—to love her and to be there.

To hold their daughter when she cries and do all the little tasks he can manage.

But the more he stays, she comes to see, the more he chips away,

like a wooden doll, worn from being caressed and wanted.

And every time he returns . . . there seems to be something about him that is lost.

Slowly, unexpectedly, she finds herself longing.

For sunshine, bright days with no rain, no gray clouds in the sky, and no winter days full of darkness.

For Cantonese, for a familiar language, for words and sentences that roll off her tongue, requiring no pretense, no practice.

For her people, even her parents and sister. Her sister, especially. Voices she's not heard in a long while.

For the feeling of being close, so incredibly close that there is no use for personal space.

For the intimacy of being known. For embraces.

For even the simplest act of sitting on the sofa with another person in silence and watching TV.

On the rare occasion when she talks to her parents in Hong Kong,

she clutches the phone in her hand like a lifeline.

"I'm fine," she always tells them. "We are fine. Everything is okay."

But when her father tells her, "Take care of yourself. We miss you,"

or when her mother asks, "When are you coming home?"

she has to bite down on her bottom lip to stop herself from crying.

She swears her mother almost catches it sometimes, the way her voice wavers ever so slightly.

But she never lets it slip. She doesn't think of home. Can't.

Because what she has in London with Tommy and Daisy . . . this has to be home.

Everything will be better soon.

TOMMY, MAY, AND CHRISTELLE

2018

Christelle has a disarming way of looking at May

as May bustles about the kitchen, trying to make her a cup of tea.

May does not think she's ever been looked at like this by anyone:

so completely transparent, without any hint of embarrassment.

The gaze destroys every layer of protection May has built up during her time in this house.

She looks down at the cup of tea she has just poured for herself.

Repeats what she has already said when she answered the doorbell and found Christelle standing there: "Tommy is not home right now. I don't know when he'll be back."

"I know, you already told me that," says Christelle.

But there is no sign of annoyance on her face, only amusement.

"I couldn't get hold of him either, but I have to drop these off and this is the only time I'm free."

She nods at the things she has brought from her travels, now scattered all over May's dining table—books, artifacts, pashminas, and intricate hand-drawn portraits in wooden frames. May says, "Tommy will love these."

"Oh, I'm sure he will." Christelle gives a smug smile and brings her cup to her lips.

"Where is he, anyway? It seems like I can't get in touch with him very much lately.

Do you have better luck as his girlfriend and . . . you know . . . the mother of his child?"

"Oh, he's . . . very busy. He has a lot going on right now." Shame twists inside May;

she feels her cheeks heating up. She has always been very intimidated by Christelle.

But to admit that she does not know where her boyfriend is—

even to admit that she has been tolerating his absences—

makes her feel as small as humanly possible. As though she has failed as a woman.

"Busy?" Christelle frowns. "With what? The university? His research projects?"

"Yes, I assume so."

"But not just with those." Christelle's bluntness is a slap across the face.

May looks down at her hands, cradling her warm cup of tea. "I wouldn't know."

"How much has he told you?"

"About what?"

"His parents."

"He told me some things . . . about how they . . . disappeared."

"How much has he told you about her?"

"Her?"

"Peggy."

So there is a name.

May lets it hang in the space between them for a minute, observing how it shifts the air within their home.

Eventually she admits, "He hasn't told me a lot."

"I figured," says Christelle. Then her expression softens; it is not pity in her eyes, but pain.

"I'm sorry. For everything. If you need me, at any time, I'm here. Do you understand?"

May nods.

"Where's Daisy?"

"Asleep upstairs."

"Can I wake her up for a bit?"

May gives her first genuine smile. "Of course."

"How are you?" Christelle asks. "Really?"

May finds that she cannot speak. Something is stuck in her throat. Sand, perhaps.

She forces herself to take a sip of tea. "I'm . . . I just . . . I miss . . ."

"Home?"

May nods, and to her horror, tears spring to her eyes.

She quickly grabs a tissue and wipes them away, apologizing. Christelle shakes her head. "It's okay, it's okay."

Then she is right next to May, her arms enveloping her in the warmest embrace.

And that is the moment May realizes how much she has missed being held.

Much later,

after Christelle has woken up Daisy, given her presents, and settled her back to sleep,

May stands waiting at the door as she puts on her boots.

"I don't want you to go," says May, surprising herself.

"Oh, babe." Christelle pulls her in for one more hug. "I'll come visit again as soon as I can."

"Hopefully next time Tommy will be here too."

"Oh, fuck Tommy," Christelle snorts. "I know you and I aren't close, but I want you to remember something, May. Tommy has a good heart.

But he is not always right. Remember that."

May feels stupid saying it, but she says it anyway: "I love him."

"Yes, I love him too. But maybe that's what makes this so hard."

Christelle squeezes May's hand one last time. "You can love someone as much as you want, but you cannot change them. Trust me, May. I've tried."

Tommy searches everywhere for Peggy—

in his dreams, in the Blitz, in records from the present, scouring every little detail for traces of her.

When he is not doing that, he is at his desk,
  writing, writing. Yet so much of what he writes
  is returned by his university colleagues,
  marked with questions and befuddled comments.
  But he keeps writing anyway;
  he cannot stop. He cannot stay still.
  He sees the messages and calls
  from Eva and Christelle, but he cannot answer them.
  He cannot stop. He cannot stay still.

He wanders through life as though he is walking through smoke.
  And most of the time he is,
  stumbling through it as it billows out—black, white, gray—
  swirling around him, a deadly ocean of fumes.

When he is not walking through that smoke,
  he slips into a deep, dark sleep,
  shadows circling around him.
  He sees his father, sometimes. His mother.
  His ah-ma, fallen on the floor, her face stricken.
  Peggy, smiling, laughing. And he thinks she might be laughing at him.

May lingers in his doorway,
  her eyes telling him: Please come to me.
  But he can't. Won't.
  His daughter, Daisy, runs up to him,
  grabbing his leg, wanting him to lift her up,
  and sometimes he does, spinning her around in the air.
  But he is afraid and ashamed; he does not know why.

He feels contaminated, as though the smoke is still clinging to his clothes.
And most of the time it is.
So he puts her down and
walks away.

Some nights, in the quiet hours before dawn,
May presses herself into him, placing kisses on the nape of
his neck,
her hands straying all over him. And sometimes he lets her,
for a few minutes, pretending, but then the light steals in and
the moment is gone.

Then he steals out of their bed,
bending down to plant a soft kiss on her temple as she
drifts back to sleep. He feels a deep tenderness toward her,
but he cannot give her what she wants. Even if he might
want to.
Maybe the person he was trying to be with May isn't who
he really is.
Smoke and fire, the pull of the past—maybe those are the
only things meant for him.
Wasn't it like this for his parents, too?
They chose to go back, time and time again.
May deserves better, he knows.
He looks in on his daughter. Her sleep is peaceful, unin-
terrupted
by monsters, fire, and history.
His daughter, too, deserves better.
And he wonders briefly if his father ever felt the same.

He imagines not.

But he has to save her: Peggy.

He must. What else is there?

He wakes, again, and sees fire. He keeps seeing fire.

And she is nowhere to be found.

The cake has two candles to mark Daisy's age.

May chose everything herself: long red candles on a chocolate cake thick with rainbow icing.

Earlier in the day, they had called her family in Hong Kong, so Daisy could hear her grandparents wish her a happy birthday in Cantonese.

Then May took her for a walk by the Thames, where they had ice cream and admired the buskers and Daisy chased her balloon.

The two presents May has bought and wrapped sit close to the cake on their dining table.

The clock ticks loudly, announcing the minutes passing by so excruciatingly.

Daisy is restless. She tries to grab one of her presents, but May disentangles her grip from the wrapping paper.

"We have to wait for your dad," she says.

The candles flicker, and they keep burning and burning.

"Maybe," May says, when the flame is nearly so low that it touches the cake, "you should blow the candles now and—"

"Daddy!" Daisy leaps down from her chair and rushes to the door.

Tommy picks her up and squeezes her tight. "Happy Birthday, my baby girl!"

But May sees it the moment he comes closer: the smoke in his eyes.

May does not say anything as their daughter blows out her candles.

Or when she opens her presents and asks Tommy to throw her up in the air one more time.

Or when they put her to bed together, watching her drift off to sleep as Tommy reads to her.

Tommy switches off Daisy's bedroom light, closes the door to her room,

and then he and May are alone in the long corridor, with his family members looking at her from their picture frames— his mother, with her sharp, mischievous eyes.

Usually those eyes make May afraid,

but tonight they give her permission to be angry. Finally.

"Tommy," May begins, "you're not here."

"I made it, didn't I?" he replies, not unkindly. He tries to give her a smile. "She had a good time. I'm sorry I was late."

May shakes her head.

She can feel her breath quickening with frustration as she repeats herself: "Tommy, you're not here."

"May, you're not making any sense. What do you mean, I'm not here? I'm here. Literally here."

"No, Tommy, you're not. You're really not. This is not you

from this time. I can see it in your eyes. You're . . . I don't know how any of this works but . . . you've been somewhere . . . I've always tried not to make a big deal of it, but today, on our daughter's birthday . . . I need you to be better."

His smile disappears as quickly as snow in spring. "May—"

"I've never once complained about what you do, Tommy. Not even when it's made me unhappy. Not once."

"May—"

"Not even when it involves Peggy."

"Who told you about . . ." He shakes his head. "Christelle."

"I've had a feeling something has been going on for a long time now. Do you think I'm stupid?"

"I never thought you were. And it's not like that with Peggy."

"Then what is it like?"

"May, I never wanted to hurt you . . ."

"It doesn't matter what you want, Tommy, it matters what you *do*."

The rage that rises up surprises her; she feels as if she has entered the skin of another person.

"I never once gave you a hard time, Tommy, because I love you. I'd do anything for you. Anything. But you can't . . . you can't do this with Daisy . . ."

"I'm not *doing* anything!"

"Tommy, today was her birthday. And you can't even be here properly for her birthday!"

But he is here, he is himself, he keeps insisting. Can't she see? Why can't she see?

"All I can see right now," she says, looking straight into his pained eyes, "is that you're not who I thought you were. It's my own fault for believing you ever were. This can't go on, Tommy. Not when we have Daisy."

He leaves in silence after their fight, and she sits on the bathroom floor, back against the tub.

She mouths the words her parents said to her daughter today on the phone:

"Happy Birthday, sweet girl. We love you."

She thinks she is out of tears.

She does not know how long she sits there, remembering. Grieving.

But later she crawls into the bedroom, exhausted.

She wraps the covers around herself,

feeling the beating of her heart as a hammering in her head.

She reaches for her phone and dials a number.

Burrowed deep in her covers, where darkness is the only thing that can touch her,

she whispers down the line: "Christelle, I'm sorry to call.

But I need your help."

———

He slips and wakes.

For a moment he thinks he must be back there, in the East End with the bombs raining down,

looking, looking, dying, but the silence presses down on him immediately, a suffocating blanket.

His eyes adjust to the light: it is late evening; he has been gone the entire night and the entire day.

Or not? He is not sure anymore.

He is lying on the small sofa in his office and the curtains are drawn.

His limbs feel waxy, every part of his body screeching like an old house.

And the silence again . . . Why is it so silent?

Something eerie dances on his skin. "May?" he calls.

But there is no answer.

He calls her name again and realizes, with a sharp feeling of guilt,

that he has not done so in a while.

He walks through the house, an underwater tunnel.

Everything in his eyesight looks blue and

tinged with gray. His world spinning in waves.

The clock inside the kitchen greets him with its momentous ticking.

He's never noticed it before: how big this room is when the house is quiet.

He finds the note on the dining room table.

It knocks him off his feet; he crumbles to the ground.

"If you want to make this work," she has written,

"come after us."

But, of course, he can't.

Won't.

EVA

Eva lives in colors:
>   dark red, ocean blue. Warm yellow, like candlelight.
>   A splash of pink. Black. Deep maroon, like blood.
>   Colors that, for a while, she forgot had existed.

Light pours in through the window, illuminating her studio: easels, canvases, palettes, brushes, and colors. So many colors.

Plants fill the flat, green leaves extending toward the ceiling and fanning out as though reaching a hand to whoever walks in.

A small kitchen with a kettle, a microwave, and a stove. A rice cooker whistling away.

She stands by it, spinning a spoon in her teacup. Takes a sip. The clock ticks comfortingly above the fridge. It is eight in the morning. Soon her first private student of the day will be arriving, clutching his sketchbooks and art supplies.

But for now . . . she still has time.

Another sip of tea. She looks at the light reflecting off her tiled floor and thinks of the painting she's currently working on: an orca rising over a foamy sea. If she could capture such a light . . .

But then her phone rings . . .

———

The little girl, her niece, looks so much like her mother; not much of Tommy is in her features. Eva has seen photographs, but of course Daisy is now much older. She recalls the baby clothes she last sent to Tommy and thinks, *Oh, I had no idea that time could pass by so quickly. But I should have known.*

Aunt Dorothy lingers in the doorway, waiting. Maa-maa Jiayi has the sleeping child in her lap, presses kisses to her forehead. May hovers over them both, her hands twisting. She looks like she is about to cry. The sight of her like this causes a fierce anger to rise up in Eva.

"What now?" Aunt Dorothy whispers to her.

"I don't know," says Eva. "I'd call Tommy, but we haven't spoken in a very long time and he keeps ignoring my messages. I don't even know if he'll take my call."

"The girl is scared to go back to her parents."

"They don't know?"

Aunt Dorothy shakes her head. "Not that she's left Tommy. You have to talk some sense into your brother."

"I'll try, but . . ." A dreadful feeling seizes Eva. "Sometimes he's like our father in that way."

"Stubborn?"

"Not just stubborn." Eva looks at the child, her cherubic features, her tiny hands, her tiny feet. The enormity of such a little thing. "Clueless."

Later, after Daisy has been put to bed on the sofa, and Aunt Dorothy and Maa-maa Jiayi have left, Eva finds May at her kitchen table.

She realizes with a jolt that the younger woman is incredibly thin. There is a haunting expression in her face, especially in her downcast eyes. A woman, Eva surmises, who has been cold for a very long time. Her thoughts, again, turn to her brother. She presses her lips together, not wishing to say anything that might upset May, and decides instead to make them oolong tea. As she moves about the kitchen, May seems unaware that she is there, her eyes kept to her hands, folded primly in her lap.

After the water is boiled and the tea is poured, Eva sits next to May and hands her a cup. Only then does May seem to notice her, mumbling "thank you" under her breath. Eva brushes away the sentiment with a hand and a small smile.

As May's hands encircle the warm drink, her expression breaks. Not a cry, perhaps. But close. As though she is about to choke on the air itself.

"I am so sorry, May," Eva says, not knowing what else she can say. "For my brother. For everything. I will try and help you as best I can. Maybe he'll come here."

The girl's head jerks up. "He will not. He doesn't care."

"I'm sure that's not true," Eva says, almost hopelessly.

May shakes her head. "You don't know. You weren't there."

"I promise that you can tell me anything. Whenever you're ready."

Eva reaches out for the younger woman's hand. At first May looks as though she might wrench away from the touch. But then she decides not to, and lets Eva grip her hand tighter.

"May, there is a family here for you and Daisy. If you want it."

May falls asleep that night on the floor of Eva's living room, next to the sofa. She is curled up on an old, thin mattress, with Eva's spare blanket wrapped around her small frame. The moonlight pours in, basking the room in a subdued white glow.

Before going to bed, Eva switches off the light in the kitchen and lingers for a while in her studio, looking at her painting. She cannot seem to get the blue just right.

TOMMY

2018

He can't. He won't. So he travels.

Sirens.
    Flames
    flickering.
    The Blitz draws him in, again and again.

Ashes.
    Smoke.
    Shattered glass.
    Screams.

His father: "Thomas, concentrate."
    His mother: Don't forget to give yourself a bit of time.

A voice: Young man, we must get you to a shelter.

A child's laugh. Daisy.
　　He looks over his shoulder, wants to run to her but
　　he forgets.
　　May's sad eyes: Do you ever think of me?
　　I do, he wants to say. I have thought of you,
　　but there is
　　fire
　　in his throat.

His ah-ma Carol: You are too much like your father, Thomas.

November. And he is twelve years old again,
　　and his parents are late.

Daisy's laughter as he picks her up.

Tommy, wake up, says Peggy.
　　Her lips on his eyelids.
　　Her hand trailing over his chest.
　　Tommy—

Christelle. Her hand on his cheek. Tommy, wake up, she says.

My daughter, he wants to say.
　　My daughter is gone.

Eva rolls her eyes: Tommy, let's be honest . . .

The entire shelter shakes
 as bombs rain down.
 A child is crying in the corner.
 His daughter is turning two today.
 She's waiting for him so she can blow out her candles.

He shuts his eyes. "Tommy," Christelle cries, "don't you dare!"

Daddy, Daisy asks, can every day be my
 birthday?
 His father: Thomas, there is so much more you can do.
 Why don't you ever do it?

May's tears:
 Tommy, you are not here.
 This is not you.

Chris, I must go. Daisy needs me. She's blowing out her candles.

Debris falls from the ceiling.
 Candles waver in the darkness.
 The entire shelter trembles.

Peggy's eyes flashing in anger.
 She laughs, smiles, and kisses him.
 Someone is screaming again.
 Is it him?

"Tommy." Christelle is crying now. He has never seen her cry
before. "Tommy, I've called Eva. May and Daisy are with her.

It's not too late—"

He tastes metal on his tongue.
    I might die here, he thinks.

Christelle shakes him. "Tommy, I don't understand what you're
saying! Wake up! Wake up!"

He cannot get up.

Peggy is ahead of him,
    but she does not turn around.
    He calls her name.
    Still
    she does not turn.

His parents are late.

A pile of wood and rubble
    and burnt bricks where there was once
    a home.

Tommy, Peggy whispers.
    Stars spinning in her eyes.
    I'm glad I've found you.

Daisy blows out her candles.

I love you.
    You don't have to say it back.

They are not coming back.

"Tommy."
   Christelle's warm hand on his cold cheek.
   "Please—
   Tommy.
   Breathe."

But he cannot get up.
   He cannot get up.
   He cannot get up.
   He cannot get up.

———

The sound of curtains being drawn open. Sunlight, blinding.

Tommy adjusts his eyes and discovers that he's lying on the sofa in his office. He moves, attempting to get up, and the thick woolen blanket slides off him and drops to the floor.

Christelle turns from the window. "Good. You're up," she says. Silhouetted against the light, her expression is hidden from view. She walks over to where he is and squats down. Only then does he see that her eyes are red, with dark circles under them. Her hair looks unwashed. Her clothes, too, look slept in.

"How long have I been asleep?" Tommy asks.

"A day or so."

His throat is impossibly dry. "How?"

"I had to give you something." Christelle bites down on her bottom lip. "It'd been days and you wouldn't stay. You kept . . . disappearing."

"Listen, Chris—"

"No, Tommy, *you* listen." Christelle closes her eyes and take a deep breath. Her voice trembles as she continues: "You have to stop this."

"Stop—?" He tries to sit up, but a bout of dizziness hits him so abruptly, he is sent crashing back down to the sofa. "Oh, fuck. What's happening to me?"

"You need rest, Tommy. You have been staying away too long, you're getting ill. I don't know what you're trying to do . . . I don't know if you're trying to find her or—"

He winces. "Chris, it's not just about that—"

"What you need to do right now, Tommy, is get on a plane and go and see your family."

He hangs his head, a deep pain, piercing and cold. "Chris, I can't do that."

Christelle's eyes flash. "Then I need you to come and stay at mine. For a week or two, at least. My parents agree with me. You should not be alone right now."

"I can't do that either."

"But . . . why?"

He cannot answer. The floor spins.

Christelle continues, a sharper edge to her tone: "Tommy, why can't you stop? Or let her go? Not just her, but"—she gestures wildly at the room they are in, his father's office—"all of this?"

His eyes remain fixed on the floor. He can hear his heartbeat thumping inside his head, a torturous battering ram.

Christelle stands up, blocking the ray of light reaching toward him through the window. "Tommy, I cannot keep seeing you like this. Please. Say something." But he doesn't.

After Christelle leaves, Tommy fools himself into thinking that this is a good thing. He can do whatever he wishes, whenever he wants, without being beholden to anyone. What does Christelle know anyway about his family and his relationships?

He already knows what Eva will say: make things right with May and Daisy, confront the weight in his heart, do what she herself is doing. So on and so forth. Similar to what Christelle told him. Deep in his heart, Tommy knows it's probably what his mother would say if she were here.

But even his mother, Tommy reasons, never abandoned her gifts. She and his father—his father, especially—made sure that they never took what they could do for granted.

"It is not enough for us to just *use* our gifts," Joshua had said. "We must nurture and test them so that they become even greater! We have a responsibility to ourselves to be the best we can be. When you're traveling, you always have to think and think! Solutions, Thomas!"

When he was younger, Tommy didn't understand why his father was so harsh. But now he thinks he does. His father never shied away from a challenge; he never took "no" for an answer, and never let emotions get in the way. If his father were in his situation, his father would not give up. He is sure of it.

But then, as the days stretch into weeks, weeks into months, and Tommy's two worlds start to blend together, his thoughts turn into an incoherent mess. A tangled ball of yarn, like the ones that used to lie around his mother's studio.

Without Christelle around, Tommy's trips to the past continue; he moves in and out of time like breathing, even though most of the time it feels like he cannot breathe at all. The Blitz. The Thames. Snow. Rain. Fire. He blinks and he's back there again, searching. Running. He lingers, far longer than he should, and when he feels his body tearing itself away from his bones, he shuts his eyes and forces himself to return.

He thinks of Peggy on that day she told him that they should never see each other again. Her expression breaking in waves. "This is not how it's supposed to be, Tommy," she'd said to him, over and over. "There's a price to what you can do and you always have to pay it. Eventually something has to break."

JOSHUA AND LILY

1999

Lily was struggling to remember a time when her ah-ma Mary had looked young. Whenever she visited Mary in the nursing home and touched her hand and spoke her name, the older woman would stare blankly back at her, lost. Her eyes, once sharp and clear as a summer sky, were now clouded, misted over like a river on a foggy day.

Ah-ma, it's me, Lily. Don't you know who I am?

But the old woman would just stare. And stare.

The very last time Lily visited her grandmother, Mary's hand lay on the edge of the bed, and she gripped it, as the older woman drew her last breath. Just like that: gone.

Carol came up behind Lily, touching her gently on the shoulder. It seemed strange, Lily thought fleetingly, that her mother's touch could ever be gentle.

She's at peace now, said Carol, her voice hollow and strained, like all the tenderness had been sucked out of it. She wouldn't want you to cry.

She wouldn't mind, said Lily, annoyance flaring up. She shrugged her mother's hands off and got to her feet.

Mary's face was vacant, drawn, and slackened by death, with none of the strength she had in life; her skin felt eerily cold when Lily brushed a hand over her cheeks.

Lily wondered about the years her ah-ma had lived—all those years she knew nothing about. The man she had loved, who was her mother's father and her very own grandfather. The man who came from across the seas and disappeared one day, never to be seen again—the one Lily tried to find in her travels sometimes but could never quite locate. Was he alive? What would he do now if he could see the woman he'd loved lying dead, all memories of him falling away from her like cobwebs?

What is it, Lilian? Carol was looking at her with a strange expression on her face. Do you have something to tell me?

Lily breathed in deeply and stifled her tears. Mum, why do you think I have anything to tell you?

You have this look on your face, said Carol. Do you think I don't know my own daughter? You know you can tell me anything.

Lily felt an unfamiliar tugging in her heart. For one split second, she was tempted to be the daughter she'd never been and fall into her mother's arms and cry and unburden her thoughts— to speak of time and memories and grief that never quite felt like grief. But she stopped herself just in time and asked: Will you bury her next to Dad?

Yes, Carol confirmed. You'll bring the children to the funeral.

I'll talk to Joshua about it first, said Lily. I'm not sure if they are too young to see their ah-lao-ma like this.

Carol shook her head. They are not too young. We all have to learn about life and death from a very young age. Bring them. They need to pay their respects.

When Lily came home later that night, the children were already asleep and her husband was locked away in his office. She didn't bother showering; instead, she curled herself into a ball in her bed. She could not even close her eyes to try and time travel. She knew she'd be able to if she really tried, if she could muster enough strength. But her grief felt like dust. And dust settled.

She heard the creak of the door opening and quickly wiped away her tears, thinking that Joshua must have finished his work earlier than usual. But the person who slid into bed with her was smaller and much, much softer.

Mum, is it Ah-lao-ma? Eva asked, grabbing her mother's hands under the duvet.

Yes, replied Lily. The tears began to sting again. I wanted to tell you and your brother in the morning. How did you know?

I felt it. While I was . . . while I was in the past.

Were you traveling again? Eva, didn't your father and I tell you that you are not allowed to travel without either him or me going with you?

Yes, you did, said Eva, but I couldn't help it, Mum. And the way her words rushed out almost broke Lily's heart. I don't think mine works like yours or Dad's. Not even Tommy's.

What do you mean?

They call me. The people from the past. Our family. I don't think they call to the rest of you in the same way.

Lily suddenly wished Joshua was here; he would want to hear all about this. She made a mental note to tell him later. Darling, she told her daughter, only your father and I are allowed to travel by ourselves because we are grown-ups.

I'll try and do better next time, Mum. I promise. But today . . . today you were calling me.

Me? Lily exclaimed in surprise. What do you mean?

I closed my eyes and I saw you, Mum. You were a little girl like me. You were walking in a park with an old woman. I thought it was Ah-ma Carol, but she didn't look like Ah-ma Carol, so I thought she must be Ah-lao-ma Mary. And Dad told me that you went to visit her, so I knew that she . . . that she must have gone.

Lily smiled despite her sadness. Little missy, what do you know about someone being gone?

Eva shrugged. Dad is gone all the time. But I think it's not the same.

No, said Lily sadly. It's not the same.

Mother and daughter lay beside each other for a while, holding hands. Lily could feel the wetness of her tears rolling silently down her cheeks.

Eva, Lily whispered. Is anyone calling you right now?

Yes. That's why I can't sleep.

Do you know who they are?

Sometimes I do, when I've heard their voices before.

Lily hesitated for a moment and then squeezed her daughter's hand. Will you take me? she asked.

Eva nodded.

Before Lily opened her eyes,

she felt the autumn chill tugging at her clothes, the wind snapping against her face.

Her daughter's hand in hers was clammy with sweat.

Mum, she heard Eva say, we're here.

Her eyes fluttered open, and, there, just down the hill in the park, beneath the orange sky, was a little girl and an old woman.

Her breath skipped. And her daughter said,

Mum, they're waiting for you.

Much, much later, after she had tucked Eva back into her own bed, Lily pulled on a dressing gown and went downstairs in search of her husband. But he was not in the office where she expected him to be. Instead, she found him in the kitchen, sipping a cup of sweet-smelling oolong tea and heating up char siu buns. On the kitchen counter were black-and-white photographs, documents, and scribbles. She recognized them from his university job, as well as from his own research.

I'm sorry I wasn't there today, he told her when he saw her standing in the doorway.

My mother appreciated your absence, she said. She walked over to him and pecked him on the cheek. She could hear the ticking of the clock above the fridge. It was nearly two in the morning.

Are you alright? Joshua asked. I'm sorry about your ah-lao-ma. She was a good woman.

I will be, Lily replied. It's been coming. She's been sick for ages. I just . . . I just wish she could have remembered us at the end. That's all.

Lily—

I'm alright, she repeated. Have you talked to Eva?

Joshua poured her a cup of the oolong. No. Why?

She traveled by herself today.

Shock was not an expression that crossed Joshua's face often, but it did now. He put down the kettle and said, I thought it would be Tommy.

You thought it would be Tommy? Lily couldn't help but scoff. Darling, how well do you know our children?

At Tommy's age, I was going back to 1950s Hong Kong and taking notes.

Tommy is not you.

Obviously. Joshua frowned and took a sip of his tea.

Lily shook her head in exasperation, grabbed a pair of chopsticks from the drying rack, and began helping herself to her husband's char siu buns. Eva is braver than Tommy, she said. But give Tommy time.

He will have to be ready soon, said Joshua. But Eva going by herself. That's . . . that's useful. Joshua looked thoughtful as he bit into the bun, revealing the pink meat of the barbecued pork inside.

Lily sipped her tea. Useful for what?

What I have planned for us.

A plan? For us? Since when?

Since tonight. With his chopsticks, Joshua gestured to the pile of photographs scattered on the counter.

Lily put down her cup and reached out for one of them. Her eyes widened when she saw who was in it. Bruce Lee, she said. The name resonated loudly in their kitchen, a reverent echo. She looked at her husband, realization dawning on her face. All of us together? As a family? Josh, are we ready?

Didn't you just tell me that Eva is? As for Tommy . . . we can get Tommy ready.

I'm not sure this is the best time to start this. Lily recalled the coldness of her grandmother's hands. Ah-ma just died. My mother—

Your mother will always behave this way. It won't matter when.

I know. I just . . . Lily sighed. She circled her hands around her cup of tea, feeling the warmth seep into her skin. I nearly told her today. About us and what we do.

Joshua's brows knitted together. Why?

I was sad, Lily replied bluntly.

But you didn't. Right?

No. I wanted to, God knows I wanted to. But I know I can't.

Exactly. And I don't want that for our children. I want this—Joshua used his chopsticks to point at the photographs and the space between them—to be something we can do together. Isn't that what you want, too?

Lily thought of Eva's hand in her own and the London of her childhood spread out before them.

Yes, said Lily. I suppose it is.

Joshua smiled one of his rare smiles, and Lily didn't know why she hadn't noticed before how like their daughter's it was. Then it is time, he said.

MAY

2018

May lingers in Eva's flat for weeks as her world begins to take shape once more.

Eva brings food, water, and company, Daisy in her arms wanting to spend time with her mother. Sometimes they move to the dining table so they can have meals together and discuss the weather, what Daisy wants to do the next day, or Eva's students' recent antics. Sometimes they stand in the studio and May marvels at Eva's skills as she adds colors to old paintings or begins sketching new ones. Eva gives Daisy her first brush, teaches her how to mix the color pink and splash it all over a blank canvas.

The three of them stroll to the nearby park on some weekend afternoons. Eat out together on evenings when Eva returns early from teaching. May brings back brochures from nurseries, flipping through and talking about them with Eva after Daisy has gone to bed. Slowly, without May realizing it, the loss turns from a shock to a constant companion; it does not hurt any less, but it does not suffocate her in the same way. Progress, of sorts.

But Daisy still asks after her father. Still questions when they can go home. Still waits by the phone for it to ring. On such occasions, May picks her up and paces around the flat, holding her tight until she falls asleep.

"She misses her dad," May tells Eva one night. She lays a slumbering Daisy down onto the extra mattress she had insisted on buying. She had rejected Eva's generous offer of her bedroom a few days in. "This is your home," May had said. "We are only guests here."

"Were they close?" Eva asks.

"When he was around, yes. He was good at playing with her. She just loved being with him."

Eva scowls. "I wish I could fly back home and shake some sense into Tommy. Maybe I should."

"You're too kind," whispers May, her fingers trailing over her daughter's forehead. "But I can't ask you to intervene."

"Do you still hope or wish that he'll . . . I don't know . . . call? Change his mind? Come after you?"

"Oh, all the time." May smiles sadly. "Mostly for Daisy. But Christelle is right: you can't force someone to change. Tommy has to find his way himself."

Eva scoffs. "Easier said than done. May, I wish I could do more."

"You're doing everything you can."

"But it is not enough."

May's hand freezes, a thought coming to her. "There is

something . . . I've been afraid . . ." She looks up at Eva a little hesitantly. "Would you come with me and Daisy . . . to see my sister?"

Much, much later, May stands by the sea and realizes this is the first time in a very long while that she is by herself. Without Tommy. Without Daisy. Just her.

Eva has taken her daughter for the day; she plans to show the little girl around the art school where she works. Yesterday, they finished moving all of May and Daisy's things to her parents', so May has the entire day to herself. At first, she did not know what to do or where to go. But a memory came into her mind: she, Tommy, and Daisy at the beach one day, a lifetime ago. And so, before she knew it, she was on the train heading out of the city, searching for the ocean.

As May sat on the train and watched the scenery whip past, she couldn't help wondering what Tommy would say if she called him up and told him that Daisy will be enrolling into a nursery very soon. That the two of them have moved into May's childhood bedroom, now painted light yellow. The brand-new bed May's sister, Anne, bought for Daisy is pushed up against the window, with a pink Hello Kitty bedspread covering it. Toys are already scattered all over the floor, and May's mother hovers nearby, always eager to babysit. Daisy is learning how to use her first set of watercolors . . .

But how could she call, again, when he himself has not done so?

And then there is Eva, who keeps telling May: "It is never too late to start over. You can still be whoever you want to be."

But who is she? May stepped off the bus with this question ringing in her ears.

May had thought herself on the verge of greatness when she first arrived in London. But what great things has she accomplished, except for bringing Daisy into the world and being her mother? Anne's greeting remark, when the sisters reunited a few weeks ago, had cut deep, even though May knew it came from a caring place: "I really hate to say I told you so, but I'm glad to see you've finally come to your senses."

May thought her time in England would provide the opportunity to become her true self, that the life she had always wanted would bloom before her very eyes. Yet here she is now, back where she first started, shattered, and defeated. Just another "I told you so" cliché.

The tide comes in and laps at her feet, its touch cold and refreshing. She lets out a deep breath as it retreats. A flash of memory. She shuts her eyes against it and feels the breeze on her face. Listens to the sound of the sea, as reliable and soothing as the way her body is now drawing air. A rare moment of perfect stillness.

She wonders, very briefly, whether Tommy has ever felt such a sense of calmness. Perhaps if he had, things would be different between them now. If he had been less damaged, if she had known better, if circumstances had not conspired against them . . . would things have worked out?

But she knows in her heart of hearts that this is wishful thinking. A useless fantasy. She forces herself to think of the house on Kennington Road, waking to an empty bed, time and time again, and Daisy forever asking where her father was, Daisy crying herself to sleep on their flight to Hong Kong . . .

Tommy's smile has gone when she opens her eyes this time. All she can see now are the waves before her, rushing in. She steps toward them readily, wishing they could engulf her whole. Her heart is completely broken. Yet she knows, as she walks on alone along the shoreline, that little by little, life will return. It has to.

PEGGY

1950

Steam billows around the platform. The train conductor is calling for them all to board. Passengers jostle each other, scrambling to get on the train. The war has robbed many families of their possessions. Instead of big crates and chests, almost everyone is clutching a bag, a basket, a satchel, anything small enough to contain what is left of their lives ever since those first few Luftwaffe bombs began dropping from the sky ten years ago. A baby is screaming murder as his mother hands him to his father, reaching for him through the train window. A teenage boy hawking newspapers swings his wares, accidentally knocking off a man's hat. The conductor blows his whistle again, the sound rising above the commotion like a sharp, shrill warning cry.

There is a crackle in the air. A spark, like tinder catching flame. Or perhaps it is just Peggy's imagination, because she knows, deep in her bones, the significance of today. Today is the day her life will change forever.

All those hours of dreaming about life outside of the East End: walks down to the beach, fresh air, books. The sea breeze. Things that grow. Her father reclining in a rocking chair by the fire as winter cocoons them inside their own cottage, snug and warm. Today is the day these dreams come within reach. For so long, despite her outward facade of bravado, she hasn't believed them possible. Merely the ramblings of a deluded dreamer. But no more. They are on the train. They are leaving London.

Peggy lets her father lean on her as he eases into his seat, his walking stick jutting out of his hand at an odd angle. "There you go," she tells him gently, as though speaking to a child. She spreads a tattered shawl over his knees. "Are you alright? Is your leg hurting?"

The old man shakes his head, resting his veined hands on his shaking knees to still them. "I'm alright," he grunts. But his walking stick slips from his grasp, hitting the ground with a dull thud. Peggy picks it up for him and sets it on her own empty seat.

Ever since the war, her father's health has been deteriorating. The destruction of their café during the Blitz is still taking a toll on him; it breaks her heart that his spirit has never been the same. His left leg, too, the one with the old knee injury, has gotten worse since that air raid on the Isle of Dogs in October 1940. While struggling to get to their shelter—an Anderson in a small churchyard—the old man took a horrible fall. If it were not for the help of their new neighbors, he and Peggy would not have made it to the shelter at all.

Another shrill whistle from the conductor. Peggy's father

grabs her hand. The small gesture of vulnerability surprises her. "Pa, what's the matter?" she asks.

The old man's jaws clench, his eyes staring straight ahead. "I never thought this day . . ."

Peggy's throat tightens. She puts her hand on top of his: she understands. "Not long now, Pa, and we'll be out of London," she says, attempting a smile. "The sea, Pa. Can you imagine? And mountains."

"I don't understand how you managed to—"

"I told you, didn't I?" Her tone is playful, but there is steel behind her words. "I'm going to take care of us now."

"But, my dear, the money. I still don't understand how we are to afford this."

"Let's say there's someone who owes me the world."

"Who could—"

"Father, we have been through this. Don't you trust me?"

"Yes, but—"

"Then I promise you that everything is fine. We'll start over. You'll see."

The old man looks as though he longs to contradict her. But then he shakes his head. "You should get in your seat, dear. We are about to be off."

"Give me a minute, Pa, I'll be back."

Peggy lets go of his hand and makes her way back down the train. Her father's insistent questioning nags at her. She had hoped that her confidence would have reassured him by now, but it seems like he will not let go of his curiosity anytime soon. This is a complication she has not foreseen. How can she ever tell her father that they're able to afford the move from London to Cornwall because of the wife who abandoned him?

Shortly after the end of the war, Peggy had written to her mother, with her new, wealthy husband in China, asking for money. Her mother had written back: "I did not think my daughter was the kind of woman who'd put a price on abandonment." And Peggy had replied: "The daughter you knew never existed. And if she did, she died during the Blitz."

For months she received no reply from her mother. Until, one day, a much smaller cream-colored envelope slipped through the letterbox in their boarding house. Inside was a check, but no letter.

Her father's pride, Peggy knows, will never allow him to stomach this truth.

The platform is beginning to empty, the last of the passengers scrambling to board the train, luggage in hand. An old Chinese man and his daughter linger nearby, waving to a loved one on the train; the old man tips his hat to Peggy as their eyes meet briefly. The young boy is still selling cigarettes and newspapers, with passengers reaching down through their windows and tossing their coins into his open hat. "All aboard! All aboard!" calls the conductor. Yet Peggy stands there, searching.

Long ago, when they were children, Tommy told her about his gift. Only London and only up to a few years after the war, he had said. Ever since she started putting her plan into motion, she's known that this moment would come. Yet the thought still devastates her: that once she leaves behind this city and this time, they will never see each other again. The two of them not being in each other's lives feels like an unfathomable, grotesque concept, something utterly unimaginable to her.

One of the very last times Peggy saw Tommy, it was after his ah-ma had just passed away. His grief and desolation made him look more like a boy than ever before, his clothes hanging rumpled and loose from his lanky frame. His eyes were downcast and pained. By then, she had already known about May and Daisy. But it was still strange to hear May's name mentioned by him when she knew more about himself than he did.

Unable to stop herself, she had said, "So you've already met May." And from then on, she knew what she must do. When she insisted that they should only be friends, he had not understood and at first refused to agree. She couldn't blame him; she wishes she could have told him everything about what awaited them. Yet that would be breaking the very same promise she had asked of him. In the end, she held her ground and got her way, like she mostly always did.

She remembers how, almost every time they kissed, she would shut her eyes and imagine what it would be like had he grown up just down the road from her, another Chinese kid lost in the East End. Perhaps his father would have worked down at the docks and his mother in a laundromat, a matronly woman with deft and skillful hands. He would still have his mother's easy smile and his father's seriousness. And the two of them could have walked down Limehouse in broad daylight, unafraid of questions and prying eyes, and he could . . . he could stay . . .

But then they always broke apart and the dream was gone. And there he was before her, a young man lost in time, unanchored, while she was forever rooted.

Once, she stared at him for a few seconds and asked, "Do you know what year it is?"

"Mine or yours?"

"Mine."

He shook his head, confused. "What does it matter?"

"Do you want to know?"

For a moment, it seemed like he might say yes. But then he faltered. "No. No, I don't think I do." And she didn't have the heart to tell him that there was already a war on.

Peggy replays these memories to herself on the platform as she scans the crowd. She has tried so hard not to hope. Not to hold on. But maybe . . . one last time . . . somehow.

But he is not there.

And she can no longer go on waiting.

When she is back in her seat on the train, Peggy takes out her notebook and pencil. Her father is already drifting off to sleep. The train lurches ahead, pulling away from the station and everything she's ever known. She looks out of the window as London begins to speed past, but all she can see is Tommy's face, broken and despairing, yet still shining with love for her. Maybe she'll never see that loving look on another man's face ever again . . .

She glances back over her shoulder, at the distant platform. The last throw of the dice. Maybe, just maybe. Just once more. What if . . .

But the blueness of the sky is beckoning her forward. It drags her gaze away from his absence and toward the lush green country ahead.

She puts her pencil to the page and begins to write.

It will be alright, she tells herself. This sadness will eventually lighten. She is alive. She is free. Life is new.

TOMMY

He finds a box of photographs in his ah-ma Carol's old bedroom.

He remembers, vaguely, that his mother had kept them in her
studio;
    Ah-ma must have disapproved and hidden them here, where
he and Eva
    would not be able to find them. His mother was keen to
document everything.
    And here were those pictures: their family, from what feels
to him
    like several lifetimes ago. He barely knew how to smile in
pictures.
    But his mother's lens captured him with so much fervor.
    His father, too, did not like being photographed.

He rarely smiled. Always a frown, a forced upward curve
of the mouth.

They were at the beach somewhere, on a rare sunny day.

His father squinting at the camera. Eva grinning.

Tommy's hair is wet from the ocean, slick and flattened
back. He is mid-jump, his toes

barely touching the sand. He has very little memory of this
day. Only that

it was the day after they went back in time as a family
and met

Bruce Lee. They drove, he remembers. Of course they drove.

They had tried to build a sandcastle, but unlike his sister,
he did not have the

patience, and the forts kept falling down. That is all he can
remember.

But it was a good day. That he knows. His head, again, is spinning;

he doesn't know when he last slept. Truly slept. He tries
to take a

deep breath, and when he does, he can taste the smoke
lingering in his throat.

He thinks of Daisy's face, glowing in the light of her birthday candles.

The anger in Peggy's eyes. He looks down again, and there
is his own childish face

staring back at him.

All he needs, he thinks, is one good day.

It is not even a realization.

Or the seed of an experiment. Or even a wish. Rather, it is a desperation.

His head is heavy. His eyes, too. His body is being pulled down, sucked into nothingness,

and he is a little boy in the ocean, a wave coming toward him to knock him over.

He smiles. Not even his usual confident smile, dripping with charm,

but a half-amused, sad smile that makes his face look young and old all at once.

What a funny thing, he ponders as he lets the tide tug him down. We never tried to build

another sandcastle ever again.

Daisy loves sandcastles.

The wave reaches him and knocks him off his feet. He stumbles backward,

shoved over like a Lego figurine.

His breath catches in his throat. The light is dying in this house, he thinks.

Or is it already getting dark outside? He closes his eyes.

It should be impossible to travel like this. It doesn't follow the rules.

But Tommy needs this more than life.

He makes a wild dash for hope.

For one good day.

The gentle rolling of the tide.
    Sea breeze.
    Salt in the air.
    The warmth of the sun.
    Heat, radiating throughout his body.
    It is impossible.
    But can it be?

His heart,
    so dormant and
    fraught before,
    begins to quicken.

He has not spoken the words in a while:
    Mum. Dad.
    But they begin to form on his lips
    as he
    opens his eyes.

It is a different beach.
    On a different day.
    And for a moment he is lost;
    he can't comprehend anything.
    Then his eyes scan the sand
    and . . . yes . . . he sees now.
    He understands.
    No, he remembers.
    He cannot fathom how
    he could have ever forgotten.
    But Christelle did tell him:

You have been forgetting
  so many things as of late.
  Especially the things
  that matter.

The quietness of the day
  is peace.
  He breathes in the air.
  Smiles. A genuine smile this time.
  He feels tears in his eyes.
  He wanders closer, but not too close.
  Thinks: I do not deserve to be that close.
  There is a bench nearby. He sits down.
  Watches himself from the past crouch down,
  the legs of his trousers rolled up, his arms scooping
  sand into a half-circle. May sits a little distance away
  on a blanket, pushing her long hair out of her face.
  He has always liked her hair. How free it makes her look.
  The sound of Daisy's giggle is so loud, it reaches where
  he is sitting on the bench. She jumps up, claps her hands,
  and squeals in excitement. There will be a castle very soon.
  Just for her. Somewhere the tide cannot reach.

He hears footsteps and turns.

Hello, she says. Can I join you?
  Their eyes lock and somehow
  he knows.

She has grown, of course. Looks to be about the same age as he is.

Maybe even older. But there is a look in her eyes,
a feeling.

He remembers his father saying:

It's in the blood.

He nods and she sits down.

There is a considerable distance between them.

You look like your mother, he says, without thinking.

She smiles a humorless smile, her eyes fixed on the family
of three in the distance.

You look the same, she says, nodding at the figure on the
beach.

I didn't expect to be here, he says. I didn't think it was possible
for me. Do you have any idea how I ended up here?

I have my theories, she replies. She frowns, still not looking at him. From what I know . . . it might have something
to do with the two of us. Our . . . bond. Or it might just be a
blip. An accident.

He, unlike her, cannot stop looking. A warmth is erupt-
ing inside his chest, a cocktail of shame and regret, but most
of all . . . pride. My mother—your ah-ma, that is—she used to
call what we can do magic. Maybe she's right. There is no rhyme
or reason to its method: it just does what it wants to. Driven
by . . . a particular emotion or experience.

Yes. A flicker in her expression. I've heard that from her before.

If he were to fall off the cliff, it would have hurt less. You have her eyes, he stammers.

A soft smile: a gift, unknowingly given. Yes, I've seen that too.

So this is how it works for you?

Yes, it's a bit like Aunt Eva's, actually.

I have . . . so many questions, he says.

Her glance drops. Maybe he does not deserve to ask them.

But she does not say anything, and so he decides to take the leap. What else has he got to lose?

Where am I, where you are? he asks. Did I ever see you again? Did I ever find you? Am I still with you now?

She turns to him, and her similarities to her mother hit him even harder. Now that her eyes are on him, her gaze burns. But he cannot look away.

I didn't expect to see you here, she says.

I just . . . I wanted . . .

One good day?

He nods. Her lips curve up into a sad smile. Me too, she says.

Tears spring to his eyes, his throat raw. Daisy—

Please. Don't.

Your mother. Can you at least tell me about her? I am . . . so, so sorry. I hope she . . . that she . . .

She knows.

And is she happy?

Tremendously.

And has she ever—

Dad. The way she says the word, too: it slips out like she has not meant it at all. Almost like a plea. Why don't we just enjoy the day?

But, Daisy—

Look. She turns back to the three of them from a lifetime

ago and nods. You're trying to build me towers, remember? I keep wanting to knock them down.

He follows her gaze, as though pulled by a string.

He gives a small laugh. Your mother wanted a moat.

Daisy smiles. And, Oh, he thinks, how beautiful she is. My little girl.

We tried to redirect the water from the sea into the moat, she says. I remember that much.

I've almost forgotten, he reflects sadly. In fact I think I did forget.

How could I have ever forgotten?

Silence.

Only the faint sounds of Daisy's giggles, floating up from the beach.

The tide, whispering.

Seagulls.

The wind.

She lays a hand on the bench in the space between them.

Dad, look! She points ahead. A little laugh. I keep wanting to run into the sea.

He chuckles. You were too fast for me. I'm struggling to keep up.

But you always caught me. In the end.

You were only little then.

True, she says, so softly he almost misses it, but I loved it . . . when you used to pick me up and hold me.

The tears begin to roll silently down his cheeks.

His hand drops to rest beside hers.

Everything, he now understands,
    has led up to her.

They sit for a long while,
    together,
    in silence,
    remembering.

JOSHUA AND LILY

2003–2004

Life gives, but it also takes away.

Two days before Joshua's father, Zhang Wei, passed away in Hong Kong, Joshua and Lily went somewhere they had never been before and had thought they would never be able to go: London, 1899.

It was a split second, just them standing in the middle of the office,

holding hands,

their eyes closed,

Lily reciting the date to herself in her mind, Joshua recalling

the black-and-white photograph he'd found in a history book.

Open your eyes, she said in awe. But he didn't need to be told:

he felt the rain on his face, the sound of carriages against cobblestone streets, the scent of smoke,

the rush.

What drew his gaze, however, was not the Victorian London around him,

but the sight of his wife, staring at him in disbelief, in excitement.

She squeezed his hands and, oh,

the rush.

But then it was over.

Darkness.

The rush of wind.

Falling, falling.

Then . . .

Light.

They opened their eyes and they were back in their own lives, their own time. The feeling of their own bodies rooted in solid ground.

Joshua was grinning from ear to ear. Lily felt laughter bubbling up inside her.

Before they knew it, they were in each other's arms.

"We did it," he said, planting kisses on the top of her head, her forehead, her eyes, and her mouth.

Everything, she thought, is worth it now.

They never thought it would be possible. That night they did not sleep, but spent hours talking, speculating, planning,

planning, planning. Would it be successful? Could they make the trip last longer than a couple of seconds? Luck, science, magic—the three things merging as one to create something new.

Joshua sprinted up from his chair and wrote the date in large letters on the blackboard: *December 31, 1899.*

Let's return there and try to stay longer! he declared, his face alight with overwhelming clarity. Just before the turn of the century! We know we can do January 1, 1900. But this . . . He grinned at Lily, lifting her heart, her world. This is big! I know it wasn't the same, but we managed to pull off the Bruce Lee trip with four people. Maybe we can do this too! I believe in us!

Her throat had constricted. For the longest time, she said, I thought we had no chance. But, Josh, we were wrong. If this works, imagine where we could go next, what we could do, what we could see! Her mind raced to the point where she began to feel lightheaded. And perhaps, in the future, she said, we might not be limited to Hong Kong and England anymore. Things could change for us!

I know! he said, still grinning. He leaned forward and captured her mouth in a kiss. She pushed into him, feeling like it was those early days when they were young and it was just the two of them in a big house and all the responsibilities of adulthood were merely a speck on the horizon.

Thank you, she whispered against his lips. For dreaming with me.

Two days later, a little after four in the morning, the phone rang.

He was the one who got out of bed to answer it. Hello, he said in English. Wang residence.

Then he heard a sob.

Ma, he said, his mouth dry. Instinctively, he grabbed the jade hanging around his neck.

He switched to Cantonese. Ma, what happened?

Your father, she said. There was an accident.

When Lily found him, he was sitting on the front porch, staring into the darkness. For the first time in years, a cigarette was clamped between his teeth. After he'd hung up the phone, he found himself making his way to the off-license at the end of the road and purchasing a pack and a lighter.

Lily sat down beside him, but he couldn't look at her. He felt . . . He didn't know what he felt. He simply continued smoking.

What's happened? she asked eventually. She didn't even touch him.

My mother called, he said, his voice sounding strange to his own ears. There was a car crash.

Your father? She did not know how she knew, but she did. Perhaps she recognized the look on his face, having seen it on her own before.

He nodded, flicked the ashes from the end of his cigarette, and put it to his lips again. The darkness was softening all around them. They could see the fences up ahead and the light from the streetlamp across the road. The cold was biting; he was in his coat, but she was wearing only her pajamas and a dressing gown.

Do you think, she asked, this has anything to do with what happened two days ago?

His head spun. Why would it?

She shrugged. She thought of her own father, and the sight

of her mother with questions in her eyes while Ah-ma Mary lay dead between them. Something twisted in her chest. Sometimes, she said, it does feel like there's a price.

A price for what? He gave a dry laugh and flicked more ash off his cigarette. There is no need to be dramatic, Lily. People die. That's life. Your father did. My ah-ma. Yours. One day we will too.

I don't know. She shook herself, wiping her moist eyes with the back of her hand. I just thought . . . maybe . . . there are correlations.

Have there ever been correlations before?

I don't know, she repeated, shaking her head. Sometimes— Josh, please don't be mad—but sometimes I feel like there's so much . . . death . . . surrounding what we do.

Death? He scoffed. What death?

Your je-je, she said. You tried to go back in time to save him.

He flinched; after he'd told her about his attempts to save his grandfather, they'd never once mentioned it again.

She pushed on: Eva keeps seeing my ah-ma Mary. Tommy goes back to the years running up to the war. Even with Bruce Lee . . . I don't know.

You're just shaken, he said, in a surprisingly leveled tone. He exhaled another column of smoke. Perhaps we both are. That's all. When have we ever been like those superstitious Chinese people, heh?

She didn't know what to say to that. As the light descended all around them, she linked her arm through his and rested her head on his shoulder. I'm sorry, she said. She sensed him tensing up.

It's okay, he said. She felt him breathe as he inhaled and then exhaled. We were not close.

Does it matter?

He shrugged. It should.

Does this change anything? she asked. And there was a pleading tone in her voice that she could not quite hide.

He shook his head. His lips thinned into a straight line. No. Why should it?

From then on, The Experiment became more than an experiment. Aside from the time he spent at university on lectures and research projects, Joshua was always in his office, preparing. When Lily wasn't taking care of the children, she was in there with him, delving into thick volumes of history textbooks. Paintings and black-and-white photographs lined the walls—of Victorian Londoners strolling down the streets, of a gray sky, of Westminster Bridge covered in fog. Clothing from that time period hung from the arms of the chairs and the sofa, a vintage shoe peeking out from under the desk, another from under the curtains. A timeline of events for the year 1899 was written on the blackboard in Joshua's minute, neat handwriting and Lily's flowing, almost indecipherable scrawl.

And then there was the day Lily intended to make a trip to January 1, 1900, only for her to end up, quite inexplicably, in the last dying moments of 1899, just before the clock struck midnight.

It's a sign! she told her husband after she had returned. The door is opening. Something is beckoning us to take the leap. Something . . . something is out there!

Joshua kissed her back in jubilation, his tense, concentrated expression widening into relief. Something is definitely at work here, he agreed. Something draws us. Just like how Eva is drawn to people in the past. Or how Tommy is always drawn to a specific time. Maybe if we go on this trip—

When we go, she said, her grin mirroring his, maybe we'll find more answers.

Is it a force? asked Joshua. Some sort of gravitational pull—

No. She shook her head, thoughtful. I wonder if perhaps there's . . . a pattern we're missing. I've been thinking it could be emotional or generational. Look at Eva. Oh, please, don't laugh. She scrutinized him with a stern look while he rolled his eyes. There's a reason she keeps being drawn to our family members. My ah-lao-ma, for example. And with Tommy—

Tommy is immature, dismissed Joshua. Maybe his abilities have not developed fully yet.

Or maybe there is something important waiting for him in that time period that he keeps going back to.

A look passed across Joshua's face. He didn't seem to have heard what Lily had just said, but then he asked, Do you think we should bring them on this trip with us?

Lily chuckled. You must be joking.

He shrugged. They came with us on the Bruce Lee trip.

But why this one too?

I have nothing else to give them, Joshua said seriously. Nothing else but this.

Josh, that is not true.

You know it is. He rubbed his forehead with the back of his thumb. Shouldn't we prepare them? When we are gone, who will carry this on?

Darling, now is not the time to think about that. Lily

pushed herself on her tiptoes and planted a kiss on the bridge of his nose, his lips. Besides . . . this is for us, remember? With your father and my father . . . my ah-ma and yours . . .

Joshua flinched. That doesn't have anything to do with—

Lily continued as though she hadn't noticed his reaction: . . . there has been so much loss. For us. Because we have been caught in the loop, forced to replay it. And I know you don't like to admit it, and you don't talk to me about it—

Joshua shook his head. There is nothing to say, he said.

The point I'm making is—she lifted a hand to cup his cheek—it's time there was some life. For us.

If someone were to ask Joshua about this time, he would say that it was the happiest of his life: he and his wife working toward the same goal, looking to the horizon, a world of possibilities and discoveries ahead of them. But of course, what he would not say—or could not say—was that even at the very height of this excitement, his father still lurked in the background, a constant shadow, taking up time and space he tried hard not to yield.

When Joshua stayed too still, or when his hands and his mind were emptied of tasks, he saw his father beyond his right shoulder, frowning. Sometimes, in the middle of the night, when he came into the kitchen for a drink or a snack, there was his father again, standing over the stove, the fire blazing into his face, beads of sweat gathering on his forehead. At night, when Joshua was in bed, he slipped in and out of dreams and reality. Memories he thought he'd forgotten kept flooding back, surprising him with how vivid every detail was. He could not understand how he could have forgotten them, and where he had managed to bury them for so long.

The two of them were together in these dreams. Sometimes Joshua was a child again, watching his father at work in the restaurant. Other times he was a teenager, his father a disapproving presence in their living room, reading a newspaper and smoking a cigarette. And there were other moments—moments he knew were not real yet felt as real as the warmth of Lily's body next to his. He and his father sitting beside each other, somewhere on a different earth, under a different sky, talking, laughing, smoking. Just talking.

But then he would wake. And there was nothing but a stone lodged somewhere in his windpipe or in one of his lungs. He knew what Lily would say about it, so he did not tell her. You need to grieve, that's what she would say. It's a whole life. And he would have to tell her, I don't have the time.

———

His son, Tommy, sat across from him, looking down. The light from the lamp on the surface of the table, slanting. Tension in the atmosphere, humming. Frustration.

Joshua flipped through Tommy's notebook, deciphering the words there. Your notes, he said to his son, are not numbered. Where are the dates? Didn't you look at your sister's?

Tommy swallowed. Yes, I did.

Annoyance pricked at Joshua. Then why didn't you do it right?

I didn't . . . It's . . .

Speak up, Tommy, Joshua said. And sit up straight. He could

not comprehend it. Did the boy not understand that this was not the way to approach the work? Explain, he said.

Tommy gulped. He straightened his posture, but his eyes kept darting away from Joshua's. A slight stammer developed. I . . . I tried to find out the date from newspapers, like you said. But it's . . . it's not that easy. I think sometimes . . . the newspapers that I find are not . . . not current.

Joshua tsked. Didn't you think of other ways? Asking someone? Looking at something else? Maybe *another* newspaper? Or . . . I don't know . . . a calendar?

Tommy's gaze snapped down to his lap again. I . . . I will do better next time, Dad.

Have you ever tried to travel outside of London?

Outside . . . outside of London?

Yes, replied Joshua, in a rather reproachful tone. Did his son not realize the scope of what he could potentially do?

I . . . I don't think I can, stammered Tommy. I don't think it works that way, Dad. We didn't even succeed with me going beyond 1950. I don't see what changing the location will do.

Do you think that's the attitude your mother and I have with the experiments we are working on?

Tommy's silence was the only answer Joshua needed. He sighed. Why could the boy not see? Tommy. He made sure to soften his voice a little. You know you can do much more, don't you?

Yes, Dad, Tommy muttered. And I will—

Try?

Yes. Try.

Don't try. Just do. More chances of success that way. Do you understand?

Yes, Dad.

Okay. Now tell your sister to come in. And your mother too. It's time.

Tommy paused. Time for what, Dad?

Your mother and I are going on a trip. It's time we explained it to you and Eva. This trip is a special one.

The way his son looked at him just then—with both fear and admiration, and then just . . . fear—Joshua saw his father again, sitting at their dining table. The reproachful look in his eyes as they swept over Joshua as he made his way out of the door.

The night before The Experiment, Lily could not sleep.

She lay on her side of the bed, looking at the telephone. Her mother, she thought, was one call away. But what could she possibly say? There were too many things that had gone unsaid, she would not even know where to begin.

Inexplicably, she remembered the look on Eva's face a few days before when she and Joshua outlined everything about the trip to them. Mum, her daughter had said, will you try and take a picture for me? I want to paint it.

Of course I will, Lily replied, beaming. Tommy. Any requests?

Her son shrugged. A sword?

Even her husband had laughed, and her boy's face glowed like the sun.

She felt Joshua's hand on her shoulder. You should get some sleep, he said.

The light from the moon and the streetlamps was sneaking

in through the cracks in their curtains. She turned her back to it so she could face her husband. His eyes were closed. In the semi-darkness he looked like marble, still and cool. Even his breaths seemed to have frozen in time, trapped somewhere inside his body before he could expel them.

She whispered, I cannot believe we are doing this.

I always knew we would, he said. From the very first day I knew we were the same.

A pause. She trailed her fingers over his brow. Josh, everything will be alright, won't it?

With us, when has it ever not been? Now sleep, Lily.

She kissed him lightly on the lips. I'll see you tomorrow, she said.

I'll see you tomorrow. Sleep.

Joshua and Lily both came to realize—separately, but both during their process of planning The Experiment—that timing ought to give you hope. If the timing of something could be wrong, there was the possibility of it someday being right. *If you tried hard enough*, thought Joshua. *Things were meant to be*, thought Lily. Everything could come together. Just like it was now.

Words were said to their children: If we are late, make sure you get your own dinner. Don't cause trouble at school. We'll see you when we get back.

Eva let Lily kiss her on the cheek and gave Joshua a small smile. Joshua ruffled his daughter's hair and patted his son on the shoulder. Tommy simply nodded as he went out the door on his way to school. See you, the boy said, over his shoulder.

And then Joshua and Lily were in the appropriate clothes, with their office made ready for the trip. They stood in the middle of the room opposite each other, breathing each other's air. Their whole existence—everything they had ever been through, all the people who had flitted in and out of their lives—and here they were. Together. It felt like destiny.

Lily took Joshua's hand. Are you ready? she asked.

He smiled. How is that even a question?

I love you, she said.

I love you too. Don't go far from me.

If I do, she said, come after me.

They closed their eyes.

And there was darkness.

TOMMY AND EVA

2019

It is raining this morning.

From her living room, where she has set up her canvas and easel, Eva can see the gray clouds hovering in the sky through her kitchen window. She has cracked it open a little, and the fresh scent of rain drifts into her flat, mingling with the smell of rice, steaming in the cooker.

She doesn't know what she is painting, except that there is a lot of blue. Her jeans are rolled up to her knees and her usual painting T-shirt—an old Spice Girls number—is spotted with all kinds of colors. But the giant paintbrush she's holding is dripping in dark navy, the canvas in front of her a swirling of oceans. Daisy will be coming around tomorrow with May, and Eva knows her niece will love the painting no matter how indecipherable or messy it is. She supposes that is a consolation.

The rice cooker whistles. Thunder rumbles in the distance. She stands for a moment, looking at the myriad of colors in her palette and at the blueness in front of her. Minutes tick by and she remains still, contemplating.

A memory stirs in the back of her mind, like a secret lover knocking discreetly on her door late at night. And then suddenly, in large strokes, she begins creating a wave, then another, then another, and before long there is a tsunami rushing into shore.

Her phone rings, but she doesn't answer. Time becomes irrelevant as she continues to paint, the rain pouring down as though the sky is weeping without restraint.

The waves are plucking a sailboat out of the depths of the ocean with their gnarly, blue fingers when her doorbell rings.

As though waking up from a trance, she shakes herself, puts down her brush and palette, wipes her hands on her grimy jeans, and goes to the door. She gasps when she opens it and sees the man standing on her doorstep.

Tommy smiles. "Hello, Ev. It's been a long time." He is holding an umbrella, but there are drops of rain on his shoulders, soaking into his jacket.

The universe comes to a standstill. Eva stumbles forward, falling into her brother's arms. There will be time, later, for loving words, updates, even painful admonitions, but for now, the twins hold each other, two halves that are whole again.

When they finally break apart, he answers the question reflected in her eyes. "Eva, I need your help," he says. "There is one last trip I need to make."

TOMMY AND JOSHUA

1987

Things take on a different meaning when you know that it will
be the last time,
    the only time.
    So he thanks his twin sister for bringing him,
    but beyond this point,
    he must go on alone.

He can see the plane parked on the runway.
    The crowd of passengers waiting to board.
    His eyes scan the crowd, searching, searching.
    and, yes, there . . . there he is:
    his father.

It is one thing for Tommy to see his father as a young man in

old photographs,
 another thing entirely to see him sitting in an airport,
 his eyes drifting toward the plane outside,
 his new life less than twenty-four hours away.

Tommy stops some distance away.
 He cannot believe that his mind is turning to the most
random details.
 Like if both of them were to stand, they would be around
the same height.
 Or that he does not think he has ever seen his father look
so nervous before.

Tommy has known that this is where he must be ever since
 he got up from the bench by the beach where he sat with
his daughter.
 Yet now that he is here, he finds he does not quite know
what to do, or what to say.

A part of him wishes he could rush forward; his father must
know him,
 he has to know him, right?
 Or if he does not . . . he can learn . . .
 Perhaps there is a second chance . . .
 And what of all the things left unsaid?
 Things he dare only whisper to himself in
 secret moments of anger,
 or moments of anger disguised as sadness?
 What if, what if, what if . . .

He thinks of his mother,
and the emotions rise up within him,
almost too big to contain.
What if, what if, what if . . .

He thinks fleetingly of Peggy,
and how she's always said things he's never been
bold enough to say. The rainclouds
outside her window and the East End docks
on a sunny day. What if, what if, what if . . .

The voice of the flight attendant pulls him back,
her pristine tone rising above the soft buzzing of light
conversation.
A song he more than recognizes is playing softly in the
background:

*Since our love ran deep,
I have longed for you . . .*

Joshua looks around him, his passport gripped tightly in
his hand,
and Tommy finds himself smiling at his father's uncertainty.
So unexpected, so human, so very much like Tommy
himself,
it compels him to make a choice.
For the first time in his life,
he knows exactly what to say.

The evening sunshine is casting pillars of

light on the floor of the departure lounge.
And Tommy walks through them,
his strides strong and steady.

There is a seat right next to his father,
    so he takes it.
    And immediately he is
    nine years old again,
    or twelve, or five,
    he cannot tell. The years he's lived all
    blending together, suddenly as real to him
    as they've never been before.

> *You ask me how deep my love for you is,*
> *how much I really love you . . .*

He sees his mother in her studio,
    turning around as she spots him lingering in her doorway.
    She smiles, her eyes warm and playful.
    Going out? she would ask him.
    Have fun. But don't be home late.
    Daisy blows out her candles.

But the song
    continues to play:

> *My affection does not waver,*
> *my love will not change . . .*

Tommy smiles.

Are you going to London? he asks. No place like it.

His father hears him and looks up.

Sees him.

And time stops.

Much later, a man stands by and watches as a plane takes off into the sky.

A woman comes up to him. How are you? she asks.

He shrugs, his tense posture unwinding like a loose spring. For a long moment he says nothing.

Sad, he finally admits. He gives a little smile. I feel sad. But everything is going to be alright.

The woman's eyes, too, are on the plane. Soon they will be together, she says. Him and Mum. At least that's something.

The plane grows smaller, a blinking light in the sky. I'm glad you're with me, he says.

I'll always be with you. She takes his hand. Are you ready?

A stillness. Unlike any other.

He squeezes her hand and nods.

Closes his eyes.

And lets the world go.

They begin to disappear as the sun does, bathing the city in a soft, golden light.

ACKNOWLEDGMENTS

The Moon Represents My Heart would be nothing without those who've believed in it from the very beginning, and those who've remained dear to my heart long before that.

My parents. There are no words to describe your unfailing love and support. Without you, none of this would've been possible. My successes are your successes. Thank you for always giving me the freedom to be who I am, and for always encouraging me to dream big and dream bravely.

My grandparents. The more I was writing this book, the more I realized that I was writing your lives. Your struggles and your triumphs, your loves and your losses. Our heritage. Even though I never got the chance to know you as well as I would have liked, I see so clearly that your love is still very much present in my life. I would not be where I am if you hadn't paved the way.

My brother, Paul. My best friend. Thank you for always being there. I really don't know what I'd do without you. Make sure you WhatsApp me straight after you read this.

My agent, Liza DeBlock. Your belief in this book has propelled it to greater heights than I could ever dream of, and I am so grateful. You're not only great at what you do, but you do it with genuine warmth and kindness, which is the most special thing.

My UK editor, Juliet Mabey, and the whole team at OneWorld; and my US editor, Vikki Warner, and Blackstone Publishing. Thank you for taking a chance on this story and on this little author from Bangkok. You've all brought this novel into the world with so much care and passion, and your attention to detail has made this story better and bolder.

My lecturers at Edinburgh Napier, David Bishop and Laura Lam. You saw this book from its inception, and I wouldn't have been able to craft it without your mentoring and guidance.

My Stockbridge Trinity, Flat Seventeen girls, and Creative Writing course mates. This book could not have been written without your generous love and encouragement. I am so proud of you all and I can't wait to give you the biggest hugs when we finally reunite!

My "tribe" in Bangkok. All my close friends and "siblings." You know who you are. Thank you for your constant love and support. For always being by my side, through the good times and the bad. I am who I am because of you. Thank you for always seeing me and my heart. This journey is never easy, but having each other has been the brightest light and the greatest pride of my life.

เพื่อน ๆ พี่ ๆ น้อง ๆ คนสนิททุกคนที่กรุงเทพ รู้ ๆ กันอยู่ว่าหมาย ถึงใคร ขอบคุณที่คอยรัก สนับสนุน และอยู่เคียงข้างกันมาตลอด

ทั้งในวันที่ดีและในวันที่แย่ พิมเป็นพิมในทุกวันนี้ก็เพราะทุกคน
ขอบคุณที่เห็นหัวใจของพิม
จริง ๆ ชีวิตมันไม่ง่ายเสมอไป แต่การที่เราได้มีกันและกัน คือ แสง
สว่างและความภาคภูมิใจที่ยิ่งใหญ่ที่สุดในชีวิตของพิมแล้ว

All the places that have given this book life: Edinburgh, where I first conceived of and began writing this story; London, where a piece of my heart will always remain; Hong Kong, where my father found his strength; and Bangkok, where I was given mine.

Researching this novel was an illuminating experience. I want to especially thank my father for his invaluable firsthand accounts of his experiences visiting the Kowloon Walled City, and the tireless research conducted by historians, journalists, and children of Liverpool's deported Chinese seamen. Trips to Limehouse, Lambeth's Imperial War Museum, and Museum of London Docklands were also particularly helpful.

Thank you to the authors, poets, filmmakers, and musical artists who've inspired me during the writing process: Wong Kar-wai, Teresa Teng, Gemma Chan, Bruce Lee, Anna May Wong, Celeste Ng, Lulu Wang, Alan Yang, Mary Jean Chan, Xiaolu Gao, Cathy Park Hong, Amanda Lee Koe, Lang Leav, Yrsa Daley-Ward, Ada Limón, Rumi, Mary Oliver, Mumford & Sons, Taylor Swift, and The Wailin' Jennys.

Last but not least, to the Most High. Thank you for continuing to carry me through the darkest of times, and for keeping my heart open so that I can always find the light.

ABOUT THE AUTHOR

Pim Wangtechawat is a Thai-Chinese writer from Bangkok with a Master's in Creative Writing from Edinburgh Napier University. Her short stories, poems, and articles have been published in various magazines and journals such as *The Mekong Review*, *The Nikkei Asian Review*, and *YesPoetry*. Through her work, she aims to tell stories that reflect our shared humanity and bring more Asian narratives to the forefront.